THE SONGS WE SANG

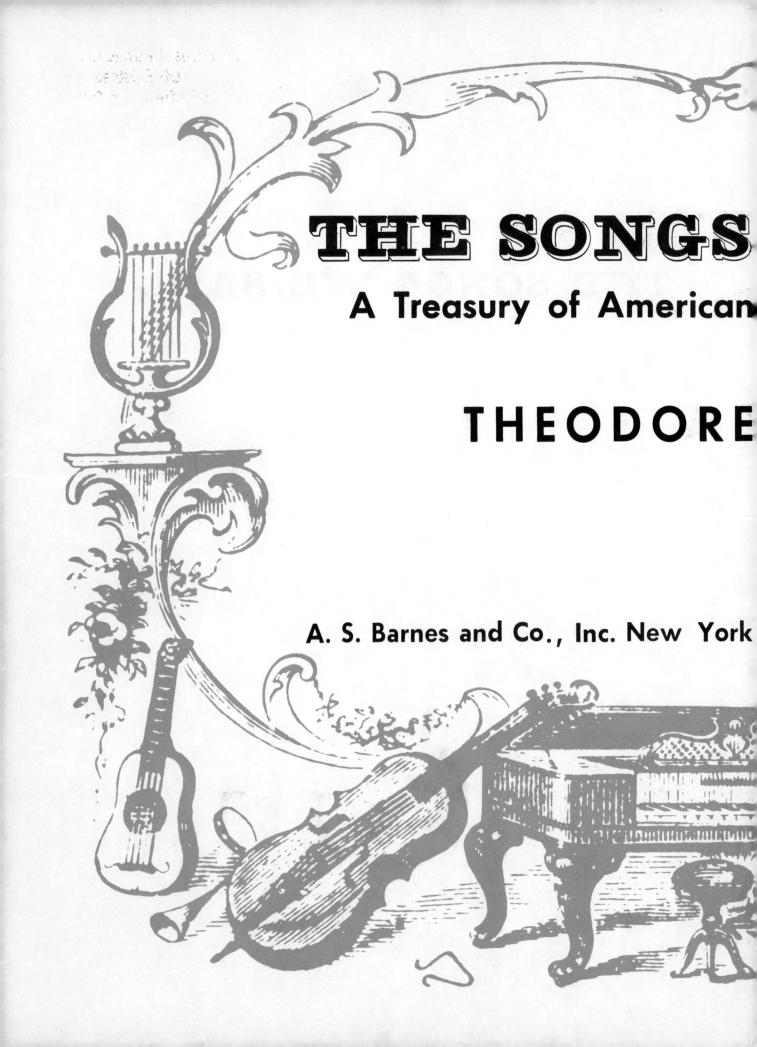

THE SONGS

A Treasury of American

THEODORE

A. S. Barnes and Co., Inc. New York

WE SANG

Popular Music

RAPH

Thomas Yoseloff Ltd London

© 1964 by Theodore Raph
Library of Congress Catalogue Card Number: 64-15203

A.S. Barnes and Company, Inc.
Cranbury, New Jersey 08512

Thomas Yoseloff Ltd
108 New Bond Street
London W1Y OQX, England

First Printing December, 1964
Second Printing April, 1967
Third Printing April, 1971

Dedicated to the fun of
singing and playing
America's best-known songs

6151
Printed in the United States of America

CONTENTS

THE SONGS WE SANG

INTRODUCTION

THIS SONGBOOK IS FORMULATED TO PROVIDE A MAXIMUM OF MUSICAL FUN AND SATISFACTION. IT combines well-known songs in sing-along keys with rich sounding easy-to-play piano arrangements, and includes chord symbols with guitar fingering, plus the story behind each of the songs.

The ever-popular sing-along tradition, an old old custom, is likely to continue for centuries to come since it offers a group activity that never fails to generate fun, excitement, and the warmth of human closeness in song. Ever since the Pilgrims landed in 1620 popular songs (songs of the people) have reflected the times, the growth, and the milestones of American history. Songs are an intimacy with most people . . . a felt experience. When a song touches enough people to become widely popular it leaves a certain influence on them, which may, in some cases, last for generations. Thus today some songs are immediately associated with the feeling and events of times gone by; one thinks of "Yankee Doodle" and the spirited pulse of the American Revolution, "Skip To My Lou" and the heroic struggles of our western pioneers, "Battle Hymn of the Republic" and our tragic Civil War, "Daisy Bell" and the rollicking Gay Nineties, "Home On the Range" and F. D. R.'s New Deal of the 1930's.

Other well-known songs are equally tied in with America's historic events but are less readily associated with them, such as "Hail Columbia" and our country's first internal crisis, "Blue-Tail Fly" and the beginning of black-faced minstrel shows, "Swing Low, Sweet Chariot" and the plight of Negro slaves, "She'll Be Comin' 'Round the Mountain" and our gigantic railroad construction era, "Hinky Dinky Parlay-Voo" and World War I.

The pages that follow contain the story behind each of the songs in the context of its historical and sociological setting. The "life history" of every song answers such questions as, How old is it? Who wrote it? Where did it come from? Etc. Although this background material is well researched, no documentation is provided since this is a songbook for fun and entertainment rather than a scholarly work.

Dates: The date next to the song title indicates the year in which the song first achieved wide popularity. A few of the dates are approximations but most are accurate.

Selection of Songs: Each song in the book is carefully selected on the basis of (1) its being well known today by most people in the United States, and (2) its having been a national hit at one time during our history. Thus every song possesses those indefinable qualities that appeal to all kinds of people in all generations.

Keys: Keys chosen for the songs are in the comfortable voice range of most people, making the songs more attractive for sing-alongs.

Verses: A full set of verses (stanzas) is provided for complete continuity. Strange words are explained in the footnotes. New lyrics are added to certain songs where the original is too short, not standardized, unprintable, etc., such as "Wabash Cannon Ball," "Pop Goes the Weasel," "Tom Dooley," "Bell Bottom Trousers." Slight lyric modifications are made in a few cases for easier singability, i. e., one syllable for each note. In certain very traditional songs where two or more notes are sung to one syllable, the music indicates this with a slur ⌒ .

Play-Along: One may play-along as well as sing-along with these songs. The chord symbols may be played by guitar, banjo, five-string banjo, ukelele, autoharp, chord organ and accordion. The system used here is that of the professionals, and the symbols are explained as follows:

C	= C major chord	C+	= C augmented chord
Cm	= C minor chord	C7+	= C 7th augmented chord
Cm6	= C minor 6th chord	Co	= C diminished 7th chord
Cm7	= C minor 7th chord	C♭5	= C flatted 5th chord
C7	= C 7th chord	C7♭5	= C 7th chord with a flatted 5th
C9	= C 9th chord	C7 (sus. 4)	= C 7th chord with a suspended 4th

Piano: All piano arrangements sound rich and full. Each one is created to fit the mood and color of the song, e. g., flowing, rhythmic, cute, sustained, etc. Piano arrangements are made at the Grade II level of proficiency, i.e., very easy to play, since most of the notes lie comfortably "under the hand." A few exceptions, not sounding well enough at Grade II, are at the Easy Grade III level. For smaller hands (including children's) omit the notes in parentheses: (♩) omit

♩ play

Use of the loud pedal is indicated thus:

(press pedal)

(release pedal)

10

Guitar: Guitar "frames" are included with the songs and the fingering is added for the convenience of beginners. Guitar may be tuned in the following manner:

Play this note

by striking this piano key

or by using a guitar pitch-pipe

and tune this guitar string to the same sound.

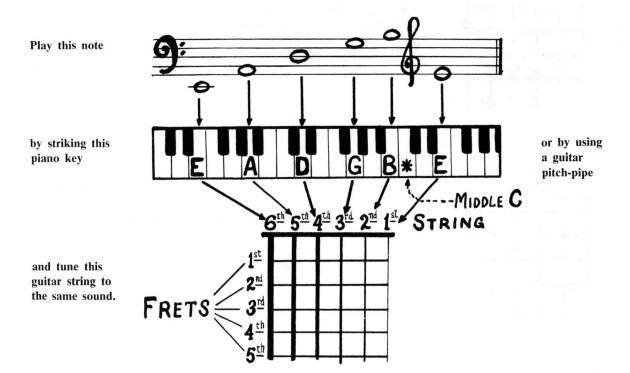

Guitar frames are read as follows:
X = do not play this string.
O = play this string open (not fingered).

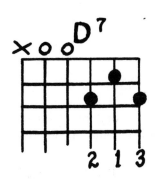

1st String: Place 3rd finger down solidly behind the 2nd fret.
2nd String: Place 1st finger down solidly behind the 1st fret.
3rd String: Place 2nd finger down solidly behind the 2nd fret.
4th and 5th Strings are open, and 6th String is not played.
When the five strings are strummed a D⁷ chord will be sounded.

11

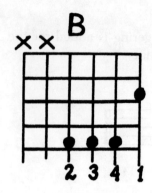

B

1st String: Place 1st finger behind 2nd fret.
2nd String: Place 4th finger behind 4th fret.
3rd String: Place 3rd finger behind 4th fret.
4th String: Place 2nd finger behind 4th fret.
5th and 6th Strings are not played.
When the four strings are strummed a B chord will be sounded.

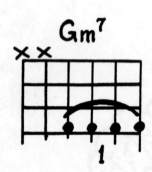

F

Place 1st finger behind 1st fret of both 1st and 2nd Strings.

Gm⁷

Place 1st finger behind 3rd fret of 1st, 2nd, 3rd, and 4th Strings.

For best guitar-playing results keep fingernails cut short. In the beginning finger tips may become tender, but after several days they will begin to develop nice protective calluses.

Several Ways in Which This Songbook May Be Used.   *Try These Suggestions.*

Type out (with carbon copies) extra lyric sheets for about a dozen songs. Use them for sing-alongs. Keep these copies with the book and use them over and over again.

Remember: In addition to piano, accompaniment for sing-alongs may be provided by guitar, banjo, five-string banjo, ukelele, autoharp, chord organ and accordion.

1. Entertain yourself or others by simply playing the songs on the piano.

2. Play the melody in octaves on the piano (both right and left hands play melody) while someone else plays guitar accompaniment.

3. Entertain yourself or others by singing the songs with piano accompaniment.

4. Sing the songs to the accompaniment of any one of the instruments listed above.

5. Sing the songs to the accompaniment of any combination of the instruments listed above.

6. Have a family sing-along accompanied by piano or any of the above instruments.

7. For an unusual twist at family reunions have a sing-along. Then, at the end of each song, ask three or four persons to describe what incidents the song reminds them of. You may get some very interesting replies.

8. Have a social-gathering sing-along accompanied by piano or any of the above instruments. Your friends and neighbors may enjoy having someone read the song's "life story" to them. Sing-alongs are particularly effective for parties such as birthdays, anniversaries, housewarmings, back-yard barbecues, Thanksgiving Day, New Years' celebrations, etc.

9. For Teenage parties this sing-along is a natural "ice-breaker."

10. Make home tape recordings of your sing-alongs and play them back.

11. A young piano student may ask his teacher to assign one of these easy pieces for his lesson.

12. When a piano student has learned a few of the songs he may then accompany sing-alongs. His guitar-playing friend could join him.

13. Nonpianists, who read music a little, can have some fun by splitting the right and left hand parts of the piano music between them.

14. This songbook (and extra lyric sheets) comes in handy on automobile trips. It provides fun and entertainment, and reduces the monotony. It is great for children and teenagers in addition to adults. Keep a copy in the car.

15. This songbook offers additional fun on picnics, boating parties, camping trips, and other kinds of outings.

Extra Fun May Be Had in Group Singing.   *Try These Vocal Effects.*

1. Sing the first chorus at normal volume. Sing the next chorus very softly. Sing the third chorus L O U D. Repeat this routine.

2. Occasionally: Sing a chorus with very short notes (like stop-time) by clipping each syllable short. Then sing the next chorus v-e-r-y s-m-o-o-t-h-l-y for contrast.

3. On multiple-verse songs you might try the following:
   Have one person sing the first verse with piano accompaniment.
   Have another person sing the second verse with guitar accompaniment.
   Continue alternating this way. It's fun.
   Any of the other instruments listed above may be substituted for piano and guitar.
   If you have a group of people you may divide them in half and alternate with groups.

4. Divide your singing group in half and separate them.
   Have one side sing two lines of the lyric, and then have the other side sing the next two lines of the lyric. Keep alternating this way.

EARLY AMERICA (1620-1810)

ON OCTOBER 12, 1492, WHEN COLUMBUS' BRAWNY SAILORS REACHED SAN SALVADOR (WATLING Island, Bahamas), they broke out in song with the popular hymn "Te Deum." Thus the first European music was heard in America. Religion was clearly the dominant influence on music during our early Colonial days. "Old Hundredth" ("Doxology") was a favorite hymn as attested to in Longfellow's "Courtship of Myles Standish." Many small bands of immigrants arrived from many countries, established churches, and sang the hymns of their fatherland. It wasn't until 1640 that the first music book was printed here on the first printing press in Cambridge, Massachusetts bearing the title *The Whole Booke of Psalmes Faithfully Translated Into English Metre*[1], later known as the *Bay Psalm Book*.

Secular songs also found their way into the daily lives of the Colonists. Some came over on the Mayflower while others arrived later. A few developed fairly good local popularity. Churchgoing people kept a vigilant ear on secular music. When risqué and bawdy songs began filtering in during the middle of the seventeenth century, the Church intervened. Recognizing the persuasive powers of music, the Church took the position, "The first and chief Use of Musick is for the Service and Praise of God, whose gift it is. The second Use is for the Solace of Men, which as it is agreeable unto Nature, so it is allow'd by God, as a temporal Blessing to recreate and cheer men after long study and weary labor in their Vocations." [2]

Virtually all our music was imported, and learned by ear in folk-song tradition. Complaints arose that no two groups sang the same song with the same melody. Thomas Symmes noted in his published pamphlet (1720), "Now singing by note is giving every note its proper pitch . . . in its proper place. Whereas, the usual way varies much from this . . . some notes are sung too high, others too low, and most too long, and many turnings with the voice are made where they should not be, and some are wanting where they should have been." Thus a movement for "regular singing" gave rise to singing schools, which paved the way for the future choral groups and community sings which are now an important part of our cultural heritage.

The early eighteenth century saw the use of music expand as our population grew. Music was everyone's property, since it knew no distinction of class, race or nationality.

---

[1] In 1947 a first edition was sold in New York for $151,000.
[2] From John Playford's *Introduction To the Skill of Musick* (London, 1655).

14

Musical instruments[1] were imported, prized, and played. Just ten years after we adopted the Gregorian calendar (1752) Benjamin Franklin invented the much-talked-about armonica, a mechanical version of musical glasses. He was partial to Scotch songs, often playing them on guitar or harp. Thomas Jefferson, gifted with a fine singing voice, frequently played violin duets with Patrick Henry. Jefferson wrote in his *Notes on Virginia* "The instrument proper to them (Negroes) is the Banjar,[2] which they brought hither from Africa." Among our earliest American composers were William Billings and Francis Hopkinson a friend of George Washington and signer of the Declaration of Independence.

When political clouds darkened, Samuel Adams organized singing groups, teaching them partisan songs denouncing unfair taxation and supporting independence. Thomas Paine often wrote the lyrics for such songs. Soon hundreds of political songs appeared, and by the time of Concord and Lexington there began a war of songs as well as gunpowder. Every military and civilian sing-along proved an important morale booster.

The end of the war touched off great immigration and migration, which resulted in an increased number of songs and a wider dispersion of the songs already established. By 1810 our population stood well over seven million[3] as the Western movement was beginning to find its stride. The most prized possessions of our frontiersmen were the rifle, an axe, the Bible, and a fiddle.

STATES ADMITTED TO THE UNION

Rank	Name	Origin of Name	Year Admitted	State Song
1.	Delaware	In honor of Lord De La Warr.	1787	Our Delaware
2.	Pennsylvania	Penn's Woodland.	1787	*
3.	New Jersey	From the Latin "Nova Caesarea" in honor of Carteret, former governor of the British Isle of Jersey.	1787	*
4.	Georgia	In honor of George II of England.	1788	Georgia
5.	Connecticut	From the Indian word "Quinnehtuk-qut" meaning "long river place."	1788	*
6.	Massachusetts	"Big hill place" from the Indian "massa" (big), "wadchu" (hill), "et" (place).	1788	*
7.	Maryland	In honor of Queen Henrietta Maria, wife of England's King Charles I.	1788	Maryland, My Maryland
8.	South Carolina	Named after Charles II of England.	1788	Carolina
9.	New Hampshire	Named after England's county of Hampshire.	1788	*
10.	Virginia	In honor of the virgin Queen Elizabeth of England.	1788	Carry Me Back To Old Virginny

[1] Violin, flute, bass, harpsichord, oboe, clarinet.
[2] Forerunner of the banjo.
[3] 90 per cent rural.

Rank	Name	Origin of Name	Year Admitted	State Song
11.	New York	Named after England's Duke of York.	1788	*
12.	North Carolina	Named after Charles II of England (from the Latin "Carolus" for Charles).	1789	The Old North State
13.	Rhode Island	Named after the Greek Island of Rhodes. (Originally named Red Island because of its red clay).	1790	Rhode Island
14.	Vermont	French, meaning "green mountain."	1791	Hail To Vermont
15.	Kentucky	From the Indian word "Kentahten" meaning "land of tomorrow."	1792	My Old Kentucky Home
16.	Tennessee	From the Indian word "Tanasi," a group of Cherokee villages on the Little Tennessee River.	1796	My Homeland Tennessee & When It's Iris Time in Tennessee
17.	Ohio	Indian word for "great river."	1803	*

* No official state song.

GREENSLEEVES
1620

THIS FOLK SONG IS WELL OVER 350 YEARS OLD AND WAS HIGHLY POPULAR IN ENGLAND THE LATTER part of the sixteenth century. It was well known to William Shakespeare who refers to it twice in "The Merry Wives of Windsor" when he has Mistress Ford say, "But they do no more adhere and keep place together than the Hundredth Psalm to the tune of 'Greensleeves'" (Act 2, Scene 1), and later, in Act 5, Scene 5, he has Falstaff say, "Let it thunder to the tune of 'Greensleeves.'"

Shakespeare could hardly have known how immensely popular his dramas and this folk song would become centuries later. Four years after his death (1616) "Greensleeves" was brought to America by the Pilgrims, and it was one of the very few secular songs frequently sung by our early settlers. Throughout Colonial America's growth this song's popularity maintained itself as one of the favorites among little and big people alike. "Greensleeves" was as well known to the man who made barrel staves as it was to George Washington. It was sung lustily by the blacksmith and more elegantly by wealthy Virginia families to the accompaniment of violins and the virginal (granddaddy of the piano).

Shortly after our Civil War this charming melody was given a brand new lyric by William Chatterton Dix, and the song became a fairly popular Christmas carol entitled "What Child Is This?" and is still sung in many places today.

Directly after World War II, America's interest in folk songs took a sharp turn upwards. Folk singers became respected artists and "Greensleeves" was one of their finest songs. Thus this song's popularity steadily increased, and when a new edition was published in 1951 the song reached hit proportions all over again.

17

GREENSLEEVES

sleeves you were my de – light Green – sleeves you're my

heart of gold No one else but my dear La-dy Green – sleeves

2. I have been ready and at your hand
   For to grant whatever your heart would crave
   And I have waged both my life and land
   Your dear love and your good will to hold and have

Chorus:

3. I bought thee kerchers to 'dorn thy head
   That were wrought so fine and so gallantly
   I kept thee well both at board and bed
   Which did cost my own purse so well favoredly

Chorus:

4. I bought thee petticoats of the best
   With a cloth so fine and soft as might be
   I gave thee jewels for thine own chest
   And yet all of this cost I did spend on thee

Chorus:

5. Well I will pray to our God on high
   So that thou my constancy mayest see
   And that yet once more before I die
   Thou so surely wilt vouch safe to love me

Chorus:

6. Greensleeves now farewell adieu adieu
   For to God I pray Him to prosper thee
   For I am still thy one lover true
   Come to me once again and do love me

Chorus:

BARBARA ALLEN
1622

THIS IS ONE OF THE OLDEST OF OLD SONGS, AND ONE OF THE FEW THAT HAS ENJOYED CONTINUAL popularity for well over three hundred years in England, Scotland, and America. This folk song originated in Scotland and dates back at least to the beginning of the seventeenth century, at which time there were both Scottish and English versions. This was a song that peasants understood, felt, and enjoyed since the lyric tells a story as old as man himself. Somewhere along the line the story became a rhyme, and the rhyme became a song. Like most folk songs it just developed, and was passed on orally from generation to generation.

"Barbara Allen" arrived in Colonial America about the time of the Pilgrims and was one of their favorites. Very shortly there were several English and Scottish variations of the song in old New England. Later, migrants from New England took this song with them to the Southern mountains where they developed a few of their own variations including extra verses to suit their own tastes. Even before the American Revolution the entire East Coast of America was covered with many variants of "Barbara Allen."

In the famous *Diary* of Samuel Pepys there is a January 2, 1666, entry conferring praise on the performance of this song by actress Mrs. Knipp at Lord Brounker's. Oliver Goldsmith (1728–1774) was often moved to tears when his diarymaid sang it. Horace Greeley (1811–1872), in his *Recollections of A Busy Life*, speaks of his mother singing this old folk song. Today there are literally hundreds of versions of "Barbara Allen;" but the central theme is always the same, and the song is always fairly popular.

20

BARBARA ALLEN

Moderately

1. In Scar-let Town where I was born There was a fair maid

dwell-in' Made ev-'ry youth cry out "Well a-day" Her name was Bar-b'ra

Al-len (Interlude) All Al-len

2. All in the merry month of May
When buds of green were swellin'
Young Jemmy Grove on his deathbed lay
For love of Barb'ra Allen

3. He sent his man unto her then
The house where she did dwell in
"You must come now to my master dear
If you are Barb'ra Allen"

4. "For death is printed on his face
   And o'er his heart is stealin'
   Then haste away for to comfort him
   Oh lovely Bar'bra Allen"

5. "Though death be printed on his face
   And o'er his heart be stealin'
   Yet not a bit better shall he be
   For I am Bar'bra Allen"

6. But slowly slowly she came up
   And slowly she came nigh him
   And all she said as he lay in bed,
   "Young man, I think you're dying"

7. He turned his face unto her straight
   With deadly sorrow sighin'
   "Oh pretty maid, come and pity me
   I'm on deathbed lyin'"

8. "If on your deathbed you do lie
   What needs the tale your tellin'?
   For I cannot keep you from your death
   Farewell," said Barb'ra Allen

9. He turned his face unto the wall
   And death was with him dealin'
   "Adieu adieu to my friends and all
   Adieu to Barb'ra Allen"

10. As she was walkin' o'er the fields
    She heard the bells a-knellin'
    And ev'ry stroke seemed to say to her
    "Unworthy Barb'ra Allen"

11. She turned her body round about
    And spied a corpse a-comin'
    "Lay down the corpse" said she with a shout
    "That I may look upon him"

12. With scornful eyes she looked at him
    Her cheeks with laughter swellin'
    Then all her friends said "Don't touch a limb,
    Unworthy Barb'ra Allen"

13. When he was dead and in his grave
    Her heart was struck with sorrow
    "Oh mother, oh make my bed, I pray
    For I shall die tomorrow"

14. "Hard hearted creature, him to slight
    Who really loved me dearly
    Oh that I would have been kind to him
    When he was 'live and near me"

15. She on her deathbed as she lay
    Begged to be buried by him
    And sore repented of ev'ry day
    That she did e'er deny him

16. "Farewell" she said "Ye virgins all
    And shun the fault I fell in
    Henceforth you take warning by the fall
    Of cruel Barb'ra Allen"

THANKSGIVING PRAYER
(We Gather Together)
1630

THIS SONG'S EVERLASTING POPULARITY DATES BACK TO THE FIRST DUTCH SETTLERS IN AMERICA. Its origin is either in the traditional folk songs of the Netherlands or was written by the Dutch composer/author Adrianus Valerius. In either case "Thanksgiving Prayer" was first published in Haarlem in Valerius' collection *Nederlandtsche Gedenck-Clanck* in the edition of 1621 or 1626.

A short time after Hendrik Hudson sailed his "Half Moon" up the Hudson River (1609), Peter Minuit arrived with a number of Dutch immigrants (1626) and bought Manhattan Island, erected a fort, and founded New Amsterdam and other settlements in surrounding areas. These Dutch people brought their culture with them, including songs, dances, and children's games. One of the songs was "Thanksgiving Prayer."

Thanksgiving Day in the Netherlands was simply a day when various churches held a special service of thanksgiving. This was a day of solemnity and simple food, even fasting, a day when farmers, in particular, gave thanks for rewarding their toil with a bountiful harvest. Here in America "Thanksgiving Prayer" became a favorite with the Dutch settlers, not only because of its beautiful melody and expressions of gratitude but also for the expressions of hope for a better life in this new world. Appreciation for this folk hymn has not diminished for over three hundred years. It is now America's Thanksgiving hymn. It is sung by millions of people today and is often heard on radio and television.

THANKSGIVING PRAYER
(We Gather Together)

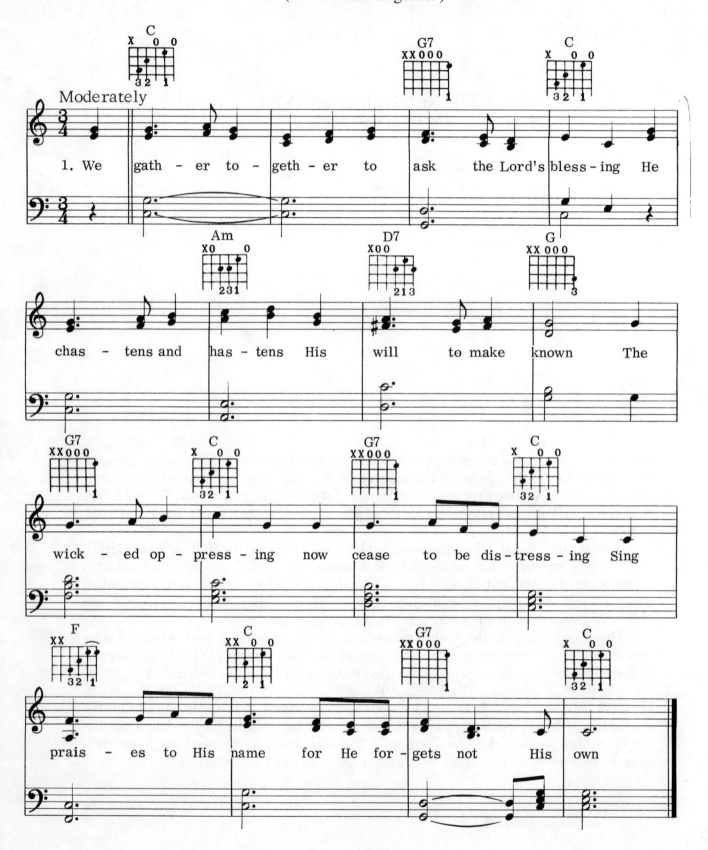

2. Beside us to guide us our God with us joining
   Ordaining, maintaining His kingdom divine
   So from the beginning the fighting we were winning
   Thou Lord wast at our side and all the glory be Thine

3. We all do extol Thee, Thou leader triumphant
   And pray that Thou still our defender wilt be
   Let thy congregation excape all tribulation
   Thy name be ever praised in glory, Lord make us free

THE GIRL I LEFT BEHIND
1650

THIS SONG HAS BEEN POPULAR IN AMERICA SINCE ABOUT 1650. ALTHOUGH IT WAS FIRST PRINTED IN 1791, in Dublin, Ireland, its origin dates back some two hundred years earlier. It was popular during Queen Elizabeth's reign, and she died in 1603. In addition to its present title it was also known in Ireland as "The Rambling Laborer" and "The Spailpin Fanach," and in England it was called "Brighton Camp."

This song was quite easy to play on the fife since it is based on the major scale, with no sharps or flats. In eighteenth-century England drums and fifes were the traditional instruments for marching soldiers, and this tune was one of their favorites. Military bands soon fell into the habit of playing it for naval and military departures.

This song was brought to America by the English and Irish immigrants who followed in the path of the Pilgrims (1620) and settled in New England around 1650. It has been popular in our country ever since. Many people associate Archibald Willard's painting *Spirit of '76* with this song. For many years West Point has used this number as a march when the graduating class is assembled for the last time in June.

26

THE GIRL I LEFT BEHIND

2. For she is as fair as Shannon's side
   And so much purer than its water
   But she did refuse to be my bride
   Though many years I had sought her

   Then to France I went and sailed away
   Her letters oft remind me
   That I promised never to gain-say [1]
   The girl I left behind me

3. Now she says "My own dear love come home
   My friends are rich and they are many
   Or abroad with you I want to roam
   A soldier's heart stout as any

   But if you'll not come nor let me go
   I'll think you have resigned me"
   Oh my heart nigh broke when I said "no"
   To the girl I left behind me

4. Never shall my only true love brave
   A life of war and heavy toiling,
   Never never as a skulking slave
   I'll tread my own native soil on

   But if it were free or to be freed,
   The battle's close would find me
   To my Ireland bound, nor message need
   From the girl I left behind me

Earlier version:

1. Come on all ye handsome comely maids
   That live near Erin's Carlow dwelling
   And beware of young men's flatt'ring tongue
   When love to you they are telling

   Now beware of the kind words they say
   Be wise and do not mind them
   For if they were talking till they die
   They'd leave you all far behind them

2. In the Carlow town I lived I own
   All free from debt and ev'ry danger
   Till a colonel Reilly listed me
   To come and join Wicklow Rangers

   Where they dressed me up in scarlet red
   And used me very kindly
   Still I thought that my poor heart would break
   For the girl I left behind me

3. I was scarcely fourteen years of age
   When I was very brokenhearted
   For I'm so in love these two long years
   Since from my love I was parted

   Now these maidens wonder how I moan
   And bid me not to mind him
   That he might have more of grief than joy
   For leaving me behind him

1. To speak against

28

A FROG WENT A-COURTING
1700

THIS SONG LANDED IN AMERICA ALMOST THE SAME TIME AS THE PILGRIMS. ALTHOUGH IT WAS FIRST printed in England in 1611 under the title "A Moste Strange Weddinge of the Ffroge and the Mouse," it was listed long before (actually 1549) in Wedderburn's *The Complaynt of Scotlande* under the title "The Frog Cam [came] to the Myl Dur [mill door]" and it was sung chiefly by the shepherds.

Despite the fact that our New England ancestors treated this as a sort of folk song, it has its roots in political satire as did the Mother Goose rhymes. It seems that Queen Elizabeth (1533–1603) gave her various suitors the amusing nicknames of animals: She called Sir Walter Raleigh her "fish," Leicester her "robin," the French Ambassador Simier her "ape," and the Duc d'Alençon was her "frog." This song refers to her romance with the Duke, which was so unpopular with her subjects.

Colonial New Englanders had no particular interest in the historical significance of this song and sang it only because they and their children liked it. Around the time of the Salem witchcraft trials, migrating New Englanders (1700) brought this song (and others) with them to their new homes in the Southern Appalachians, and for a long time afterwards the Blue Ridge mountaineers kept this song's popularity alive. During our period of national expansion (nineteenth century) this song spread over the entire country, and today there are hundreds of versions and verses.

A FROG WENT A-COURTING

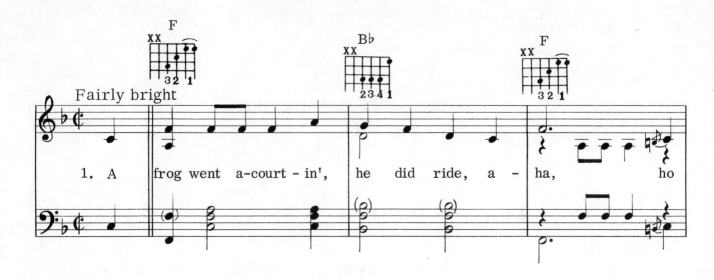

Fairly bright

1. A frog went a-court-in', he did ride, a - ha, ho

ho   A frog went a-court-in', he did ride, With

sword and pis-tol by his side, a - ha, ho ho

2. He rode till he reached Miss Mouse's door, aha, ho ho
   He rode till he reached Miss Mouse's door,
   Where he had often been before, aha, ho ho

3. He sat little mousie on his knee, aha, ho ho
   He sat little mousie on his knee,
   And said "Miss Mousie, marry me," aha, ho ho

4. She said "I will ask my Uncle Rat," aha, ho ho
   She said "I will ask my Uncle Rat,
   And see what he will say to that," aha, ho ho

5. Hence old Uncle Rat did ride to town, aha, ho ho
   Hence old Uncle Rat did ride to town,
   To buy his niece a wedding gown, aha, ho ho

6. Now where will the wedding supper be, aha, ho ho
   Now where will the wedding supper be,
   Down yonder in the hollow tree, aha, ho ho

7. The first to arrive was big Brown Bug, aha, ho ho
   The first to arrive was big Brown Bug,
   He drowned in the molassas jug, aha, ho ho

8. The next to arrive was Parson Fly, aha, ho ho
   The next to arrive was Parson Fly,
   He ate so much he nearly died, aha, ho ho

9. The next to arrive was big Tom Cat, aha, ho ho
   The next to arrive was big Tom Cat,
   He chased Miss Mouse and Uncle Rat, aha, ho ho

10. The last to arrive was Dick the Drake[1], aha, ho ho
    The last to arrive was Dick the Drake,
    Who chased the frog into the lake, aha, ho ho

11. Now go put the songbook on the shelf, aha, ho ho
    Now go put the songbook on the shelf,
    If you want more go sing yourself, aha, ho ho

1. "Dick the Drake" probably refers to Sir Francis Drake.

DRUNKEN SAILOR
1740

THIS IS A WELL-KNOWN SEA CHANTEY, POPULAR IN COLONIAL AMERICA DURING THE EARLY DAYS OF sailing vessels, shanghaied sailors, and pirates. Chanteys are chiefly work songs which not only provide pleasant diversion but aid the men in working together by supplying a rhythm for their movements. The word "chantey" is from the French "chanter" (shań-tay) meaning "to sing." The melody seems to have been borrowed from an ancient Irish dance or marching tune. Over the centuries there have been many parodies to this song, several unprintable.

"Drunken Sailor" was used as a real work song by sailors operating out of our Colonial ports. It was known as a "stamp-'n'-go" type of chantey. As they sang in rhythm, a few sailors took firm hold of the fall (rope) connected to the heavy sail. Then, on the words "Way, hey, and up she rises," they stamped their feet on the deck for a solid footing, and together they pulled hard on the fall while taking three or four steps. Thus the massive sail was raised. "Drunken Sailor" was one of their favorite walkaway (stamp-'n'-go) chanteys.

This song became equally popular on the British Indiamen (large sailing ships of the East India Company) engaged in commerce between England and the Far East around the time of the Pilgrims (1620) and up to the War of 1812. Although American sailors used this sea chantey long before our American Revolution, it has since developed into one of our delightful songs of humor and has been heard and sung right up to the present day.

DRUNKEN SAILOR

1. Old time sailors pronounced this: Earl-lie.

2. What can we do with a drunken sailor
   What can we do with a drunken sailor
   What can we do with a drunken sailor
   Early in the mornin'

   Into the scuppers, ahoy there sailors
   Into the scuppers, ahoy there sailors
   Into the scuppers, ahoy there sailors
   Early in the mornin'

Chorus:

3. What can we do with a drunken sailor
   What can we do with a drunken sailor
   What can we do with a drunken sailor
   Early in the mornin'

   Give him a lick o' the bosun's flipper
   Give him a lick o' the bosun's flipper
   Give him a lick o' the bosun's flipper
   Early in the mornin'

Chorus:

4. What can we do with a drunken sailor
   What can we do with a drunken sailor
   What can we do with a drunken sailor
   Early in the mornin'

   Take him an' shake him an' try to wake him
   Take him an' shake him an' try to wake him
   Take him an' shake him an' try to wake him
   Early in the mornin'

Chorus:

5. What can we do with a drunken sailor
   What can we do with a drunken sailor
   What can we do with a drunken sailor
   Early in the mornin'

   Into the brig till he gets up sober
   Into the brig till he gets up sober
   Into the brig till he gets up sober
   Early in the mornin'

Chorus:

YANKEE DOODLE
1754

HERE IS PERHAPS THE MOST OUTSTANDING SONG IN THE HISTORY OF AMERICA'S PEOPLE. IT HAS been continually popular for over two hundred years and there have been countless parodies on the melody.

Although the origin of "Yankee Doodle" has been claimed by France, Spain, the Netherlands, Germany, and Hungary, the melody seems to have come from England where it was a children's game song called "Lucy Locket." It is also quite likely that "Lucy Locket" was based on another English melody "Fisher's Jig." Legend has it that when Oliver Cromwell rode his horse (*circa* 1653) he wore an Italian-style hat crowned with a long feather known as a "macaroni." In derision his enemies made up a rhyme ending with "stuck a feather in his cap and called it macaroni" which they sang to the melody of "Fisher's Jig." This seems to have been the first version brought to America by the English soldiers who fought in the French and Indian War (1754–1763), and it caught on with the Colonists right away. Before long each settlement seemed to have had its own set of lyrics combined with certain variants of the melody. Meanwhile "Lucy Locket" arrived in New England where it became quite popular.

Some years later "Yankee Doodle" developed into the most important song of the American Revolution. British soldiers used a crude derisive set of lyrics with which they mocked the shabby Colonist soldiers, and the Colonists in turn used another set of lyrics which eventually became their battle cry. "Yankee Doodle" was a favorite with fife and drum bands since it was so catchy and so easy to play. The shabby Colonists sang this song at their Concord victory (1775), and the Colonial army sang it at Yorktown (1781) when General Cornwallis surrendered his sword to George Washington.

The word "Yankee" was a contemptuous nickname the British soldiers applied to New Englanders. It derived either from the Dutch word "Janke" meaning "Little John," or from the Indian pronunciation of the word "English"—"Yenghis." The word "doodle" was a derisive term meaning "dope, half-wit, a fool."

YANKEE DOODLE

2. There was Captain Washington
   Upon a slapping stallion
   A-giving orders to his men
   There must have been a million

Chorus:

3. Then I saw a swamping gun
   As large as logs of maple
   Upon a very little cart
   A load for father's cattle

Chorus:

4. Ev'ry time they shot it off
   It took a horn of powder
   And made a noise like father's gun
   Only a nation louder

Chorus:

5. There I saw a wooden keg
   With heads made out of leather
   They knocked upon it with some sticks
   To call the folks together

Chorus:

6. Then they'd fife away like fun
   And play on cornstalk fiddles
   And some had ribbons red as blood
   All bound around their middles

Chorus:

7. Troopers too would gallop up
   And shoot right in our faces
   It scared me almost half to death
   To see them run such races

Chorus:

8. I can't tell you all I saw
   They kept up such a smother
   I took my hat off, made a bow
   And scampered home to mother

Chorus:

THE RIDDLE
(I Gave My Love A Cherry)
1785

ALTHOUGH THIS SONG ENJOYED A RECENT REVIVAL THROUGH OUR GREAT FOLK SINGERS, IT IS A VERY old ballad indeed. It seems to have originated in the rural areas of Britain. The lyric is based on four of the riddles in the ancient ballad "Captain Wedderburn's (or Walker's) Courtship."

This song was brought to our country around the middle of the eighteenth century and for a number of years was known only to the Kentucky mountaineers who followed Daniel Boone westward. However, during America's great expansion period many of these mountaineers migrated further westward, exposing countless others to the beauty, simplicity and charm of the song. And even before our War of 1812 it had already become known over a wide area of the United States.

While pioneer children enjoyed all kinds of games and riddles to pass the time away on their long trek to the West, this was a riddle they could sing, and thus it became one of their favorites. Their hardy parents too could be heard singing this song whether building a homestead, on the move in covered wagons, fording a river, or climbing the mountain. "They sang it in the beating sun, they sang it in the rain, they sang it on the broad prairie, and over rough terrain." With the recent revival of this song (since World War II) there is now hardly a person who has not heard it at least once.

THE RIDDLE

2. How can there be a cherry that has no stone?
   How can there be a chicken that has no bone?
   How can there be a ring that has no end?
   How can there be a baby with no cryin'?

3. A cherry when it's bloomin' it has no stone
   A chicken in an eggshell it has no bone
   A ring when it is rollin' it has no end
   A baby when it's sleepin' has no cryin'

OH DEAR, WHAT CAN THE MATTER BE?
1795

WHILE THIS SONG HAS BEEN POPULAR HERE FOR OVER 250 YEARS IT IS REALLY ENGLISH. ALTHOUGH its origin is obscure, it is known to have achieved wide distinction in England around 1792 through duet performances at the fashionable Harrison concerts. Within a couple of years the song made its way to this country along with the many waves of immigration shortly after the American Revolution. During the early nineties it was frequently performed in theatres of New York and Philadelphia and became quite popular before our country was ten years old. This charming song has some special appeal for Americans everywhere since its fame has steadily increased during the past 165 years or so.

OH DEAR, WHAT CAN THE MATTER BE?

Fairly bright

1. Oh dear, what can the mat - ter be?

Dear, dear, what can the mat - ter be?

Oh dear, what can the mat - ter be?

John - ny's so long at the fair _____ He

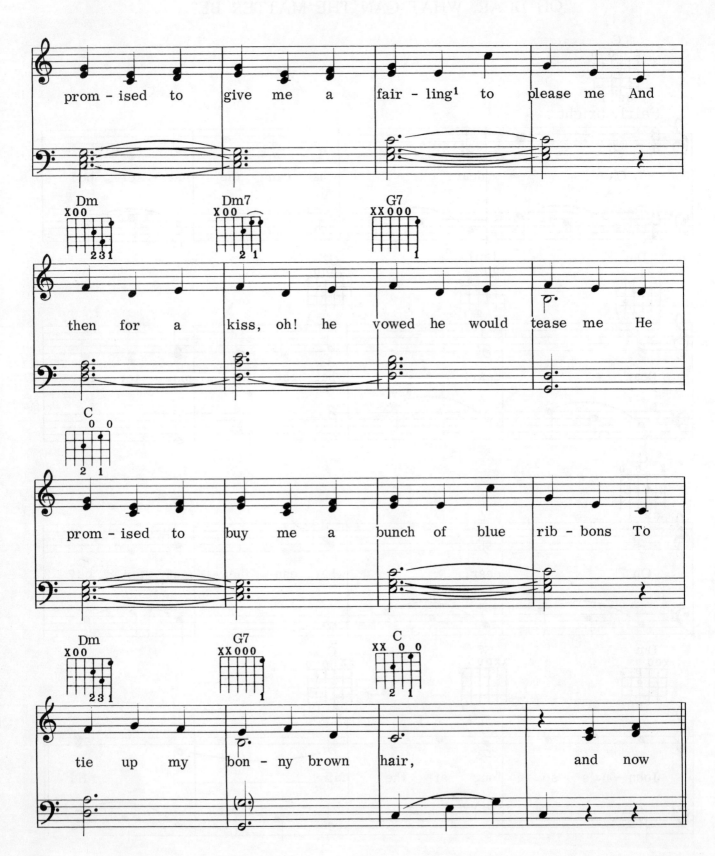

1. "FAIRLING" means a gift from the fair.

2. Oh dear, what can the matter be?
   Dear, dear, what can the matter be?
   Oh dear, what can the matter be?
   Johnny's so long at the fair

   He promised he'd buy me a basket of posies
   A garland of lilies, a garland of roses;
   A little straw hat to set off the blue ribbons
   That tie up my bonny brown hair, and now

   Oh dear, what can the matter be?
   Dear, dear, what can the matter be?
   Oh dear, what can the matter be?
   Johnny's so long at the fair

HAIL COLUMBIA
1798

THIS SONG WAS BORN NINE YEARS AFTER OUR COUNTRY BECAME A SOVEREIGN NATION. IT WAS JUST after John Adams completed his first term of the presidency in Philadelphia that there was hot political unrest here. France and England were at war against each other and great pressures were put upon our new government by French and English partisans both in and out of government. This situation was further aggravated in the spring of 1798 when Congress passed the Alien and Sedition Act.

About the time party strife reached its high tension point, Gilbert Fox, an eminent singer, was scheduled to give a benefit performance. He needed new material but his search was in vain. In despair he visited his lawyer friend, Joseph Hopkinson, and explained that since twenty boxes at the theatre were still unsold the performance would be a failure unless he could get a new and stirring patriotic song adapted to "The President's March," a popular march composed (by Philip Fayles) and played for George Washington's first inauguration in New York, 1789. Hopkinson promised to do what he could.

Joseph Hopkinson firmly believed that loyalty to our new nation should be held above the passions and interests of partisan groups, and in light of the political turmoil he worked on a lyric designed to arouse the American spirit. He delivered his song to Fox the following afternoon. Advertisements were placed in Philadelphia newspapers and on performance night (April 25) the theatre was packed. In the audience were President John Adams and his entire cabinet. After several songs Gilbert Fox was ready for the main feature, the well publicized "Hail Columbia." He began singing it to the accompaniment of a chorus and brass band. As he continued his audience became more and more deeply involved as the song triggered the spirit of American independence and patriotism. When Fox reached the final note his audience burst forth with acclamation. Encore after encore was demanded as the enthusiasm continued to mount, and by the seventh encore the entire audience rose and joined Gilbert Fox in singing the chorus.

Performances were extended and night after night "Hail Columbia" met with the same kind of response. News of this song spread quite rapidly in those days of slow transportation and communication. Within one week the song was performed in New York City. People were heard singing it in the streets during public assemblies, and in a short time "Hail Columbia" reached every part of our young country. For the next twenty or thirty years this song was performed at flag-lowering ceremonies on American ships. When Major R. Anderson first raised the American flag over Ft. Sumter the band played "Hail Columbia" to the accompaniment of loud cheers from all hands present. Even today, this song stirs the hearts of singing Americans everywhere.

HAIL COLUMBIA

2. Immortal patriots, rise once more
   Defend your rights, defend your shore
   Let no rude foe with impious hand
   Let no rude foe with impious hand
   Invade the shrine where sacred lies,
   Of toil and blood, the well-earned prize
   While off'ring peace, sincere and just
   In heav'n we place a manly trust
   That truth and justice may prevail
   And ev'ry scheme of bondage fail

Chorus:

3. Sound, sound the trump of fame
   Let Washington's great name
   Ring through the world with loud applause
   Ring through the world with loud applause
   Let ev'ry chime to freedom dear
   Listen with a joyful ear
   With equal skill, with steady pow'r
   He governs in the fearful hour
   Of horrid war, or guides with ease
   The happier time of honest peace

Chorus:

4. Behold the chief who now commands
   Once more to serve his country stands
   The rock on which the storm will beat
   The rock on which the storm will beat
   But armed in virtue, firm and true
   His hopes are fixed on heav'n and you
   When hope was sinking in dismay
   When gloom obscured Columbia's day
   His steady mind, from changes free
   Resolved on death or liberty

Chorus:

48

AULD LANG SYNE
1799

"AULD LANG SYNE" IS ONE OF AMERICA'S THREE TOP SONGS OF ALL TIME (THE OTHER TWO ARE "Happy Birthday" and "For He's A Jolly Good Fellow") and will probably remain forever our most popular convivial song. The melody is built on what is called the pentatonic scale (only five notes) and can be played on the piano using only the five black keys.

This is a very ancient Scottish folk song. Its earliest beginnings trace back to Britain's King Charles (Stuart) I, who reigned from 1625 until his execution in 1649, at which time the expression "auld lang syne" was popular. From then on there appeared several poems using this expression, some coupled with "should auld acquaintance be forgot." Certain of these verses were set to music and at least one of them was published the latter part of the seventeenth century. None of these songs survived, however, except the one version which began, "Should old acquaintance be forgot and never thocht upon" and ended "On old long syne." This seems to have been the version that was changed over the years and improved upon until it developed into the first verse of our present-day song.

Around 1793 or so the Scotch poet Robert Burns wrote verses 2 and 3, and his friend George Thomson set it to the melody of an old Scottish Lowland tune that was used for "I Fee'd (Hired) A Lad At Michaelmas," "The Miller's Wedding," and also "The Miller's Daughter." This is the "Auld Lang Syne" of today.

During the 1790's America was undergoing mass immigration from the British Isles, and it was during these cradle days of America that "Auld Lang Syne" entered our country, achieved almost immediate popularity, and became a part of our country's singing life.

Besides being the theme song of New Year's Eve, this song is widely used at reunions, partings, graduations, and other types of sentimental celebrations. Until about 1900 this was the melody of Princeton University's alma mater "Old Nassau," and was also used for Vassar's "The Rose and Silver Gray." There have been many many parodies for political and other purposes, but the original is certainly the most enduring.

AULD LANG SYNE

1. Auld Lang Syne = for old time's sake

2. We twä [2] hāe [3] run about the brāes [4]
   And pū'd [5] the gowans [6] fine
   We've wandered mŏny [7] a weary foot
   Sĭn' [8] Auld Lang Syne

Chorus:

3. We twä hāe pāi-dled [9] ĭ' [10] the bûrn [11]
   From morning sun till dīne [12]
   But seas between us brāid [13] hāe roared
   Sĭn' Auld Lang Syne

Chorus:

4. And there's a hand, my trust fiere [14]
   And gīe's [15] a hand of thine
   We'll tăk [16] a right guide-willie [17] waught [18]
   For Auld Lang Syne

Chorus:

5. And surely ye'll be your pint-stowp [19]
   And surely I'll be mine
   We'll take a cup of kindness yet
   For Auld Lang Syne

Chorus:

2. Twä = two
3. Hāe = have
4. Brāes = hillsides
5. Pū'd = pulled
6. Gowans = daisies
7. Mŏny = many
8. Sĭn' = since
9. Pāidl'd = waded
10. Ĭ' = in
11. Bûrn = a small river
12. Dīne = dinner, noontime
13. Brāid = broad
14. Fiere (Fēr) = close friend, brother
15. Gīes = give us (me)
16. Tăk = take
17. Guide-willie (Gĭd-wĭllē) = good-will
18. Waught (Wâkt) = draft, a drink
19. Pīnt-stoōp = a container holding a bit over 3 pints

BILLY BOY
1800

THIS IS A FOLK SONG OF OUR SOUTHERN MOUNTAINEERS. WHILE THE MELODY PROBABLY ORIGINATED
somewhere in the British Isles centuries ago, the lyric idea and pattern seem based on the
old English ballad "Lord Randall." There is good reason to believe that this song made its
first American appearance in New England right after the Revolution through the many
immigrants pouring in from the British Isles.

As the East became fairly well settled, many of the Irish, Scots, and English began
moving south and westward. A great number of these migrants decided not to go beyond
the Appalachians and made their homes in the Blue Ridge chain, quite shut in by the mountains. This is the area in which the song became firmly established. It was widely sung by
these mountain people, and it was not until after the Louisiana Purchase (1803) that some
of them began migrating again—this time westward. Their songs went with them, and it
wasn't long before the pioneers all along the Ohio River were singing this song and even
adding their own versions. They in turn spread its popularity to all points west.

Today there are many versions of this song, and many parodies too. It has even been
used as a sea chantey, with several off-color verses.

52

BILLY BOY

2. Did she ask you to come in, Billy Boy, Billy Boy?
   Did she ask you to come in, charming Billy?
   Yes she asked me to come in, with a dimple in her chin
   She's a young thing and cannot leave her mother

3. Did she set for you a chair, Billy Boy, Billy Boy?
   Did she set for you a chair, charming Billy?
   Yes she set for me a chair, she has ringlets in her hair
   She's a young thing and cannot leave her mother

4. Can she bake a cherry pie, Billy Boy, Billy Boy?
   Can she bake a cherry pie, charming Billy?
   She can bake a cherry pie, quick's a cat can wink an eye
   She's a young thing and cannot leave her mother

5. Can she make a feather bed, Billy Boy, Billy Boy?
   Can she make a feather bed, charming Billy?
   She can make a feather bed, put the pillows at the head
   She's a young thing and cannot leave her mother

6. Just how old can she be, Billy Boy, Billy Boy?
   Just how old can she be, charming Billy?
   Three times six or four times sev'n, two times twenty and elev'n
   She's a young thing and cannot leave her mother

THE WAYFARING STRANGER
1807

ORIGINALLY THIS WAS A DEEPLY MEANINGFUL RELIGIOUS SONG, BORN IN THE SOUTHERN APPALACH-ian Mountains about the time of the American Revolution. The freedom-loving mountaineers of this region, chiefly of English, Scottish, Irish and Welsh stock, endured enormous hardships in their determination to build homes and protect their loved ones. Day by day they fought the wilderness, poor equipment, the soil and weather, Indians, wild animals, rugged terrain, and most of all the loneliness deep inside of them, longing for some reward for their hard labors, in this world or in the next. Many of their songs expressed the pain of their daily lives and their hopes and dreams of a beautiful hereafter. This song is a good example. Woodrow Wilson once said "In these mountains is the original stuff of which America was made."

These early Americans, leaning on their faith to sustain them in adversities, joined together occasionally for religious revival meetings, and "The Wayfaring Stranger" was one of their favorite spirituals. After the American Revolution some of these people began leaving their mountain homes as they headed westward, joining with other pioneers who had experienced the same kinds of hardships. Thus even before our War of 1812 this song had already become quite widely known among these Americans westward bound. Of recent years, since World War II, "The Wayfaring Stranger" has been revived by our very fine folk singers.

THE WAYFARING STRANGER

2. My father lived and died a farmer
   A-reapin' less than he did sow
   And now I follow in his footsteps
   A-knowin' less than he did know

   I'm goin' there to see my father
   I'm goin' there, no more to roam
   I'm just a-goin' over Jordan
   I'm just a-goin' over home

3. I know dark clouds will gather 'round me
   My way is steep and rough, I know
   But fertile fields lie just before me
   In that fair land to which I go

   I'm goin' there to see my brother
   I'm goin' there, no more to roam
   I'm just a-goin' over Jordan
   I'm just a-goin' over home

BELIEVE ME, IF ALL THOSE ENDEARING YOUNG CHARMS
1810

IN THIS SONG THE MUSIC CAME FIRST WITH THE WORDS FOLLOWING PERHAPS ONE HUNDRED YEARS later. Either the melody was brought from England to Ireland where it underwent certain changes or, as some authorities believe, it originated in Ireland. Whichever the case may be, it bore the title "My Lodging Is In the Cold Ground" and was probably sung a good many years before its publication. Its first printing seems to have been in a 1737 London ballad opera the year George Washington was a little boy of five. Since printing techniques were fairly crude and transportation difficult in those days, the song's popularity spread very slowly, although surely, through Ireland and England. Scotland soon had its own version entitled "I Lo'ed Ne'er A Laddie But Ane."

The great Irish poet Thomas Moore knew and loved this melody which he considered as Irish as the shamrock. At the time of our Louisiana Purchase (1803) Moore was a government official in Bermuda but returned a year later (by way of the United States) to England and then Ireland. Here he began formulating a collection of Irish melodies. To the melody of "My Lodging Is On the Cold Ground" he composed the beautiful lyrics of "Believe Me If All Those Endearing Young Charms," which was first published in London 1808. Moore's new version reached America almost immediately and seems to have become a hit in all eighteen states between the time James Madison took office (1809) and the War of 1812.

During the year Sam Houston, Davy Crockett and Jim Bowie fought the battles of the Alamo, this melody received another brand new set of lyrics in celebration of Harvard University's Jubilee (1836). It became Harvard's song with the title "Fair Harvard."

BELIEVE ME, IF ALL THOSE ENDEARING YOUNG CHARMS

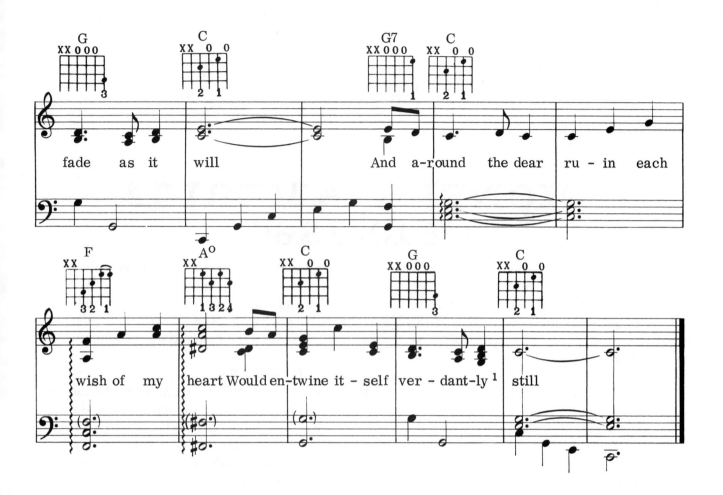

fade as it will And a-round the dear ru-in each

wish of my heart Would en-twine it-self ver-dant-ly[1] still

2. It is not that while beauty and youth are thine own
   And thy cheeks unprofaned by a tear
   That the fervor and faith of a soul can be known
   To which time will but make thee more dear
      No, the heart that has truly loved never forgets
      But as truly lives on to the close
   As the sunflower turns on her God when he sets
   The same look which she turned when he rose

1. With green vegetation

PIONEER AMERICA (1810-1860)

DURING THIS FIFTY-YEAR SPAN AMERICA MOVED FORWARD IN GIANT STRIDES WITH THE SPRING AND resilience of an adolescent. Our physical size doubled and our population quadrupled. We gained greater sophistication politically, intellectually, and commercially. Despite our growing internal problems we managed to become more cohesive as a sovereign nation. Popular music went hand in hand with these developments since it was so closely woven into our daily lives.

In 1811 the first steamboat saw service on the Mississippi River where many a river-traveling planter, trader, gambler and pretty woman transported Southern songs to the North and East. The number of musically literate people increased so rapidly that the piano industry came into being with Chickering (1823) and Steinway (1853), an important factor in the founding of music stories in our cities. While we still imported songs we also sang many of our own, which gave rise to the music publishing industry. Several songsters were published, one of the more popular ones being *The Missouri Songster,* frequently sung from by Abraham Lincoln and Ann Rutledge.

During this historical period important contributions to American popular music were made by many composers amongst whom were Septimus Winner,[1] Henry Russell,[2] and Lowell Mason.[3] Such music was circulated throughout our cities and frontier towns largely by traveling entertainers. The more cultural type of music was disseminated by singing families such as the Hutchinsons,[4] the Bakers, the Cheney family, and the Rainer family.[5] Popular music was generally given to the public by singers and minstrels.

Black-faced minstrel shows were an important part of America's entertainment and singing life. This form of amusement was begun in 1828 by Daddy Rice (Thomas D. Rice) who performed as a single actor. The first black-faced minstrel-show group was born in the depression of 1842 when Dan Emmett[6] combined his talent with that of three other actors. Their first performance as the Virginia Minstrels was at the Chatham Square Theatre in New York City on February 17, 1843. This group immediately became a theatrical sensa-

[1] Composer of "Whispering Hope" and "Where Has My Little Dog Gone."
[2] Composer of "Life On the Ocean Wave" and "Woodman Spare That Tree."
[3] Composer of "America" and "Nearer My God To Thee."
[4] Hutchinson, Minnesota, was named after this family.
[5] They did much toward popularizing "Silent Night."
[6] Composer of "Dixie."

tion and was followed by many imitators. One of the imitators was Ed Christy[7] who organized the greatest of all minstrel shows in 1846. It was Ed Christy who developed the organized pattern for minstrel shows which was to be followed for the next sixty years.

Minstrel shows varied in size from four to almost any number. The performers blackened their faces with burnt cork, wore colorful striped shirts, light pantaloons, swallowtail jackets, and white gloves. They seated themselves either in a straight line or more often in a semicircle. The two end men were known as Mr. Tambo (he played the tambourine) and Mr. Bones (he played the bones), both of whom generally told the jokes. The middle man was Mr. Interlocutor, a sort of M. C. who ran the show. The performance consisted of singing and dancing, amusing patter, playing instruments, and telling jokes. Minstrel shows traveled all over the land bringing wide popularity to many a song in their repertory.

One of the greatest events of the whole era came about quite by accident in California. Early in 1848 as a Captain Sutter was building a mill in the Sacramento Valley he became curious about the odd "stones" he found in the water. A San Francisco mining prospector, identifying them as pure gold, swiftly took off for Sutter's Mill. Within weeks Sutter struck a rich gold deposit. The news spread like lightning. By May of 1848 Sacramento was swarming with over two thousand rugged prospectors. In September the *Baltimore Sun* reported the gold discoveries with other newspapers following suit. People all over the country buzzed with excitement. There followed in 1849 the greatest migration in American history. Thousands of people rushed to California in covered wagons, buggies, horseback, in ships around Cape Horn, and even on foot. All brought their songs with them and all sang throughout torturous months of incredible hardships. The intermingling of songs among the many different groups helped lighten their daily burdens a little, and in the process they learned more songs. Within a year California had over 100,000 hopeful prospectors, and for good reason too, since more than $60,000,000 worth of gold was uncovered by 1853.

Toward the end of the 1850's the antislavery issue was becoming increasingly acute. As the political atmosphere grew more threatening America's singing was reduced a little—but only a little.

TERRITORIAL ACQUISITIONS

A.	Louisiana Purchase	1803	United States (Thomas Jefferson) bought from France (Napoleon Bonaparte) 828,000 sq. miles for $15,000,000—or less than 3 cents per acre.
B.	Florida	1819	Acquired from Spain by treaty.
C.	Texas	1845	Annexed by request.
D.	Territory of Oregon	1846	Acquired from Great Britain by treaty.
E.	Mexico's Cession	1848	Acquired through peace terms of the Mexican War.
F.	The Gadsden Purchase	1853	General Gadsden purchased 29,644 sq. miles from Mexico, in behalf of the United States, for $10,000,000—or just under 53 cents per acre.

[7] Stephen Foster wrote many of his songs for Christy's minstrels.

STATES ADMITTED TO THE UNION

Rank	Name	Origin of Name	Year Admitted	State Song
18.	Louisiana	Named after France's King Louis XIV	1812	Song of Louisiana
19.	Indiana	Land of the Indians	1816	On the Banks of the Wabash
20.	Mississippi	From the Indian "misi" (big) and "sipi" (river).	1817	Way Down South In Mississippi
21.	Illinois	Combination of French and Indian words meaning "Land of the Illini" (Land of men, or warriors).	1818	Illinois
22.	Alabama	Indian derivative meaning "I make a clearing" or "tribal town."	1819	Alabama
23.	Maine	From the ancient French province Mayne.	1820	State of Maine Song
24.	Missouri	Algonquin Indian word for "Land of big canoes."	1821	Missouri Waltz
25.	Arkansas	French prefix added to "Kansas," a Sioux Indian word meaning "South wind people."	1836	The Arkansas Traveler
26.	Michigan	Algonquin Indian word for "Great lake."	1837	Michigan, My Michigan
27.	Florida	Spanish word for "feast of flowers."	1845	Suwannee River
28.	Texas	Indian word meaning "friends."	1845	Texas, Our Texas
29.	Iowa	Indian word for "sleepy people."	1846	Song of Iowa
30.	Wisconsin	From the Algonquin Indian word "wishkonsing" meaning "place of the beaver or muskrat hole."	1850	On Wisconsin
31.	California	From a mythical island mentioned in 1510 Spanish book by Garcia Ordonez de Montalvo.	1850	I Love You California
32.	Minnesota	From a Dakota–Sioux Indian word meaning "sky-tinted cloudy water."	1858	Hail Minnesota
33.	Oregon	From the Indian name "Ourigan" given to the Oregon River.	1859	Oregon, My Oregon

THE BLUE BELL OF SCOTLAND
1815

THIS SONG DATES BACK TO THE YEAR 1799. NO ONE SEEMS TO KNOW WHERE THE MELODY CAME from although it is thought to be an old Scotch or English tune. Mrs. James Grant (née Annie McVicar) originally wrote the lyrics in honor of the departure of the Marquis of Huntly's Scottish troops for Europe in 1799, the year George Washington died. Mrs. Grant had entitled the song "The Bells of Scotland."

Almost immediately an Irish actress–singer, Mrs. Dorothy Jordan, modified the lyrics, changed the title to the present one, and introduced it to the public for the first time at the famous Theatre Royal, Drury Lane, London, 1800. From that time on the song rose to great heights of popularity and quite rapidly spread to young America, where it was published in Baltimore in that same year. Through theatre performances and publications in the cities of our growing country, this song became well known to the public by 1820, and has since sustained a steady popularity.

THE BLUE BELL OF SCOTLAND

2. Oh where, please tell me where does your highland laddie dwell?
   Oh where, please tell me where does your highland laddie dwell?
   He dwells in merry Scotland at the sign of the blue bell
   And my blessing went with him on the day he went away

3. Oh what, please tell me what does your highland laddie wear?
   Oh what, please tell me what does your highland laddie wear?
   A bonnet with a proud plume, 'tis the gallant badge of war
   And a plaid 'cross his bold breast that will one day wear a star

4. Suppose, oh supposing that your highland lad should die
   Suppose, oh supposing that your highland lad should die
   The bagpipes shall play o'er him and I'd lay me down and cry
   But it's oh! in my heart that I do wish he may not die

ALL THROUGH THE NIGHT
1825

THIS OLD MELODY IS A TRULY GENUINE AND DISTINCTIVE WELSH FOLK SONG. ITS FIRST APPEARANCE in print was in 1784 (just after the American Revolution) in a collection entitled *Musical and Poetical Relicks of the Welsh Bards*. The composer is unknown. The first set of lyrics to embrace this melody was probably written by the English authoress Amelia Opie on the subject of "Poor Mary Ann," and published together with five other Welsh songs around 1800.

Just how and when this song reached America and in what area is still a mystery. But we do know this song gained some fairly good popularity here around 1825, when John Quincy Adams became President of the twenty-four United States.

Many decades later Opie's lyrics were replaced by the English lyricist, Harold Boulton, those of "All Through The Night" instead of "Poor Mary Ann." Boulton's words are the lyrics sung today. The subject of Boulton's lyrics and his beauty of expression, coupled with the peaceful plaintiveness of the melody, have made this song one of the standards for singing groups and concert soloists. Thus its popularity has grown very slowly but quite steadily, and it is today a symbol of beauty and of the song-loving Welsh people.

ALL THROUGH THE NIGHT

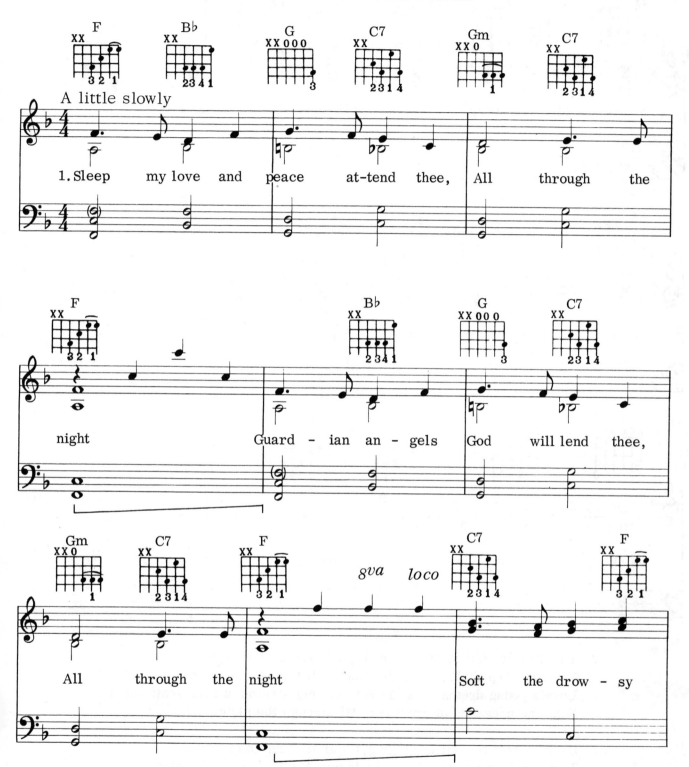

A little slowly

1. Sleep my love and peace at-tend thee, All through the

night Guard - ian an - gels God will lend thee,

All through the night Soft the drow - sy

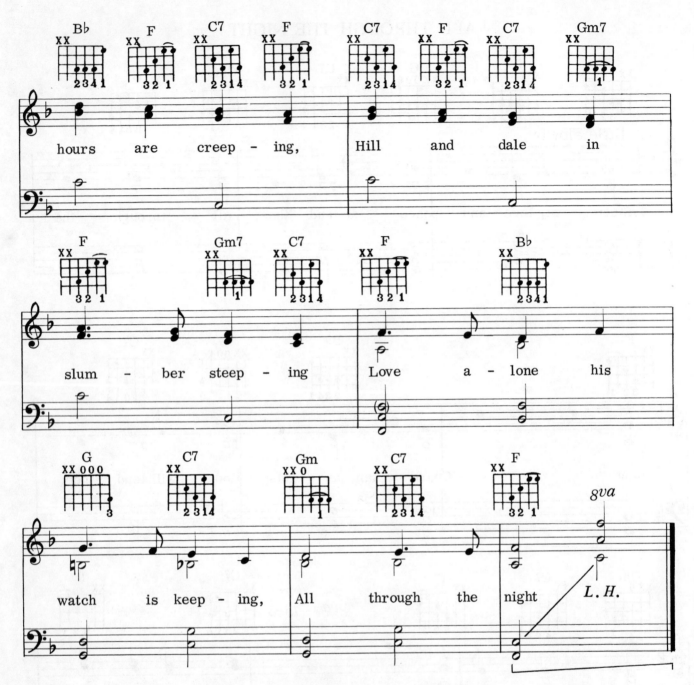

2. Though I roam a minstrel lonely, All through the night
   My true harp shall praise thee only, All through the night
   Love's young dream alas is over, Yet my strains of love shall hover
   Near the presence of my lover, All through the night

3. Hark! a solemn bell is ringing, Clear through the night
   Thou my love are heav'nward winging, Home through the night
   Earthly dust from off thee shaken, Soul immortal thou shalt waken
   With thy last dim journey taken, Home through the night

CHARLIE IS MY DARLING
1830

THE "CHARLIE" REFERRED TO IN THIS SONG WAS THE ENGLISH PRINCE CHARLES EDWARD, WHO WAS also known as the "Young Chevalier." In 1745, when New England colonists helped the British capture Louisburg (Nova Scotia) from the French, Prince Charles attempted to restore the Stuart monarchy to the throne of England. He left France and went to Scotland, where he had many sympathizers (Jacobites), to form an invasion force.

The daughter of one of his most fervent admirers was a Baroness Carolina Nairne. Among her most cherished possessions were a lock of Charles' hair, his spurs, and other keepsakes. It was Baroness Nairne (of Perthshire, Scotland) who wrote the lyrics of this song (about 1820) in his memory, describing the sentiment of the Scottish people who watched with great hope as he prepared for his ill-fated invasion (1745) through Northern England. This song had a magnetic effect on the common folk who took it to their hearts and treated it as a folk song. Almost immediately the song was transported to the shores of young America where it developed a growing popularity, chiefly in the cities.

CHARLIE IS MY DARLING

Charlie is my dar - ling, my dar - ling, my dar - ling
Charlie is my dar - ling, the young chev - a - lier

2. Charlie is my darling, my darling, my darling
   Charlie is my darling, the young chevalier
   As he came marching up the street the pipes played loud and clear
   And all the folks came running out to meet our chevalier
   Charlie is my darling, my darling, my darling
   Charlie is my darling, the young chevalier

3. Charlie is my darling, my darling, my darling
   Charlie is my darling, the young chevalier
   With highland bonnets on their heads and claymores [1] bright and clear
   They came to fight for Scotland's right and our young chevalier
   Charlie is my darling, my darling, my darling
   Charlie is my darling, the young chevalier

1. "Claymores" are large double-edge swords used by the Scottish Highlanders.
They were often held with both hands.

4. Charlie is my darling, my darling, my darling
   Charlie is my darling, the young chevalier
   They've left their bonnie highland hills, their wives and bairnies[2] dear
   To draw the sword for Scotland's lord, who's our young chevalier
   Charlie is my darling, my darling, my darling
   Charlie is my darling, the young chevalier

5. Charlie is my darling, my darling, my darling
   Charlie is my darling, the young chevalier
   Oh there were many beating hearts and many hopes and fears
   And many were the pray'rs put up for our young chevalier
   Charlie is my darling, my darling, my darling
   Charlie is my darling, the young chevalier

2. "Bairnies" means "children".

74

SKIP TO MY LOU [1]
1832

THIS IS ONE OF THE CELEBRATED FOLK SONGS OF ALL TIME HERE IN AMERICA, ALTHOUGH NO ONE seems to know anything of its origin. It has been continually popular with our people since the early nineteenth century, and was featured in the 1944 Hollywood movie *Meet Me In St. Louis.* This folk song was well used by our frontiersmen settling down in their homesteads and those still traveling westward over covered wagon trails. It was sung by bear hunters, Indian fighters, wild cowboys and miners on their night off.

"Skip to My Lou" was quite a favorite song with the teenage children of our American pioneers. In those days the young people were faced with strong religious taboos against dancing, holding a girl by the waist, and lovemaking, which resulted in their inventing the "play-party," an innocent type of game-with-song which entailed a minimum of physical contact between boy and girl. Thus they gained the approval of their elders.

The play-party generally took the form of couples holding hands in a large ring, and they sang as they skipped around and around in rhythm. One boy was left in the center of the ring seeking to "steal" (choose) a partner.

Some of the nonplaying young folks joined in with their elders in singing, clapping hands in rhythm, and stamping the floor with the heel of their heavy boots. Although musical instruments were not permitted, this did make quite a lively scene and was thoroughly enjoyed by all. This song was perhaps the best play-party song, an "icebreaker" for such an inhibited and restricted group of people.

[1] The word "Lou" means "sweetheart" in the South, and "Loo" is the Scottish word for "love."

SKIP TO MY LOU

With a lilt

Lost my part - ner, what - 'll I do

Lost my part - ner, what - 'll I do   Lost my part - ner,

what - 'll I do   Skip to my lou, my dar - ling

2. I'll get 'nother one, pretty one too
   I'll get 'nother one, pretty one too
   I'll get 'nother one, pretty one too
   Skip to my lou, my darling

3. Can't get a red bird, jay bird'll do
   Can't get a red bird, jay bird'll do
   Can't get a red bird, jay bird'll do
   Skip to my lou, my darling

4. Lou lou, skip skip skip
   Lou lou, skip skip skip
   Lou lou, skip skip skip
   Skip to my lou, my darling

5. Flies in the buttermilk, shoo shoo shoo
   Flies in the buttermilk, shoo shoo shoo
   Flies in the buttermilk, shoo shoo shoo
   Skip to my lou, my darling

6. Gone again, what'll I do
   Gone again, what'll I do
   Gone again, what'll I do
   Skip to my lou, my darling

7. I'll get a partner better than you
   I'll get a partner better than you
   I'll get a partner better than you
   Skip to my lou, my darling

8. Can't get a blue bird, black bird'll do
   Can't get a blue bird, black bird'll do
   Can't get a blue bird, black bird'll do
   Skip to my lou, my darling

9. I got another one, skip skip skip
   I got another one, skip skip skip
   I got another one, skip skip skip
   Skip to my lou, my darling

10. Flies in the sugar bowl, shoo fly shoo
    Flies in the sugar bowl, shoo fly shoo
    Flies in the sugar bowl, shoo fly shoo
    Skip to my lou, my darling

11. Cat's in the cream jar, ooh ooh ooh
    Cat's in the cream jar, ooh ooh ooh
    Cat's in the cream jar, ooh ooh ooh
    Skip to my lou, my darling

12. Off to Texas, two by two
    Off to Texas, two by two
    Off to Texas, two by two
    Skip to my lou, my darling

DOWN IN THE VALLEY
1835

THIS, ONE OF OUR NATION'S FINEST HILLBILLY SONGS, MAY HAVE ORIGINATED CENTURIES AGO IN THE British Isles. But the version we know today was born in our Southern mountains and was developed by the Kentucky mountaineers—most of whom were English, Scotch, and Irish—about the time of the Louisiana Purchase in 1803. Later on it was widely sung by the followers of Daniel Boone as they made their hazardous journey westward over the highlands of Tennessee and Kentucky into the Ozarks of Arkansas and Missouri. Enroute this song was quickly picked up by other families migrating north and west, and it became quite well known during this period. It was taught by rote (in true folk-song tradition) from generation to generation and Americans everywhere loved it every step of the way.

So widely popular has this song become that Kurt Weill wrote an American folk opera bearing its title, with music based on this song. During the 1950's it broke out into great popularity all over again when it appeared in the 1951 movie *Along the Great Divide* and again in the 1952 movies *The Last Musketeer* and *Montana Territory*.

There have been many different versions of this song, and in certain regions it is known as "Birmingham Jail," "Barbourville Jail," and "Powder Mill Jail."

78

DOWN IN THE VALLEY

2. Bird in a cage dear, bird in a cage
   Dying for freedom, ever a slave
   Ever a slave dear, ever a slave
   Dying for freedom, ever a slave

3. If you don't love me, love whom you please
   Throw your arms 'round me, give my heart ease
   Give my heart ease dear, give my heart ease
   Throw your arms 'round me, give my heart ease

4. Write me a letter, send it by mail
   Send it in care of Birmingham jail
   Birmingham jail dear, Birmingham jail
   Send it in care of Birmingham jail

5. Writing this letter containing three lines
   Answer my question: "will you be mine?"
   "Will you be mine dear, will you be mine?"
   Answer my question: "will you be mine?"

6. Roses love sunshine, vi'lets love dew
   Angels in heaven know I love you
   Know I love you dear, know I love you
   Angels in heaven know I love you

SHENANDOAH
1837

FEW SEA CHANTEYS ORIGINATED IN THIS COUNTRY SINCE WE WERE A BRAND NEW NATION IN THE days of sailing vessels, but "Shenandoah" is genuinely American. The song seems to have originated in the early nineteenth century as a land ballad in the areas of the Mississippi and Missouri Rivers, with the story of a trader who fell in love with the daughter of the Indian Chief Shenandoah. This enchanting song was taken up by sailors plying these rivers in keel and Mackinaw boats, and thus made its way down the Mississippi to the open ocean. The song had great appeal for American deep-sea sailors, and its rolling melody made it ideal as a capstan chantey, where a group of sailors push the massive capstan bars around and around in order to lift the heavy anchor.

The song reached its first height of popularity perhaps a little before the 1840's, the beginning of the fast clipper ship era that added so much to American growth. The song was traditional with the U.S. Army cavalry who called it "The Wild Mizzourye."

When steamboats replaced the sailing vessels, sailors and landlubbers alike were reluctant to give up this best-of-all chanteys, and so it has remained to this day one of our most beautiful and popular folk songs.

SHENANDOAH

2. Oh Shenandoah, I love your daughter
   Away you rolling river
   I'll take her 'cross that rolling water
   Away, I'm bound away
   'Cross the wide Missouri

3. This white man loves your Indian maiden
   Away you rolling river
   In my canoe with notions laden
   Away, I'm bound away
   'Cross the wide Missouri

4. Farewell, goodbye, I shall not grieve you
   Away you rolling river
   Oh Shenandoah, I'll not deceive you
   Away, we're bound away
   'Cross the wide Missouri

ANNIE LAURIE
1839

THIS OLD SONG SAW ITS FIRST AMERICAN PUBLICATION (1838) DURING RALPH WALDO EMERSON'S time, when music was first taught in public schools (Boston) and when antislavery pressures were becoming increasingly strong. Within one year "Annie Laurie" became nationally popular despite the nationwide economic depression that started with the Panic of 1837.

For many people "Annie Laurie" has come to mean "a soldier's sweetheart," the girl he left behind. But there once was a real Annie Laurie who was much celebrated for her beauty. She was the daughter of Sir Robert Laurie, first baronet of Maxwellton, Scotland, born almost a hundred years before the American Revolution. It is believed the original verses were written by Annie's unlucky suitor, William Douglas of Fingland (Scotland). However, the song as we know it today was written (words and music) by Lady John Douglas Scott of Berwickshire, Scotland.

Lady Scott was a musically gifted person, having composed many other songs, and she was also somewhat of a fanatic in upholding Scottish customs. When she heard that her song "Annie Laurie" was a sensation with the British troops in the Crimean War she was truly amazed. She probably would have been doubly amazed had she known how popular it was to become in America for well over a hundred years.

84

ANNIE LAURIE

1. Max - well - ton's braes[1] are bon - nie Where ear - ly falls the dew And it's there that An - nie Lau - rie Gave me her prom - ise true Gave

1. Braes = hillsides, slopes of a hill.

2. Her brow is like the snowdrift
   Her throat is like the swan
   And her face it is the fairest
   That e'er the sun shone on
   That e'er the sun shone on
   And dark blue is her eye
   And for bonnie Annie Laurie
   I'd lay me doon and dee

3. Like dew on gowans[2] lying
   The fall of her fairy feet
   And like winds in summer sighing
   Her voice is low and sweet
   Her voice is low and sweet
   She's all the world to me
   And for bonnie Annie Laurie
   I'd lay me doon and dee

2. Gowans = daisies

DRINK TO ME ONLY WITH THINE EYES
1840

THIS SONG HAS BEEN KNOWN HERE SINCE THE BIRTH OF OUR COUNTRY. ITS FIRST AMERICAN PUBLI-cation was in the year of George Washington's first election to the Presidency, 1789. Alexander Reinagle brought it out in his *Collection of Favorite Songs*.

The words of this song were originally those of a third-century Greek poet, Philostratus the Athenian, in his *Letters*. Approximately thirteen centuries later England's great dramatist Ben Jonson translated almost literally portions of "Letter 33," addressed it to "Celia," and published it in England in 1616 in a volume of lyrics and epistles of *The Forest*.

The origin of the music is uncertain for lack of proof. It has been credited to a Colonel Mellish as well as to Mozart. The latter seems a slight possibility since Sir Walter Scott also used the very same music for his song entitled "County Guy," and Scott (1771–1832) was a contemporary of Mozart's (1756–1791). But if the music were Mozart's, one wonders how it was combined with Ben Jonson's poem published over 150 years earlier. After its first American publication this song became a favorite concert selection among baritones. Other publications soon followed and within a few decades its popularity grew to sizable proportions, particularly in our American cities.

DRINK TO ME ONLY WITH THINE EYES

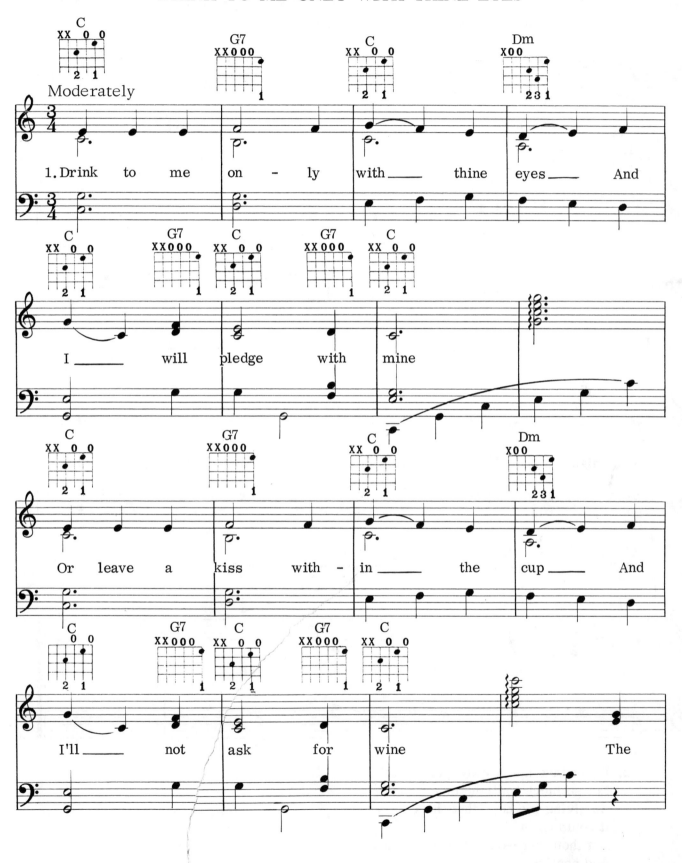

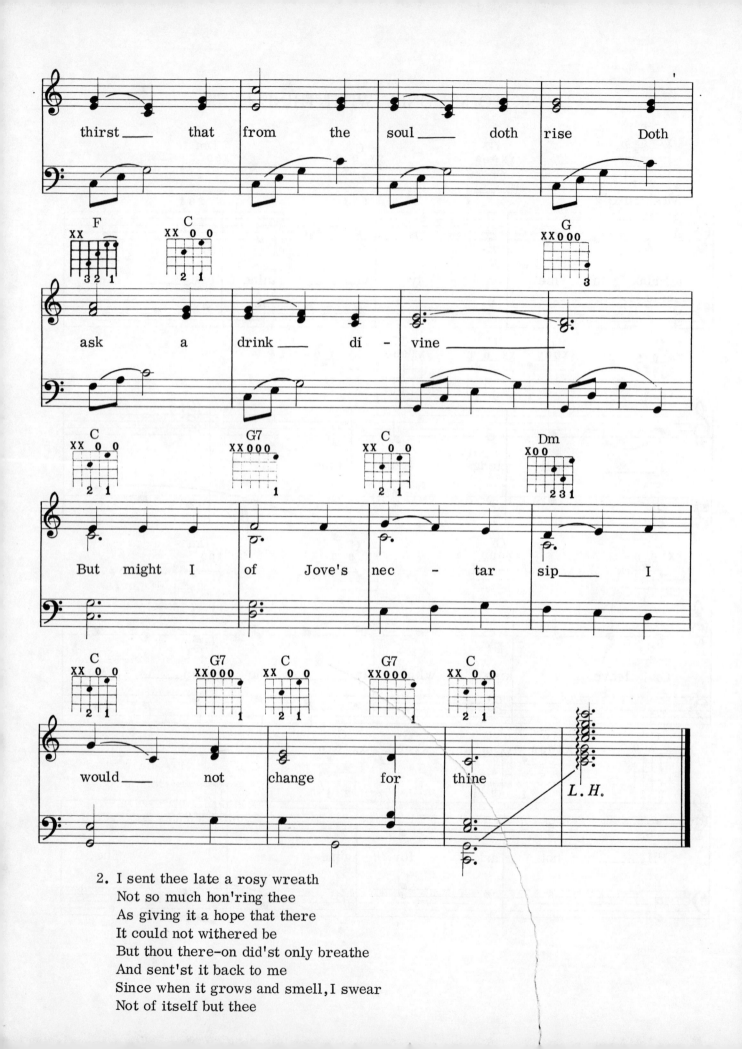

thirst ____ that from the soul ____ doth rise Doth

F C G

ask a drink ____ di - vine ____

C G7 C Dm

But might I of Jove's nec - tar sip ____ I

C G7 C G7 C

would ____ not change for thine

L.H.

2. I sent thee late a rosy wreath
   Not so much hon'ring thee
   As giving it a hope that there
   It could not withered be
   But thou there-on did'st only breathe
   And sent'st it back to me
   Since when it grows and smell, I swear
   Not of itself but thee

ON TOP OF OLD SMOKY
1841

DIRECTLY AFTER THE AMERICAN REVOLUTION MANY THOUSANDS OF IMMIGRANTS POURED INTO THIS country, most of them from the British Isles. As communities began to get "crowded" many of these people felt they had nothing to lose and everything to gain by moving to newer lands and better opportunities. Thus a large number of them migrated southward through Pennsylvania and into the highlands of Kentucky, Tennessee, North Carolina, and Virginia where they became fairly shut in by the mountains. Here they settled down and stayed, and later became known as our mountaineers of the Southern Appalachians. These song-loving people kept many of their old ballads alive, and it was with these English–Scottish–Irish people that "On Top of Old Smoky" came into being. The song, however, does bear certain traces of an old New England song "The Wagoner's Lad." The mountaineers called it a "lonesome tune" and it was one of their favorites. Old Smoky refers to one of the large hazy-looking peaks in the Blue Ridge chain, a few miles from Asheville, North Carolina.

During America's big push to the West (the first half of the nineteenth century) scores of these mountain people packed their belongings and joined the movement. For self protection they mingled with people from other regions of the East, and traveling together they sang their songs. "On Top of Old Smoky," a plaintive and appealing song, caught on very quickly and its popularity fanned out in many directions. It was not long before most everyone on the Southwest Trail knew and loved it, and this song now became firmly established as a nationally popular song.

Today there are a great number of recordings on the market, folk singers love to perform it, the song has appeared in the Gene Autry movie *Valley of Fire*, and with the 1950 revival it once again became one of the leading popular songs in America.

ON TOP OF OLD SMOKY

2. A-courtin's a pleasure
   A-partin' is grief
   A false-hearted lover
   Is worse than a thief

3. A thief he will rob you
   And take what you have
   But a false-hearted lover
   Sends you to your grave

4. They'll hug you and kiss you
   And tell you more lies
   Than the leaves on a willow
   Or the stars in the skies

5. My sad heart is aching
   I'm weary today
   My lover has left me
   I'm a-feelin' this way

6. It's rainin', it's pourin'
   The moon gives no light
   My horse he won't travel
   This dark lonesome night

7. I'm goin' away, dear
   I'll write you my mind
   My mind is to marry
   And to leave you behind

8. Come all you young people
   And listen to me
   Don't place your affection
   On a green willow tree

9. The leaves they will wither
   The roots they will die
   You will be forsaken
   And never know why

10. Same as 1.

FLOW GENTLY SWEET AFTON
1842

THE WORDS OF THIS SONG CAME FIRST, AND WERE WRITTEN ABOUT FIVE YEARS AFTER THE AMERican Revolution by Scotland's great poet, Robert Burns. Burns wrote the poem and set it to the music of an old Scottish tune in honor of Mrs. Dugald Stewart, wife of the Scottish philosopher. Mrs. Stewart was the first aristocrat to recognize his talent and she encouraged him in his work. Robert Burns wrote this song inspired by Lady Stewart's home in Afton Lodge on the banks of Afton River in Ayrshire, Scotland. The Mary in the lyric is said to have been the object of Burns' unsuccessful romance. The song was entitled "Afton Water."

About half a century later, the year steam navigation across the Atlantic was established, a Philadelphian, James Spilman, gave this beautiful poem an improved musical setting and the work was first published in 1838. Within the next four years or so the song achieved considerable popularity, and with subsequent publications this popularity has been sustained to the present day.

94

FLOW GENTLY SWEET AFTON

1. Braes = Slopes or hillsides, as in a river bank, a hill, or a valley.

stock-dove [2] whose ech-o re-sounds from the glen Ye

wild whist-ling black-birds in yon thorn-y den Thou

green-crest-ed lap-wing [3], thy scream-ing for-bear I

charge you, dis-turb not my slum-ber-ing fair

2. Stock-dove = A European wild pigeon.
3. Lapwing = A species of bird with a shrill wailing cry.

2. How lofty sweet Afton, thy neighboring hills
   Far marked with the courses of clear winding rills
   There daily I wander as morn rises high
   My flocks [4] and my Mary's sweet cot [5] in my eye

   How pleasant thy banks and green valleys below
   Where wild in the woodlands the primroses blow

   There oft as mild evening creeps over the lea
   The sweet-scented birk [6] shades my Mary and me

3. Thy crystal stream Afton, how lovely it glides
   And winds by the cot [7] where my Mary resides
   How wanton thy waters her snowy feet lave [8]
   As gath'ring sweet flow'rets, she stems thy clear wave

   Flow gently sweet Afton, among thy green braes
   Flow gently sweet river, the theme of my lays [9]

   My Mary's asleep by thy murmuring stream
   Flow gently sweet Afton, disturb not her dream

4. Flocks = locks of hair.
5. Cot = a lock of tangled hair.
6. Birk = Birch tree.
7. Cot = also means cottage.
8. Lave = bathe.
9. Lays = simple lyrics or short narrative poems.

LONG, LONG AGO
1843

THIS WAS THE SMASH SONG HIT OF 1843 WHEN OUR COUNTRY WAS TWENTY-SIX STATES STRONG and Daniel Webster dedicated the Bunker Hill Monument near Boston.

The song was composed in England all of ten years earlier (1833) by the songwriter–dramatist Thomas Haynes Bayly, who also composed other songs including "Gaily the Troubadour." Bayly called this song "The Long Ago" and it remained in his possession and out of circulation for several years. Finally the editor of a Philadelphia magazine, Rufus Griswold (who replaced Edgar Allan Poe), made a collection of Bayly's poems and songs. He edited them and publication was in 1843. "The Long Ago" was in this collection, and it is very likely Griswold who changed the title to "Long, Long Ago."

Popularity-wise, this song was Thomas Bayly's masterpiece. The American public took his beautiful song to its heart, and succeeding generations have cherished it. It is interesting to note that the 1942 song hit "Don't Sit Under the Apple Tree" strongly resembles a "swing" version of "Long, Long Ago." This song was featured in the 1942 movie *Calling Wild Bill Elliot*.

LONG, LONG AGO

2. Do you remember the path where we met? long, long ago, long, long ago
   Ah yes, you told me you ne'er would forget, long, long ago, long ago
   Then to all others, my smile you preferred
   Love when you spoke gave a charm to each word
   Still my heart treasures the praises I heard, long, long ago, long ago

3. Though by your kindness my fond hopes were raised, long, long ago, long, long ago
   You, by more eloquent lips have been praised, long, long ago, long ago
   But by long absence your truth has been tried
   Still to your accents I listen with pride
   Blest as I was when I sat by your side, long, long ago, long ago

VIVE LA COMPAGNIE [1]
(Vive l'Amour) [2]
1845

THIS CONVIVIAL SONG CAME UPON THE AMERICAN SCENE THROUGH ITS PUBLICATION IN BALTIMORE, Maryland, the same year in which Samuel Morse demonstrated his wireless to the United States Congress, 1844.

The composer of music and words of "Vive La Compagnie" is unknown since its first publication carried no names. The song's first burst of popularity was among college students and it has since appeared in many college song books. When students wished to honor someone they substituted that person's name for *compagnie* in the lyric.

The song was also frequently performed by the Maryland cadets at the brand new Naval Academy which came into being in 1845. Confederate soldiers in the Civil War sang a parody on this song entitled "Chivalrous C.S.A." (Confederate States of America) in celebration of their victory at Manassas (Bull Run) on July 21, 1861.

This robust song has gained in popularity for over a century. It received a big lift recently (in the 1940's) through the operatic voice of Lauritz Melchior who featured it at concerts and in his 1945 movie *Thrills of Romance*.

[1] *Vive la Compagnie* = Long live companionship, good fellowship.
[2] *Vive l'Amour* = Long live love.

102

VIVE LA COMPAGNIE
(Vive l'Amour)

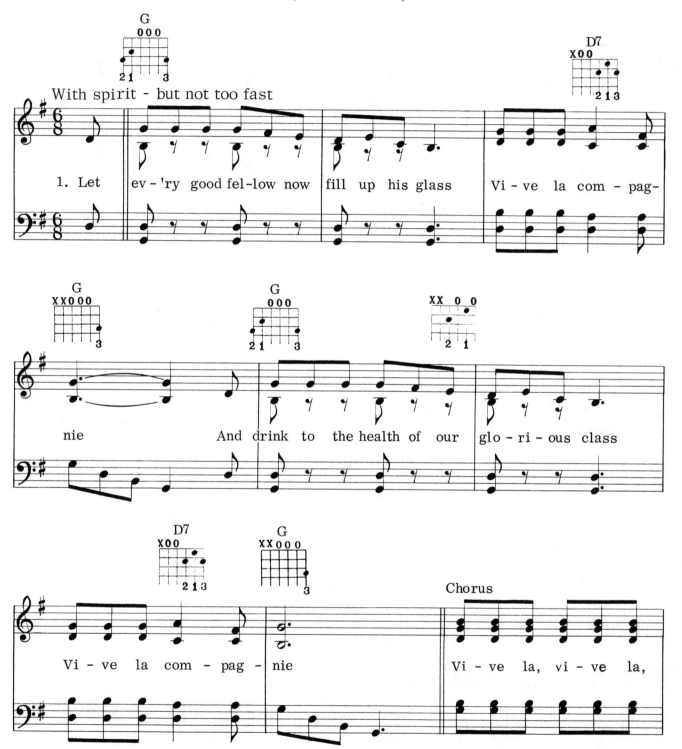

With spirit - but not too fast

1. Let ev-'ry good fel-low now fill up his glass Vi-ve la com-pag-

nie   And drink to the health of our glo-ri-ous class

Vi-ve la com-pag-nie

Chorus

Vi-ve la, vi-ve la,

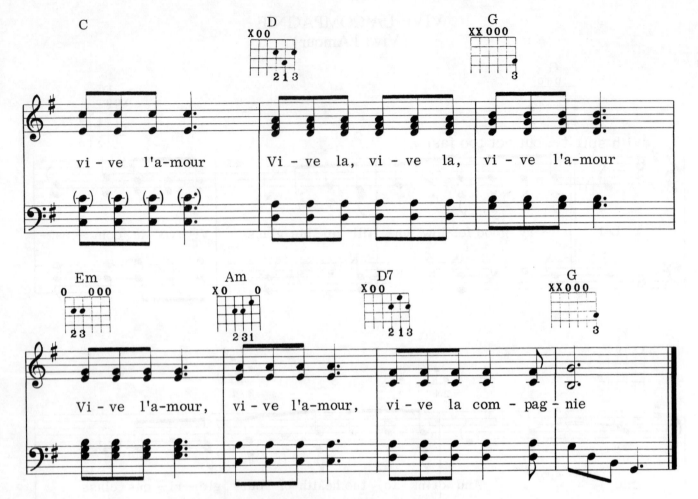

2. Now let every married man drink to his wife
   Vive la compagnie
   The joy of his bosom and plague of his life
   Vive la compagnie

Chorus:

3. Come fill up your glasses, I'll give you a toast
   Vive la compagnie
   A health to our dear friend, our kind worthy host
   Vive la compagnie

Chorus:

4. Since all with good humor I've toasted so free
   Vive la compagnie
   I hope it will please you to drink now with me
   Vive la compagnie

Chorus:

THE CAMPBELLS ARE COMING
1847

THIS SONG HAS A DIRECT BEARING ON SCOTTISH HISTORY. THE CAMPBELL FAMILY HAD A LONG succession of earls and dukes of Argyll. The Campbells referred to in this song were loyal Scots under the leadership of John Campbell, second duke of Argyll and Greenwich.

During the Jacobite[1] uprising in 1715, John Campbell was commander-in-chief of the numerically inferior forces in North Britain, and as a man of high principles he succeeded in putting down the Scottish rebellion with hardly any bloodshed. His praises were voiced by everyone including Sir Walter Scott, and John Campbell became known as the "Great Argyll."

The melody is that of an old Irish folk song, "An Seanduine" (meaning "old man") probably originating in the glens of West Cork toward the end of the seventeenth century. There had been several variations of this song until its first publication about 1745. Other printings followed in 1747, 1756, and 1761. In England the song was called "Hob" or "Nob." Somewhere in this period the Scotch appropriated the melody, and it became "The Campbels Are Coming" with certain variants. The standardized version was produced by the Scottish musician Finlay Dun the early part of the nineteenth century. This song probably reached America some time before the California Gold Rush (1849) during swells of heavy immigration from the British Isles. Its popularity grew quite rapidly.

[1] Supporters of the Stuart claim to the English throne after the Scottish Revolution of 1688.

THE CAMPBELLS ARE COMING

1. The Camp-bells are com-in', o - ho o - ho, The Camp-bells are com-in', o-

ho o - ho The Camp-bells are com - in' to bon - nie Loch-le - ven [1] The

Camp-bells are com - in', o - ho o - ho Up - on the lo-monds [2] I

lay, I lay Up - on the lo-monds I lay, I lay I

1. Lochleven = A lake in southern Scotland
2. Lomonds = High ground

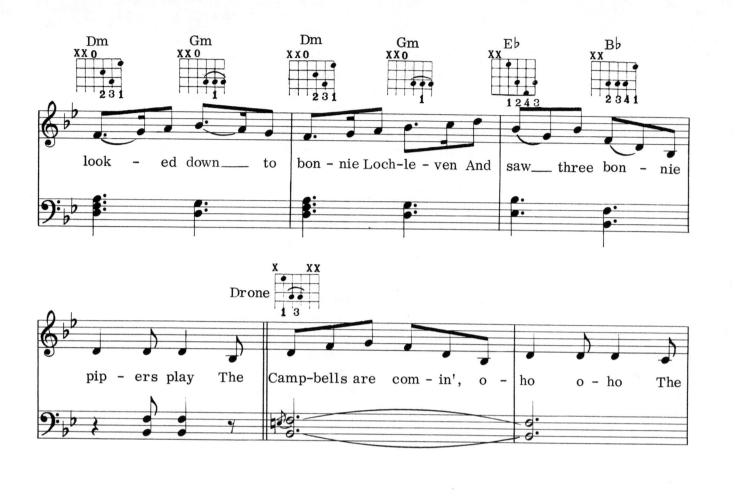

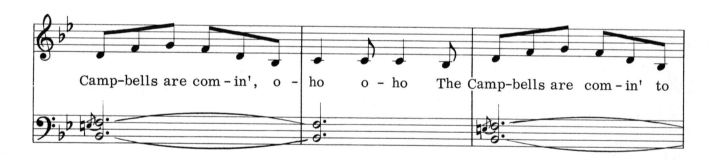

2. The Campbells are comin', o-ho o-ho
   The Campbells are comin', o-ho o-ho
   The Campbells are comin' to bonnie Lochleven
   The Campbells are comin', o-ho o-ho
   Great Argyll goes before, before
   He makes the cannons and guns to roar
   Wi' sound o' trumpet, pipe and drum
   The Campbells are comin', o-ho o-ho
   The Campbells are comin', o-ho o-ho
   The Campbells are comin', o-ho o-ho
   The Campbells are comin' to bonnie Lochleven
   The Campbells are comin', o-ho o-ho

3. The Campbells are comin', o-ho o-ho
   The Campbells are comin', o-ho o-ho
   The Campbells are comin' to bonnie Lochleven
   The Campbells are comin', o-ho o-ho
   The Campbells they are a'[3] in arms
   Their loyal faith and truth to show
   Wi' banners rattlin' in the wind
   The Campbells are comin', o-ho o-ho
   The Campbells are comin', o-ho o-ho
   The Campbells are comin', o-ho o-ho
   The Campbells are comin' to bonnie Lochleven
   The Campbells are comin', o-ho o-ho

3. A' = All

BLUE-TAIL FLY
1848

THIS SONG WAS ONE OF ABRAHAM LINCOLN'S FAVORITES, AND HE CALLED IT "THAT BUZZING SONG." It is very likely that he played it on his harmonica. The song was also a favorite of the black-faced minstrels and their audiences. Although the song may have originated among the plantation Negroes, it was not until about 1846 that Dan Emmett (the daddy of minstrel shows) wrote it down on paper. Other black-faced minstrel shows picked up this song and performed it in hundreds of frontier towns and settlements, and from there it seems to have traveled every covered-wagon trail. Wherever it went it was sure to capture the people's fancy through its strong folk appeal. The song became a national hit just before the California Gold Rush got going. Today this song is treated as a novelty folk song and is frequently heard over radio, television, in the street, in concert halls, and on recordings. It is also known as "Jimmy [or Jim] Crack Corn."

BLUE-TAIL FLY

2. Then after dinner he would sleep
   A vigil I would have to keep
   And when he wanted to shut his eye
   He told me "Watch the blue-tail fly"

Chorus:

3. One day he rode around the farm
   The flies so num'rous, they did swarm
   One chanced a-bitin' him on the thigh
   The devil take the blue-tail fly

Chorus:

4. The pony run, he jump and pitch
   And tumble master in the ditch
   He died, the jury they wondered why
   The verdict was the blue-tail fly

Chorus:

5. They laid him 'neath a 'simmon[1] tree
   His epitaph is there to see:
   "Beneath this stone I'm forced to lie
   A victim of the blue-tail fly"

Chorus:

6. Ol' master's gone, now let him rest
   They say that things are for the best
   I can't forget till the day I die
   Ol' master and the blue-tail fly

Chorus:

1. Persimmon

OH SUSANNA
1849

ALTHOUGH THIS SONG WAS COMPOSED IT IS TODAY CONSIDERED AN AMERICAN FOLK SONG. It has been highly popular for over a hundred years,—there have been many parodies— and it was the theme song of the Forty-niners during the California Gold Rush. Words and music are by Stephen Foster.

Stephen Foster was a Fourth of July baby in 1826, the very day John Adams and Thomas Jefferson died, when our country was about fifty years old. Stephen was the son of the wealthy pioneer Colonel William Barclay Foster, and during his lifetime he wrote some two hundred songs. He composed "Oh Susanna" when he was only twenty years old.

This song had its first public performance as a novelty number with banjo accompaniment on September 11, 1847, at the Eagle Ice Cream Saloon in Pittsburgh, Pennsylvania, and his audience loved it. Stephen Foster gave this and another song to a friend William Peters who published them in 1848 and wound up making over $10,000 on them. It is doubtful that Foster received any of the money.

"Oh Susanna" became an immediate hit throughout the entire country, which at that time extended all the way to the Mississippi River. It became a favorite with the minstrels (whom Foster loved so dearly) and of the people. This song is well known throughout our country, any time and any place. It was used in the 1951 movie *Overland Telegraph* and in the same year another movie bore its title. "Oh Susanna" will probably last forever in America.

112

OH SUSANNA

2. When I jumped aboard the telegraph
   And travelled down the riv'r
   The electric fluid magnified
   And killed five hundred chigg'r

   When the bullgine[1] bust the horse run off
   I really thought I'd die
   So I shut my eyes to hold my breath
   Susanna don't you cry

Chorus:

3. Now I had a dream the other night
   When ev'rything was still
   And I thought I saw Susanna
   She was comin' down the hill

   Now the buckwheat cake was in her mouth
   The tear was in her eye
   So I says "I'm comin' from the South
   Susanna don't you cry"

Chorus:

4. Now I soon will be in New Orleans
   And then I'll look around
   When at last I find Susanna
   I will fall upon the ground

   But if I can never find her
   Then I think I'd surely die
   When I'm dead and gone and buried deep
   Susanna don't you cry

Chorus:

1. Dialect for "engine"

114

BLOW THE MAN DOWN
1849

THIS SEA CHANTEY MOST LIKELY ORIGINATED WITH THE ROUGH AND TOUGH SAILORS WHO WORKED on the Black Ball Line sailing from Boston, New York, and Philadelphia to Liverpool during America's expansion period from 1816 to 1878. As with most all work songs this one helped put the sailors' work movements into rhythm and lifted their spirits at the same time. (See "Drunken Sailor" for further explanation.) There are many versions of this song, both words and melody.

During the Gold Rush days many of our more well-to-do pioneers made their way to California by boat around Cape Horn. This trip took about five months and was quite expensive in those days, costing around $200. Boat passengers learned this song from the sailors and it became a most familiar one with the forty-niners who sang it for diversion when they were not too busy dreaming of the gold they would find in California. It has been one of our more popular songs ever since. Our Naval Academy in Annapolis uses its own version as a football song.

BLOW THE MAN DOWN

Moderately fast

1. Come all ya young fel - lers that fol - low the sea With a

ho ho, blow [1] the man down Now

just pay at - ten - tion and lis - ten to me

Give me some time to blow the man down

1. "Blow" means "knock"

2. Aboard the Black Baller I first served my time
   With a ho ho, blow the man down
   But on the Black Baller I wasted my time
   Give me some time to blow the man down

3. We'd tinkers and tailors and sailors and all
   With a ho ho, blow the man down
   That sailed for good seamen aboard the Black Ball
   Give me some time to blow the man down

4. 'Tis larboard and starboard, on deck you will crawl
   With a ho ho, blow the man down
   When kicking Jack Williams [2] commands the Black Ball
   Give me some time to blow the man down

5. Now when the Black Baller's preparin' for sea
   With a ho ho, blow the man down
   You'd bust your sides laughin' at sights that you see
   Give me some time to blow the man down

6. But when the Black Baller is clear of the land
   With a ho ho, blow the man down
   Old kicking Jack Williams gives ev'ry command
   Give me some time to blow the man down

7. Aboard the Black Baller I first served my time
   With a ho ho, blow the man down
   But on the Black Baller I wasted my time
   Give me some time to blow the man down

2. Jack Williams was actually one of the rugged skippers
   on the Black Ball Line.

BUFFALO GALS
1850

ONE OF OUR EARLIEST BLACK-FACED MINSTRELS, COOL WHITE (BORN JOHN HODGES), COMPOSED and published this song in 1844 under the title "Lubly Fan." He performed it throughout the country with his Virginia Serenaders and the song caught on with audiences everywhere. Within a couple of years other minstrel shows began using this song, including the famous Christy Minstrels, giving it various titles such as "Charleston Gals," "Pittsburgh Gals," "Louisville Gals," "Texas Gals," etc., depending on the town in which the show was playing. In 1848 the well-known Ethiopian Serenaders stuck to the title "Buffalo Gals" and eventually all other titles were dropped.

By 1850 this song was enormously popular. It was no longer minstrel-show property alone. It now belonged to the people. It was picked on the banjo, sawed by country fiddlers, blown on squeaky fifes, clapped out at dances, and sung by all kinds of people east and west of the Mississippi. Mark Twain even used it in Tom Sawyer. This song's popularity never seemed to diminish over the years. Since it uses catchy, syncopated beats, it was one of the forerunners of jazz. In 1944 (exactly one hundred years after Cool White wrote it) it was made into the song hit "Dance With A Dolly."

BUFFALO GALS

Moderate and bouncy

1. As I was lumb'ring down the street Down the street, down the street A

hand-some gal I chanced to meet Oh she was fair to view

Chorus

Buf-fa-lo gals won'-cha come out to-night Come out to-night, come out to-night

Buf-fa-lo gals won'-cha come out to-night And dance by the light of the moon

2. I asked her if she'd have a talk
   Have a talk, have a talk
   Her feet took up the whole sidewalk
   As she stood close to me

Chorus:

3. I asked her "Would you want to dance
   Want to dance, want to dance"
   I thought that I would have a chance
   To shake a foot with her

Chorus:

4. Oh I danced with the gal with a hole in her stockin'
   And her hip kept a-rockin' and her toe kept a-knockin'
   I danced with the gal with a hole in her stockin'
   And we danced by the light of the moon

Chorus:

5. I wanna make that gal my wife
   Gal my wife, gal my wife
   Then I'd be happy all my life
   If I had her with me

Chorus:

SWEET BETSY FROM PIKE
1851

THE HEIGHT OF THIS SONG'S POPULARITY WAS DURING THE CALIFORNIA GOLD RUSH DAYS. IT WAS A great wagon song and could be heard on almost any prairie schooner or around the camp fire. The song was a natural for our pioneers since it reflected with a sense of humor the hardships of our westward-bound ancestors. Betsy and Ike were from Pike County, Missouri.

The lyrics were, no doubt, made up by the pioneers themselves, with verse added to verse. The melody seems to date back to early nineteenth-century Britain and the song "Vilikins (or Willikins) and His Dinah" which was also a narrative type of song. And, in turn, this tune was a variation of an old Scottish melody sung to "Lord Randall," the lyrics of which seem to have been the granddaddy of the folk song "Billy Boy." As with most folk songs during their earlier days the melody to "Lord Randall" underwent numerous changes. There were English and Irish variants of the Scottish melody and still further variants of these. By the time "Vilikins and His Dinah" became rather well known in New England (around 1840 or so) the general melody was fairly well established, and today there are only slight melodic variations of "Sweet Betsy From Pike." This song's popularity was paralleled in Great Britain, and it is probably as well known there today as it is here in America.

SWEET BETSY FROM PIKE

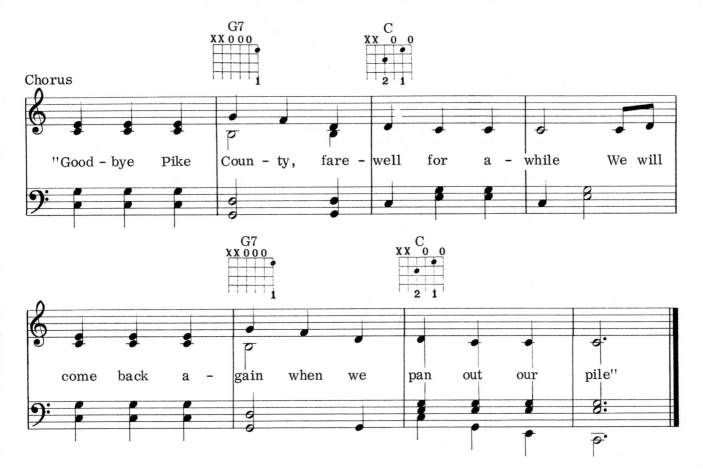

Chorus

"Good - bye Pike Coun - ty, fare - well for a - while We will

come back a - gain when we pan out our pile"

2. The Shanghai ran off an' the oxen all died
   That morning the last piece of bacon was fried
   Poor Ike got discouraged an' Betsy got mad
   An' the dog wagged his tail an' looked wond'rously sad

Chorus:

3. The wagon broke down with a terrible crash
   And out on the prairie rolled all sorts of trash
   A few little baby clothes done up with care
   Looked a little suspicious but all on the square

Chorus:

4. The Injuns came down in a wild yellin' horde
   And Betsy was skeered they would scalp her adored
   Behind the front wagon wheel Betsy did crawl
   It was there she fought Injuns with musket and ball

Chorus:

5. They soon reached the desert where Betsy gave out
   An' down in the sand she lay rollin' about
   While Ike in great horror looked on with surprise
   Saying "Betsy get up,you'll get sand in your eyes"

Chorus:

6. Sweet Betsy got up with a great deal of pain
   An' said she'd go back to Pike County again
   But Ike gave a sigh and they fondly embraced
   An' they travelled along with his arm 'round her waist

Chorus:

CAMPTOWN RACES
1851

THIS DELIGHTFUL NONSENSE SONG, CONSIDERED AN AMERICAN FOLK SONG, WAS CREATED BY Stephen Foster during a happier period of his life, when he was only twenty-four years old, around 1850. This was the year in which he married, in which Millard Fillmore became our thirteenth president, Harriet Beecher Stowe was completing *Uncle Tom's Cabin,* and the mad California Gold Rush was already in full swing.

The song was first published in 1850 under the title "Gwine To Run All Night." Stephen Foster, wild about minstrels, got Ed Christy's Minstrels to feature the song, and thus in a short time it became a big hit. People from New York to San Francisco sang and whistled this tune on the street, at work, and in their homes without ever knowing who wrote it. In spite of this enormous popularity it was not much of a money-maker, since in seven years it sold only some 5000 copies and Foster's royalties totaled slightly over a hundred dollars. Thus in 1857 Stephen Foster sold all his rights to the song.

The Forty-niners, traveling overland and by sea, loved this song and often added their own parodies. "Camptown Races" achieved sizable popularity in England after being introduced by Ed Christy's Minstrels. This song was featured in the 1952 movie *I Dream of Jeanie.* As time and American popular-song history have gone on, this song has taken its place as one of Stephen Foster's best.

CAMPTOWN RACES

2. The long-tail filly and the big black horse, doo-dah doo-dah
   They fly the track and they both cut across, oh doo-dah day
   The blind horse stickin' in a big mud hole, doo-dah doo-dah
   Can't touch bottom with a ten-foot pole, oh doo-dah day

Chorus:

3. Old muley cow come on the track, doo-dah doo-dah
   The bobtail fling her over his back, oh doo-dah day
   Then fly along like a railroad car, doo-dah doo-dah
   And runnin' a race with a shootin' star, oh doo-dah day

Chorus:

4. See them a-flyin' on a ten-mile heat, doo-dah doo-dah
   Around the racetrack, then repeat, oh doo-dah day
   I win my money on the bobtail nag, doo-dah doo-dah
   I keep my money in an old tow bag, oh doo-dah day

Chorus:

WAIT FOR THE WAGON
1852

HERE IS ANOTHER OF THE COMPOSED POPULAR SONGS WHICH HAS GONE INTO THE AMERICAN folk-song category. "Wait For the Wagon" was born coincidentally with the first published version of *Uncle Tom's Cabin* as a magazine serial, at a time of mounting antislavery pressures.

The song was written by George P. Knauff and R. Bishop Buckley (the organizer of Buckley's Minstrels) and was first published in Baltimore in 1851. Within a year "Wait For the Wagon" became quite a hit in the East and then gradually made its way down into the South through the performances of traveling minstrel shows, including Buckley's Minstrels. Here the song's popularity hung on for years, particularly in the Ozarks and regions of Mississippi. By the time our Civil War began this song was so well known in these areas that the melody was appropriated by Southerners for a parody called "The Southern Wagon."

Although "Wait For the Wagon" has enjoyed occasional revivals and parodies through the years, its basic simplicity and catchy melody has real folk appeal for most people. The song was featured in the 1943 movie *Black Market Rustlers*. It is frequently heard on television and radio, and is often sung and enjoyed right in our own homes today.

POP GOES THE WEASEL
1853

MANY THINK THIS SONG IS GENUINELY AMERICAN WHILE SOME CONSIDER IT ENGLISH. OTHERS believe it came from a children's song while still others associate it with a country dance. All are correct in a way.

"Pop Goes the Weasel!" did originate in England centuries ago although no one knows precisely when or where, or if it simply developed as a folk song. It is known, however, that the song was quite popular as a child's singing game in England during the exodus of Pilgrims to America (1620–1640). Somewhere during the next century the song made its first American appearance in Colonial New England where it was used mainly as a contra dance, and it became quite a favorite during the middle 1700's.

As many New Englanders began migrating (after the Revolution) to other parts of the country this tune went with them. The nonsensical humor of the song intrigued all who heard it, and thus "Pop Goes the Weasel" joined the musical life of many a rural community. Country fiddlers in particular made this their favorite number giving it the same playing style as any other American country tune. Wherever the tune was popular, people made up their own lyrics; but the one stanza that seemed to stabilize itself was the one beginning with "All around the cobbler's bench."

Until the middle 1800's this song's popularity remained chiefly in a few isolated regions. But when "Pop Goes the Weasel" was finally published in 1853 it immediately rose to great popular heights throughout our thirty-one states. Parodies followed including many that were political, nonsensical, or unprintable.

The song's title has nothing to do with a small explosion or an animal. The word "pop" is British slang meaning to "pawn" something, and "weasel" was British slang meaning "the tools of one's trade." If a person were a tailor his weasel would be scissors, needles, thimble and tape measure, or a carpenter's weasel would be his saw, hammer, plane, and square. Therefore, the expression "pop goes the weasel" simply means one's money is gone and something will have to be pawned.

America has always had its share of nonsense songs but "Pop Goes the Weasel" is one of the very few to have become an all-time favorite. Since the first chorus and a half is the only standardized version a few original stanzas have been added.

POP GOES THE WEASEL

2. A nickel for a spool of thread
   A penny for a needle
   That's the way the money goes
   Pop goes the weasel

   You may try to sew and sew
   And never make something regal
   So roll it up and let it go
   Pop goes the weasel

3. I went to a lawyer today
   For something very legal
   He asked how much I'm willing to pay
   Pop goes the weasel

   I will bargain all my days
   But never again so feeble
   I paid for ev'ry legal phrase
   Pop goes the weasel

4. A painter would his lover to paint
   He stood before the easel
   A monkey jumped all over the paint
   Pop goes the weasel

   When his lover she did laugh
   His temper got very lethal
   He tore the painting up in half
   Pop goes the weasel

5. I went hunting up in the woods
   It wasn't very legal
   The dog and I were caught with the goods
   Pop goes the weasel

   I said I don't hunt or sport
   The warden looked at my beagle
   He said to tell it to the court
   Pop goes the weasel

6. My son and I we went to the fair
   And there were lots of people
   We spent a lot of money, I swear
   Pop goes the weasel

   I got sick from all the sun
   My sonny boy got the measels
   But still we had a lot of fun
   Pop goes the weasel

7. I went up and down on the coast
   To find a golden eagle
   I climbed the rocks and thought I was close
   Pop goes the weasel

   But alas I lost my way
   Saw nothing but just a sea gull
   I tore my pants and killed the day
   Pop goes the weasel

8. I went to a grocery store
   I thought a little cheese'll
   Be good to catch a mouse in the floor
   Pop goes the weasel

   But the mouse was very bright
   He wasn't a mouse to wheedle
   He took the cheese and said "goodnight"
   Pop goes the weasel

MY OLD KENTUCKY HOME
1854

THIS IS THE OFFICIAL SONG OF THE STATE OF KENTUCKY, A LAND FIRST DISCOVERED BY MARQUETTE and Joliet in 1673 and explored a century later by Daniel Boone.

"My Old Kentucky Home" was composed by Stephen Foster during the most carefree and productive period in his life, at age 27. He wrote it during the time our country was experiencing an ever-growing antislavery movement. *Uncle Tom's Cabin* (published in 1852) had sold over 300,000 copies and its sentiment was already widely felt. Stephen Foster, not particularly interested in the abolitionist movement, seemed to have developed "My Old Kentucky Home" from a poem entitled "Poor Uncle Tom, Good Night," which in turn may have been influenced by the book *Uncle Tom's Cabin.*

Foster wrote this great song one morning while on a visit to Bardstown, Kentucky, at the charming, attractive mansion of his uncle, Senator Rowan. The sun shone brightly, the birds sang, Foster saw the cute little Negro children playing, and he composed the words and music of "My Old Kentucky Home." It was in his nature to treat the Negro with affection and sensitive understanding.

Not long after its publication in 1853 the song became a popular success. It was introduced to the public for the first time by the Ed Christy Minstrels, and it earned for Foster almost $1,400, a nice sum of money in those days when rents were around five dollars a month and a full-course restaurant dinner cost about 50 cents. Stephen Collins Foster was without a doubt the best writer of what was then called Ethiopian songs, and "My Old Kentucky Home" is a good example.

MY OLD KENTUCKY HOME

2. They hunt no more for the 'possum and the coon
   On meadow, the hill and the shore
   They sing no more by the glimmer of the moon
   On the bench by that old cabin door
       The day goes by like a shadow o'er the heart
       With sorrow where all was delight
       The time has come when the darkies have to part
       Then my old Kentucky home, good night

Chorus:

3. The head must bow and the back will have to bend
   Wherever   the darky may go
   A few more days and the trouble all will end
   In the field where sugar-canes may grow
       A few more days for to tote the weary load
       No matter, 'twill never be light
       A few more days till we totter on the road
       Then my old Kentucky home, good night

Chorus:

POLLY WOLLY DOODLE
1855

THIS IS A MUCH-FUN AND LITTLE-KNOWN-ABOUT AMERICAN FOLK SONG. IT HAS BEEN POPULAR
since the mid-1850's, the era of Longfellow and Walt Whitman, *Uncle Tom's Cabin*, hoopskirts, and President Franklin Pierce. The song seems completely anonymous although some
believe it to be of Negro origin.

This was one of the most performed songs of the black-faced minstrels. Every troupe
sang it, and every audience loved it. Just before the Civil War this song was heard in every
theatre, on every riverboat, and in every town.

During the 1880's the song became one of the favorites among college glee clubs, and
from the 1890's to this day it has been on the "preferred" list of barber shop quartets. For
nearly a century most songbooks have included this song. It is today one of our all-American
nonsense songs. "Polly Wolly Doodle" was used in the 1946 movie *Tangier*.

POLLY WOLLY DOODLE

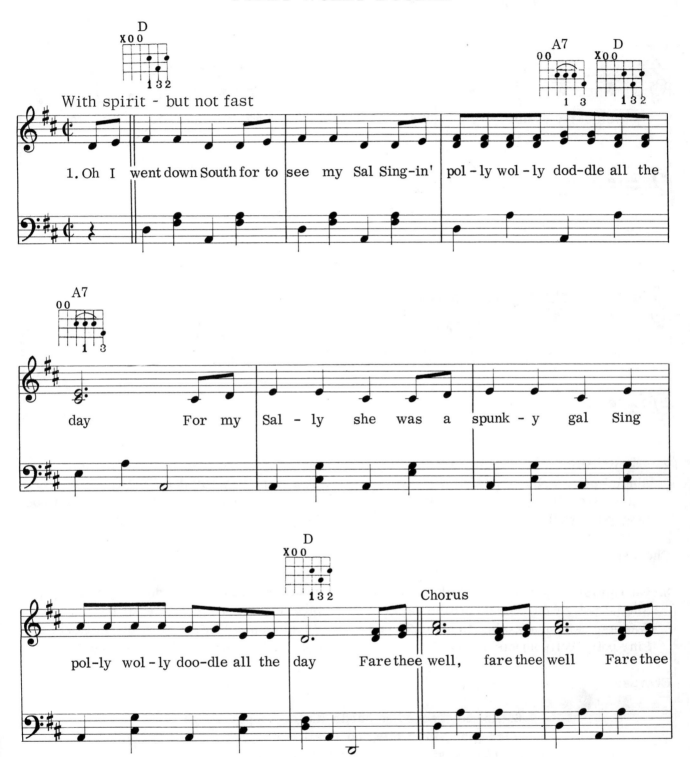

1. Oh I went down South for to see my Sal Sing-in' pol - ly wol - ly dod-dle all the

day For my Sal - ly she was a spunk - y gal Sing

pol-ly wol - ly doo-dle all the day Fare thee well, fare thee well Fare thee

Chorus

well my fair - y fay For I'm off to Lou'-si - an - a for to

see my Sus-y An - na Sing-in' pol - ly wol - ly doo-dle all the day

2. Oh my Sally was such a maiden fair
   Singin' polly wolly doodle all the day
   With her curly eyes and her laughing hair
   Sing polly wolly doodle all the day

Chorus:

3. Oh a grasshopper sat on a railroad track
   Singin' polly wolly doodle all the day
   Was a-pickin' his teeth with a carpet tack
   Sing polly wolly doodle all the day

Chorus:

4. Oh I went to bed but it weren't no use
   Singin' polly wolly doodle all the day
   'Cause my feet stuck out for a chicken roost
   Sing polly wolly doodle all the day

Chorus:

5. From behind the barn, down upon my knees
   Singin' polly wolly doodle all the day
   I could swear I heard that ol' chicken sneeze
   Sing polly wolly doodle all the day

Chorus:

6. An' he sneezed so hard with the hoopin' cough
   Singin' polly wolly doodle all the day
   That he sneezed his head an' his tail right off
   Sing polly wolly doodle all the day

Chorus:

LISTEN TO THE MOCKING BIRD
1856

A BOY WHISTLED; ALICE HAWTHORNE HEARD IT; THIS SONG WAS BORN; AND PEOPLE EVERYWHERE whistled it.

In the year this song was composed (1854) some Whigs, Democrats and Free Soilers got together in Jackson, Michigan, and formed the Republican Party. Most of their wives wore the latest thing in fashion—hoopskirts. Though we were a song-loving nation we were also a serious nation moving ever closer toward abolition of slavery.

"Listen To the Mocking Bird" was written by Septimus Winner, the man who also gave us "Whispering Hope," "Ten Little Indians," the words to "Where, Oh Where Has My Little Dog Gone," and a score of other songs. He was twenty-seven years old at the time, a music teacher and the owner of a music store in Philadelphia. Winner was acquainted with a young Negro boy, Dick Milburn (called Whistling Dick), a beggar who collected coins for his whistling and guitar playing on the streets. His whistling often turned to a beautiful imitation of a mocking bird, and this attracted Winner's attention and thought. It gave him an idea for a song and he promptly went to work on it. He finished "Listen To the Mocking Bird," gave Whistling Dick a job in his store, and published the composition in April, 1855, using the pseudonym Alice Hawthorne. Pseudonyms were common practice in those days, for example Mark Twain (Samuel Clemens) and Artemus Ward (Charles Browne). Winner chose Hawthorne after his mother's maiden name. He never explained the "Alice" part of it.

Within months this song hit all parts of our nation and people everywhere went wild over it, especially in the South where the mocking bird is a common sight. For years afterwards Southern mothers named their baby girls Hally (or Hallie) after this song. President Abraham Lincoln said of this song "It is as sincere as the laughter of a little girl at play," and King Edward VII of England remarked, "I whistled 'Listen To the Mocking Bird' when I was a little boy."

The song became popular all over Europe and it is estimated that by 1905 total sheet copies sold ran approximately twenty million. This song's immense popularity has stuck solidly for over a century. It is truly one of our old-time, all-time song hits.

LISTEN TO THE MOCKING BIRD

2. Ah well I yet can remember, I remember, I remember
   Ah well I yet can remember
   When we gathered in the cotton side by side
       'Twas in the mild mid-September, in September, in September
       'Twas in the mild mid-September
       And the mocking bird was singing far and wide

Chorus:

3. When charms of spring are awaken, are awaken, are awaken
   When charms of spring are awaken
   And the mocking bird is singing on the bough
       I feel like one so forsaken, so forsaken, so forsaken
       I feel like one so forsaken
       Since my Hallie is no longer with me now

Chorus:

144

CINDY
1857

THIS IS A TYPICAL FOLK SONG, BORN OF AMERICAN PIONEERS, THAT CAME INTO BEING SOMEWHERE around Thomas Jefferson's time (1805) when we were a nation of only seventeen states. The song originated in the mountains of Alabama, Georgia, the Carolinas, Kentucky, and Tennessee. It was one of their best play-party songs and a favorite with mountaineer fiddlers and banjo pickers.

For some time this tune was locked up in the Appalachians until some of the mountaineers began moving westward the early part of the nineteenth century. It took a while for this tune to catch on with other migrants, and not until about the mid-50's was its popularity firmly established. But catch on it eventually did—with cowboys, miners, railroad men, homesteaders, prospectors, and all the rest of our pioneer people. This turned out to be a great tune for the square dance, the reel, for banjo-playing minstrels, and for people who liked to sing, stamp, and clap their hands. It is a gay, foot-tapping folk song, and fully enjoyed today wherever it is heard. Many recordings are available.

CINDY

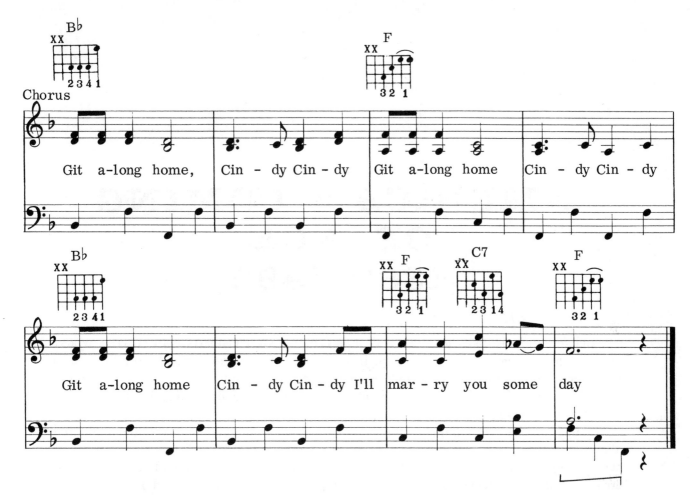

Chorus

Git a-long home, Cin-dy Cin-dy Git a-long home Cin-dy Cin-dy

Git a-long home Cin-dy Cin-dy I'll mar-ry you some day

2. I wish I was an apple
   A-hangin' on a tree
   An' ev'ry time that Cindy passed
   She'd take a bite of me

   If I were made of sugar
   A-standin' in the town
   Then ev'ry time my Cindy passed
   I'd shake some sugar down

Chorus:

3. My Cindy got religion
   She had it once before
   But when she heard my ol' banjo
   She leaped upon the floor

   She took me to her parlor
   She cooled me with her fan
   She said I was the purt-iest thing
   The shape of mortal man

Chorus:

4. Now Cindy is a sweet girl
   My Cindy is a peach
   She threw her arms around me tight
   An' hung on like a leech

   She kissed me an' she hugged me
   She called me sugar plum
   She hugged so tight I hardly breathed
   I thought my time had come

Chorus:

5. If I had thread an' needle
   If I knew how to sew
   I'd sew that gal to my coat tail
   An' down the road I'd go

   I want my Cindy Cindy
   Her lips an' arms an' feet
   I never seen another gal
   That Cindy couldn't beat

Chorus:

AMERICA'S COMING OF AGE (1860-1890)

THE OPENING OF THIS HISTORICAL ERA WAS SIGNALED BY A SHOT FIRED ON FORT SUMTER. WORRY and excitement reigned in every family. In the efforts of both governments to rally men to the colors it was learned that songs were among the more potent and effective means. Songs were used throughout the war to generate martial spirit and dedication to the cause, in addition to maintaining a high morale.

Songs appeared and disappeared during our four-year struggle but two of them endured above all others. They became the outstanding battle songs. "Dixie" was in the heart of every fighting Southerner. "Battle Hymn of the Republic" stirred the blood of every Northerner. Paradoxically however, "Dixie" was composed by a Northerner[1] while the militant music for "Battle Hymn of the Republic" was composed by a Southerner.[2] Both songs became favorites of President Abraham Lincoln. He praised "Dixie" as one of the best songs he had ever heard, promptly asking the band to play it for him. Upon hearing "Battle Hymn of the Republic" for the first time, it is said the President's eyes welled up with tears, and he asked for a repetition.

In the quarter of a century following the Civil War our most popular music was influenced by many different elements as our nation's maturity gradually picked up speed. Such elements as railroad building, traveling circuses, minstrel shows, increased college singing, medicine show wagons and tents, variety shows and vaudeville all contributed their influence to our growing wealth of songs. Encouraged by the Homestead Act[3] and aided by the railroads, a large part of our population was on the move, with the westward migration in full swing. Several now-forgotten songs were written in glorious praise of the health-and-wealth benefits in the Golden West. Simple songs of the pop-tune variety held favor throughout the country while the more complex type, such as Gilbert and Sullivan songs, enjoyed the much smaller audience of our few large cities.

[1] Dan Emmett of Ohio.
[2] William Steffe of South Carolina.
[3] 1862. This act gave 160 acres of land in the West to all who filed declaratory papers.

The year 1867 saw the first publication of Negro songs,[1] those songs which had been in the making for over two hundred years. In earlier times a few of these songs had managed to trickle up the Mississippi and turn east; but it was not until 1871 that Americans by the thousands thrilled to the simple nobility of Negro folk songs when the Fisk (University) Jubilee Singers began their famous concert tour in the United States and abroad. Many of these same songs stand high today in national popularity. Before the century's end the roots of jazz would already have taken shape in the form of ragtime and the blues.

Within this period of thirty years our population doubled, standing at nearly sixty-three million in 1890. One-third of the increase (over ten million) were immigrants, mostly of the lower classes. The bulk of immigrants were from the British Isles, Germany, Scandinavia, Austria–Hungary, Italy, and Russia. All sang their native songs, and all songs had equal opportunity to become popular. A few of the songs that made the grade were "Funiculi, Funicula," "Blue Danube Waltz," "In the Gloaming," "Killarney," "Silent Night," and "Nancy Lee." America's accommodation of such large numbers of diverse immigrants, coupled with an enormous national energy, resulted in a modified social complexion. This in turn influenced to some degree a change in our musical taste, and this change is reflected in the kinds of songs that rose to popular heights during the next two decades (1890–1910).

STATES ADMITTED TO THE UNION

Rank	Name	Origin of Name	Year Admitted	State Song
34.	Kansas	From the Sioux Indian word meaning "South wind people."	1861	Home On the Range
35.	West Virginia	Same as for Virginia. "West" was applied when these counties refused to secede during the Civil War.	1863	West Virginia Hills
36.	Nevada	Spanish word meaning "snow-clad."	1864	Home Means Nevada
37.	Nebraska	From the Indian name for the Platte River meaning "flat water."	1867	My Nebraska
38.	Colorado	From the Spanish for "red," first applied to the Colorado River.	1876	Where the Columbines Grow
39.	North Dakota	From the Dakota Indian word meaning "allies."	1889	North Dakota Hymn
40.	South Dakota	Same as for North Dakota.	1889	Hail South Dakota
41.	Montana	Latin, meaning "mountainous."	1889	Montana
42.	Washington	Named in honor of George Washington.	1889	Washington, My Home

[1] Slave Songs of the United States, edited by Allen, Ware and Garrison.

BEAUTIFUL DREAMER
1864

THIS, ONE OF OUR STANDARD SONGS OF EVERLASTING POPULARITY, IS THE PRODUCT OF AN UN-trained but gifted intuitive composer. Both words and music of "Beautiful Dreamer" were composed by the great Stephen Collins Foster in 1864. It is one of his best sentimental songs, and it was his very last composition.

That this song should have such fine quality is rather fortunate considering the circumstance under which it was written. Having achieved fame at an early age, Foster in this period of his life was experiencing increasing difficulty; in writing successful songs, in supporting his family, and in maintaining his emotional equilibrium. Since he had left Pittsburgh three years before and had come to New York his life seemed to go from bad to worse, and he frequently became depressed and lonely. During this period, it is said, many of his last songs were written down on brown wrapping paper in the back room of an old grocery store. Very likely this is the way in which "Beautiful Dreamer" was written.

In 1864, the year before our Civil War ended, this song was published posthumously and it was advertised as "Stephen Foster's last song, written only a few days before his death." Although it developed great popularity and established itself as a definite success, Foster never knew it.

150

BEAUTIFUL DREAMER

Gone are the cares of life's bus-y throng Beau-ti-ful dreamer, a-wake un - to

me Beau-ti-ful dream-er, a-wake un-to me

2. Beautiful dreamer, out on the sea
Mermaids are chanting the wild Lorelei
Over the streamlet vapors are borne
Waiting to fade at the bright coming morn
    Beautiful dreamer, beam on my heart
    E'en as the morn on the streamlet and sea
Then will all clouds of sorrow depart
Beautiful dreamer, awake unto me
Beautiful dreamer, awake unto me

ST. PATRICK'S DAY
1865

MANY RECOGNIZE THIS SONG BUT FEW KNOW THE TITLE. THE MELODY READILY PRODUCES ASSOCIA-
tions with the emerald green of Ireland. So typically Irish does it sound that it is hard to
believe the melody is actually English. Originally this was a folk melody born in old rural
England toward the end of the sixteenth century or the early 1600's. Its first appearance in
print was in John Playford's famous collection of country fiddle tunes entitled *Dancing
Master,* published in England in the year 1650.

Over a century and a half later (just before our War of 1812) the Irish poet Thomas
Moore wrote the present three verses to this melody for a gala celebration in England honor-
ing the birthday of the Prince of Wales. This, and many others of Moore's works, exposed
through song and poetry the injustices Irishmen suffered at the hands of England. Picture,
if you will, the lyric content of this great song, dedicated to the guest of honor, and performed in the presence of royalty and powerful dignitaries. So politically effective were
Moore's songs and poetry that eventually he became Ireland's national hero.

During the ensuing years "St. Patrick's Day" filtered into Ireland where it achieved some
modest degree of circulation. However, after Ireland's tragic famine of 1846 coupled with
continuing political unrest, wholesale evictions, and the Irishman's great love of freedom,
many thousands left Ireland and emmigrated in huge waves to the United States from about
1850 to around 1870 or so.

While Irish immigrants enjoyed a new found freedom here in America, and where they
even gained political strength through their ability to speak English, their hearts were still
in the Old Country where many loved ones remained. Singing often provided comfort and
memories, and since Thomas Moore's lyrics expressed so well the heart and spirit of these
sorrowed people "St. Patrick's Day" burst forth into great popularity among these new Irish-
Americans.

Today, around a century later, this song is familiar to practically everyone; especially on
St. Patrick's Day parades where it is one of the most played marches. The melody of "St.
Patrick's Day" is a natural for bagpipes and fifes for there are no sharps or flats.

ST. PATRICK'S DAY

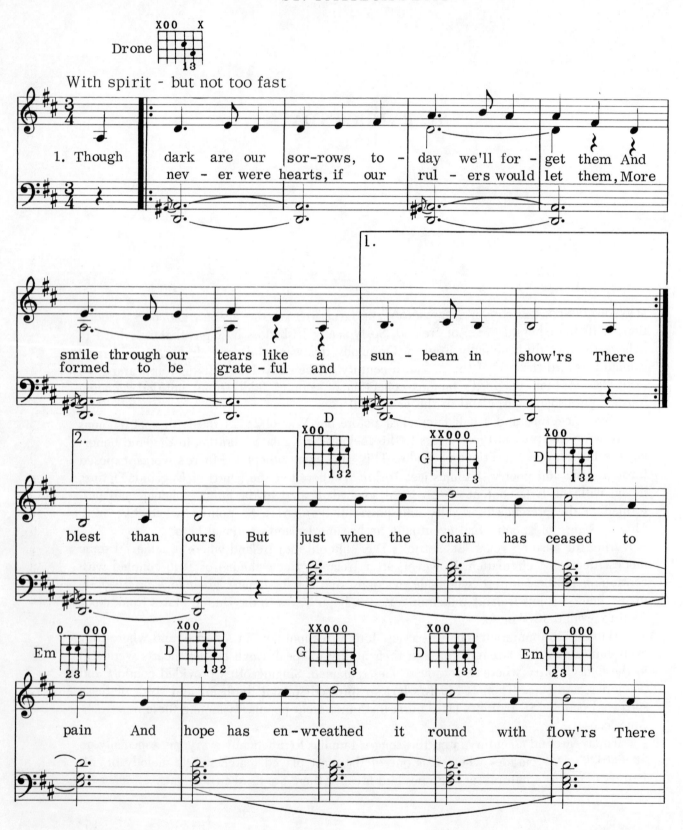

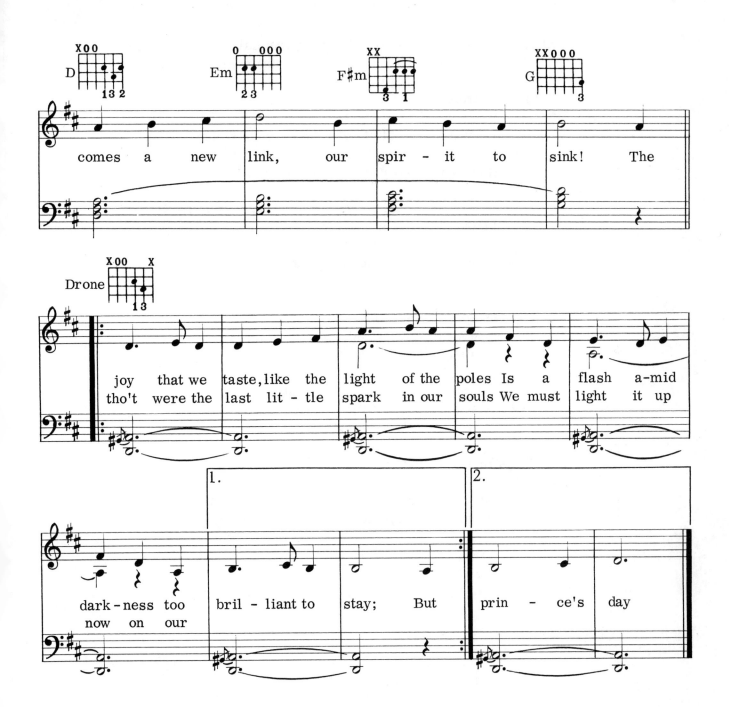

comes a new link, our spir - it to sink! The

Drone

joy that we taste, like the light of the poles Is a flash a-mid
tho't were the last lit - tle spark in our souls We must light it up

1.
dark-ness too bril - liant to stay; But
now on our

2.
prin - ce's day

2. Contempt on the minion who calls you disloyal!
   Though fierce to your foe, to your friends you are true;
   The tribute most high to a heart that is loyal
   Is love from a heart that loves liberty too

   While cowards who blight your fame, your right,
   Would shrink from the blaze of battle array,
   The standard of green in front would be seen

   My life on your faith! were you summoned this minute,
   You'd cast ev'ry bitter rememb'rance away,
   And show what the arm of old Erin has in it
   When roused by the foe on her prince's day

3. He loves the Green Isle and his love is recorded
   In hearts which have suffered too much to forget
   And hope shall be crowned, and attachment rewarded,
   And Erin's gay jubilee shine out yet

   The gem may be broke by many a stroke
   But nothing can cloud its native ray
   Each fragment will cast a light to the last

   Thus Erin, my country, though broken thou art
   There's a luster within thee that ne'er will decay
   A spirit which beams through each suffering part
   And now smiles at all pain on her prince's day

WHEN YOU AND I WERE YOUNG, MAGGIE
1866

THIS SONG WAS BORN THE YEAR AFTER OUR CIVIL WAR ENDED. ALSO BORN IN THE SAME YEAR WAS Christian Science (originated by Mary Baker Eddy), Fisk University (Nashville, Tenn.) for Negro men and women, and the YWCA (in Boston). We were still a growing nation of only thirty-six states. Croquet was the popular outdoor game in those days, women used mascara and men wore pork-pie hats.

"When You and I Were Young, Maggie" first came into being through a man's sincere expression of love and devotion to his sweetheart. The form of his expression was a poem, written by Canadian George W. Johnson, a school teacher and poet. Before coming to the United States, Johnson courted his pretty student, Maggie Clark, at a mill by a creek near her home. In his poem Johnson visualizes the kinds of memories he and Maggie will have in their old age together. This poem was published in a collection entitled *Maple Leaves* (named after Canada's national emblem).

This poem attracted the interest of Englishman James Austin Butterfield, then living in Chicago. Butterfield, an accomplished composer–singer–teacher–publisher–conductor, gave Johnson's poem a top-notch musical setting and published the song himself in 1866.

Needless to say, the song rose to great heights of popularity, and for nearly a hundred years now "When You and I Were Young, Maggie" has remained one of America's great songs of love, devotion, and reminiscence. This song was used in the 1944 movie *Swingtime Johnny.*

WHEN YOU AND I WERE YOUNG, MAGGIE

2. A city so silent and lone, Maggie
   Where young and gay and best
   In polished white mansions of stone, Maggie
   Where they each found a place for their rest
      Is built where the birds used to play, Maggie
      And join in songs that were sung
      We sang just as gay as did they, Maggie
      When you and I were young

Chorus:

3. They say I am feeble with age, Maggie
   My steps less sprightly than then
   My face is a well-written page, Maggie
   Then but time, time alone was the pen
      They say we are aged and gray, Maggie
      As spray by white breakers flung
      To me you're as fair as you were, Maggie
      When you and I were young

Chorus:

WEARING OF THE GREEN
1867

THIS SONG, THE VERSION WE KNOW TODAY, HAS THE MANTLE OF A FOLK SONG. THE MELODY SEEMS to be an adaptation of "The Tulip," a Scottish melody composed by James Oswald in 1757 (when George Washington was only twenty-five years old). The words are credited to a French–Irish–American playwright Dion Boucicault, who wrote them in 1865 (the year our Civil War ended) for the song of "Shaun The Post" in his successful play *Arrah-Na-Pogue*.

Since America was in the midst of large waves of Irish immigrants arriving (1850–1870), and since the words of this song reflected so well their feelings about Ireland, the shamrock,[1] and the pressures from which they fled, the song circulated rather quickly thus achieving great popularity (around 1867) which has been sustained to the present day.

[1] The shamrock is a trefoil plant, a clover that grows abundantly in Ireland and has been the national (and sometimes religious) symbol. Irish soldiers used it as an emblem from the time of the American Revolution until they ran into stern English opposition. When Queen Victoria forbade them to display it, Irish resentment ran high. The shamrock was thought by many to be a favorite of Saint Patrick, since the three leaves symbolize the Trinity, and they also resemble somewhat the Cross. In addition, for some unknown reason the number 3 has always had a special significance for the Gaelic people.

162

WEARING OF THE GREEN

2. Then since the color we must wear is England's cruel red
   Sure Ireland's sons will ne'er forget the blood that they have shed
   You may take the shamrock from your hat and cast it on the sod
   But 'twill take root and flourish still, though under foot 'tis trod

   When the law can stop the blades of grass from growing as they grow
   And when all the leaves in summertime their verdure[1] dare not show

   Then I sure will change the color that I wear in my caubeen[2]
   But till that day, please God, I'll stick to wearin' of the green

3. But if at last our color should be torn from Ireland's heart
   Her sons with shame and sorrow from the dear old soil will part
   I've heard whisper of a country that lies far beyond the sea
   Where rich and poor stand equal in the light of freedom's day

   Dear old Erin must we leave you, driven by the tyrant's hand
   Must we ask a mother's welcome from a strange but happy land

   Where the cruel cross of England's thraldom[3] never shall be seen
   And where, thank God, we'll live and die still wearin' of the green

1. Greenness and freshness of vegetation.
2. A shabby old hat.
3. Bondage, slavery.

THE MAN ON THE FLYING TRAPEZE
1868

AMERICAN PEOPLE NEVER SEEM TO TIRE OF THIS SONG, NOW ALMOST A HUNDRED YEARS OLD. EACH time its popularity has sagged a bit some famous personality came along and picked it right up again. During the nineteenth century the rescuer was Tony Pastor, the father of vaudeville (from the French, meaning a light form of comedy). In this century Walter O'Keefe, Rudy Vallee and the movies were the benefactors.

The song was first published anonymously in 1868 whereupon it enjoyed a good round of popularity. America was still weary from its recent Civil War, and people in all thirty-seven states needed relaxation from their daily tasks of rebuilding and re-unifying the nation. "The Flying Trapeze," as it was then called, contributed some of this relaxation.

Several of our post-Civil War songs were written by Englishmen, and this song is one of them. The words are by the English actor–singer–comedian George Leybourne, and the music by Alfred Lee, also English. It seems they forgot to copyright their song in the United States since three competing publishers brought it out in 1868. Leybourne very likely was the first to introduce it with his fine singing voice, and the song quickly became a favorite with singing circus clowns who performed to small audiences in those days. Some years later the singer–minstrel–entrepreneur–former clown, Tony Pastor, attached himself to this song and gave its popularity quite a lift.

Through the years this song has undergone certain changes in melody and lyrics, which accounts for the few variations we have today. And, of course, the title became "The Man On the Flying Trapeze." This song's popularity was revived again in 1931 when Walter O'Keefe sang it with his nasal twang in the *Third Little Show* on Broadway, and popularity was boosted still further when the song was featured in the 1935 movie *The Man On the Flying Trapeze* starring W. C. Fields. Rudy Vallee performed the song frequently and effectively on his famous radio show during the 1930's, and the song was used again in the 1941 movie *Too Many Blondes*. This song, a perpetual reminder of circus days, is one of America's great songs of humor, ideal for "gang" singing, and people always seem to enjoy the long "Oh! . . ." just before going into the chorus, the same as in "Alouette."

166

THE MAN ON THE FLYING TRAPEZE

2. Now this man by name was Signor Boni Slang
   Tall, big and handsome, as well made as Chang
   Where'er he appeared, why, the hall loudly rang
   Ovations from ev'ryone there
       Now he'd smile from the bar on the people below
       And then one night he smiled on my love
       Then she winked back at him and she shouted "Bravo!"
       As he hung by his nose up above. Oh!

Chorus:

3. Her father and mother were both on my side
   And very hard tried to make her my bride
   Her father he sighed and her mother she cried
   To see her whole life thrown away
       But 'twas to no avail, she went there ev'ry night
       And she threw him bouquets on the stage
       Which had caused him to meet her, how he ran me down
       But to tell it would take a whole page. Oh!

Chorus:

4. One night I, as usual, went to her home
   Found there her mother and father alone
   I asked for my dear love and soon 'twas made known
   Oh horror! she just ran away
       Packed her bags and eloped after midnight
       And with him with the greatest of ease
       Up from two stories high he had lowered her down
       To the ground on his flying trapeze. Oh!

Chorus:

5. Some months after that I went into a hall
   To my surprise I found there on the wall
   A bill in red letters which did my heart gall
   That she was appearing with him
       He had taught her gymnastics and dressed her in tights
       She would help him to live at his ease
       He had made her assume a more masculine name
       And by now she went on the trapeze. Oh!

Final Chorus: She floats through the air with the greatest of ease
              You'd think her a man on the flying trapeze
              She does all the hard work while he takes his ease
              That is what has become of my love

LITTLE BROWN JUG
1869

FOUR YEARS AFTER THE CIVIL WAR, THE YEAR ULYSSES GRANT BEGAN HIS FIRST TERM OF OFFICE, this humorous song had its first publication. These post-Civil War days were difficult ones in American history—the beginning of reconstruction, adjustment to an America re-united, and the continuation of our expansion period symbolized by the driving of a golden spike in a laurel tie joining the continent by railroad.

"Little Brown Jug" was another of the songs to provide just the right kind of humor and relief from these hard times. The song is simple, honest, and earthy, and very suitable as a polka which was quite popular in those days. The song shortly became a national hit to the surprise of its composer, Joseph Winner, who wrote it under the pseudonym R. A. Eastburn. Joe Winner was rather envious of his older brother Septimus Winner who had written "Listen To the Mocking Bird," "Whispering Hope," and other successful songs. Full of determination, he announced to his family one day that he was going to write a song that would become so popular it would outshine any of Septimus'. His family simply laughed—sympathetically. Americans everywhere have never lost sight of this song. It always produces a laugh and has been played and sung continually for almost a century. It is today one of our standard songs of humor.

LITTLE BROWN JUG

2. 'Tis you who makes my friends and foes
   And it's you who makes me wear old clothes
   Now here you are so near my nose
   So tip her up and down she goes

Chorus:

3. When I go toiling on my farm
   I will take the brown jug in my arm
   I place it 'neath a shady tree
   My dear brown jug, 'tis you and me

Chorus:

4. If all the folks in Adam's race
   Were they here together in one place
   Then I'd prepare to shed a tear
   Before I'd part from you, my dear

Chorus:

5. If I'd a cow that gave such milk
   I would clothe her in the finest silk
   I'd feed her on the choicest hay
   And milk her forty times a day

Chorus:

6. The rose is red, my nose is too
   But the vi'let's blue and so are you
   And yet I guess before I stop
   We'd better take another drop

Chorus:

SHE'LL BE COMIN' 'ROUND THE MOUNTAIN
1870

THIS SONG WAS BORN OUT OF RAILROADING FOLKLORE. DIRECTLY AFTER THE CIVIL WAR RAILROAD-building swung into full stride. The Union Pacific tracklaying westward was to meet the east-bound Central Pacific at Ogden, Utah (they joined May 10, 1869). Other railroads, as well, were expanding as the iron horse needed more and more track. Many a tracklaying foreman was hired chiefly for his singing ability since his singing made the work go smoother and kept the men in better spirits. These are the men who gave us this song as we know it today.

The melody of this song was originally both the old folk hymn "The Old Ship of Zion" and the still older spiritual "When the Chariot Comes" (well known to our Southern moun-taineers). Railroad men gave this melody a snappy, hillbilly kind of twist, and it is probably these same men who also made up the repetitious words of the song.

Because Americans like an occasional good nonsense song, and because railroad workers covered a good deal of territory in those days, this song rapidly caught on. At first it became popular east of the Mississippi and later in the West as railroads expanded. The 1951 Abbott and Costello movie was named after this song, and the song itself was used in the 1946 movie *Tangier*.

174

SHE'LL BE COMIN' 'ROUND THE MOUNTAIN

2. She'll be drivin' six white horses when she comes, etc.

3. She'll be shinin' just like silver when she comes, etc.

4. Oh we'll all go out to meet her when she comes, etc.

5. She'll be breathin' smoke an' fire when she comes, etc.

6. We'll be singin' "hallelujah" when she comes, etc.

7. We will kill the old red rooster when she comes, etc.

8. We'll have chicken an' some dumplin's when she comes, etc.

GO DOWN MOSES
1873

IN THE BEGINNING THIS WAS AN AMERICAN NEGRO FOLK SONG. FOR ABOUT A HUNDRED YEARS IT underwent changes and refinement, as is the case with folk songs.

"Go Down Moses" probably originated in its simplest form around 1795, during George Washington's administration, and came into being in the following way. Bishop Francis Asbury of the newly organized Methodist Episcopal Church in 1784, a horseback-traveling clergyman, was a man dedicated to the worth and salvation of every person regardless of race or position in life. His daily work brought him in close contact with Negroes whom he taught, helped, and treated as worthwhile people. He devoted a great deal of time and energy to these people, and in this connection he noted in his diary September 18, 1797, "The will of God be done." Negroes lavished praise upon the Bishop in their most articulate and expressive manner, *i.e.*, through song. He was their personal Moses and, using metaphors from the bible, Negro slaves in the East made up a song about their Moses and deliverance.

The next important phase in the development of this song occurred in the decade prior to our Civil War when the Fugitive Slave Laws (1850) and the "underground railroad" were in operation. The abolitionist movement was rapidly gaining momentum and the Pennsylvania Quakers played an important role in it, perhaps even initiating the "underground railroad" through which at least 40,000 Negro slaves escaped into Canada and freedom. One of the most colorful and courageous figures in this operation was a Negro woman, Harriet Tubman, referred to as General Tubman by John Brown and as "Moses" by fellow Negroes. At great personal risk she made many trips into the South, bringing back with her countless numbers of slaves. Her fame and legend spread among Negroes everywhere, and their singing of "Go Down Moses" was now an ardent tribute to their hero, Harriet Tubman. This song now took on the added dimension of hope, and it was widely sung by Negro regiments during the Civil War (1861–65). Directly after the war certain black-faced minstrels included "Go Down Moses" in their acts, thus popularizing the song still further.

Although the song was now widely popular among Negroes and a scattering of whites, it wasn't until the Fisk Jubilee Singers made their famous concert tours, beginning in 1871, that this song's popularity swelled to national proportions. America at large was for the first time exposed to all the wonders and beauty of Negro spirituals. By this time "Go Down Moses" was fairly set in words and melody.[1] This song received an unexpected boost just before World War I when Henry Thacker Burleigh, a distinguished Negro singer–com-

[1] In 1871 the Fisk Jubilee Singers performed "Go Down Moses" for President Grant in Washington, and in 1874 they sang it for Queen Victoria of England.

poser–arranger, made brilliant arrangements of several spirituals, including "Go Down Moses" for which he received the Spingarn medal in 1917. Since FDR's days (1930's) in Washington "Go Down Moses" has been sung by countless fine artists, both Negro and white, and it has been continually performed by prominent name bands and popular singers. This song may be found in most song books, and in some under the titles "Let My People Go" or "Down In Egypt Land." Today this song is no longer American Negro; it is American . . . from coast to coast.

GO DOWN MOSES

Tell ol' Phar - aoh, ____ let my peo-ple go

2. Thus spoke the Lord, bold Moses said
Let my people go
If not, I'll smite your first-born dead
Let my people go
Go down, Moses, way down in Egypt land
Tell ol' Pharaoh, let my people go

3. No more shall they in bondage toil
Let my people go
Let them come out with Egypt's spoil
Let my people go
Go down, Moses, way down in Egypt land
Tell ol' Pharaoh, let my people go

4. The Lord told Moses what to do
Let my people go
To lead his people right on through
Let my people go
Go down, Moses, way down in Egypt land
Tell ol' Pharaoh, let my people go

5. 'Twas on a dark and dismal night
Let my people go
When Moses led the Israelites
Let my people go
Go down, Moses, way down in Egypt land
Tell ol' Pharaoh, let my people go

6. Oh Moses, clouds will cleave the way
Let my people go
A fire by night, a shade by day
Let my people go
Go down, Moses, way down in Egypt land
Tell ol' Pharaoh, let my people go

7. When Israel reached the water side
Let my people go
Commanded God, "It shall divide"
Let my people go
Go down, Moses, way down in Egypt land
Tell ol' Pharaoh, let my people go

8. "Come Moses, you will not get lost"
Let my people go
"Stretch out your rod and come across"
Let my people go
Go down, Moses, way down in Egypt land
Tell ol' Pharaoh, let my people go

9. When they had reached the other shore
Let my people go
They sang a song of triumph o'er
Let my people go
Go down, Moses, way down in Egypt land
Tell ol' Pharaoh, let my people go

10. Now Pharaoh said he'd go across
Let my people go
But Pharaoh and his host were lost
Let my people go
Go down, Moses, way down in Egypt land
Tell ol' Pharaoh, let my people go

11. Oh take your shoes from off your feet
Let my people go
And walk into the golden street
Let my people go
Go down, Moses, way down in Egypt land
Tell ol' Pharaoh, let my people go

I'LL TAKE YOU HOME AGAIN, KATHLEEN
1876

"I'LL TAKE YOU HOME AGAIN, KATHLEEN" WAS ONE OF THE TWO BIG SONG HITS OF 1876 (THE other was "Grandfather's Clock") in the 38 United States of America, published the same year that Alexander Graham Bell patented the telephone. The song was written the previous year by Thomas Westendorf, a public-school music teacher in Plainfield, Indiana, and publicly performed for the first time in the town hall.

Westendorf, deeply in love with his wife Jennie, wrote the song on the occasion of feeling lonesome for her while she was visiting her home town, Ogdensburg, New York. For reasons best known to Westendorf, he changed the name of the girl to Kathleen. The song has a kind of dream-fantasy quality whereby the composer's feeling of loneliness places his wife "across the ocean wild and wide," and leaps forward in time to their old age where he lovingly promises her his protection.

This song was quite a favorite of Thomas Edison, and Henry Ford liked it so well he obtained Westendorf's autographed song copy for his museum in Detroit and distributed photostatic copies to his friends.

Many people have the impression this is an Irish song, perhaps because of the name Kathleen, but it is obviously American. This song's great tenderness, sincerity, and beauty has kept its popularity alive to the present day.

180

I'LL TAKE YOU HOME AGAIN, KATHLEEN

2. I know you love me, Kathleen dear
   Your heart was ever fond and true
   I always feel when you are near
   That life holds nothing, dear, but you
   The smiles that once you gave to me
   I scarcely ever see them now
   Though many many times I see
   A dark'ning shadow on your brow

Chorus:

3. To that dear home beyond the sea
   My Kathleen shall again return
   And when thy old friends welcome thee
   Thy loving heart will cease to yearn
   Where laughs the little silver stream
   Beside your mother's humble cot [1]
   And brightest rays of sunshine gleam
   There all your grief will be forgot

Chorus:

1. Cottage

CARRY ME BACK TO OLD VIRGINNY
1878

"CARRY ME BACK TO OLD VIRGINNY," A GREAT ALL-TIME FAVORITE, WAS WRITTEN (WORDS AND music) by a Negro, James Bland, who was born not in Virginia, but in Flushing, New York in 1854, just ten years before the Emancipation Proclamation. Later, his family moved to Washington, D.C. During the boy's youth he worked as a page in the House of Representatives during Ulysses Grant's administration. Here Bland frequently entertained statesmen with his own compositions, singing and playing the banjo. He subsequently studied music more formally while attending Howard University.

Before Bland was twenty years old he had written "Carry Me Back To Old Virginny" as a result of a visit he made to a plantation in Virginia. He was moved by the soft peaceful atmosphere of cotton and cornfields and while strumming on his ever-present banjo, he translated his feelings into the familiar and poignant plea of the aging person who longs to return to the scenes of his childhood. Since Bland was crazy about minstrels he gave this song over to them before it was copyrighted. Thus it became fairly popular before its first publication, after which it became an overnight hit.

This song may be found in most song books. In 1940 it was voted the official song of the state of Virginia. It was featured in the 1952 movie, *With A Song In My Heart,* and before that, in the 1940 movie *Hullabaloo.*

CARRY ME BACK TO OLD VIRGINNY

2. Carry me back to old Virginny
   There let me live until I wither and decay
   Long by the old Dismal Swamp have I wandered
   There's where my old weary life will pass away
   Master and Mistress have long gone before me
   Soon we will meet on that bright and golden shore
   There we'll be happy and free from all sorrow
   There's where we'll meet and we will never part no more

OH, DEM GOLDEN SLIPPERS
1879

THIS SONG HAS ENJOYED A STEADY POPULARITY SINCE F. W. WOOLWORTH OPENED HIS FIRST five-and-ten-cent store (Utica, New York) in 1879. It was the feature song in the 1940 western movie *Tulsa Kid*. James Bland, an educated and highly gifted Negro, composed both words and music a few weeks before his 20th birthday. Later that same year (1874), when young Bland met with and auditioned for the famous star of Skiff & Gaylord's Minstrel Show, he played this song (and others) for George Primrose and exclaimed that he wanted more than anything else to become a minstrel himself. Although Primrose failed to offer a job, he was so enthusiastic about Bland's compositions that he immediately began to use them in his show.

The following year Bland succeeded in joining a company of Negro minstrels, known as the Original Georgia Minstrels. He became an end man in which he sang, played banjo, and composed songs. It wasn't until four years later (1879) that "Oh, Dem Golden Slippers" was published since music-loving James Bland was quite casual about copyrighting and publication. After publication, however, other minstrel shows began using this song and very quickly its popularity blossomed into a national hit.

As a member of the Georgia Minstrels, James Bland entertained audiences with many of his own compositions throughout all thirty-eight states of the Union. In 1884, the year Grover Cleveland was elected president and the Washington National Monument was completed, the Georgia Minstrels went to Europe where their performances became something of a sensation among royalty and commoners. Many an Englishman could be heard whistling or singing "Oh, Dem Golden Slippers."

During the 1890's here in America this song was a favorite with most minstrel shows, and since it was such a good "gang" song the man-on-the-street kept it very much alive right up to the present day. James Bland is considered one of the most important contributors of Ethiopian songs on the American scene, and "Oh, Dem Golden Slippers" is a shining example.

188

OH, DEM GOLDEN SLIPPERS

1. Oh my gold-en slip-pers they are laid a - way I was sav - in' them un-til my wed - ding day An' my long tail coat that I love so well I will wear up in the char-iot in the morn And my long white robe that I had

189

bought last June I am gon - na change it 'cause it fits too soon An' the

old grey horse that I used to drive I will hitch him to the char-iot in the morn

Chorus

Oh dem gold-en slip-pers Oh dem gold-en slip-pers

Gold-en slip-pers I'm gon-na wear Be-cause they look so neat

Oh dem gold-en slip-pers Oh dem gold-en slip-pers

Gold-en slip-pers I'm gon-na wear To walk the gold-en street

2. Oh my old banjo it hangs upon the wall
   'Cause it ain't been tuned up ever since last fall
   But the folks say we'll have a real good time
   When we ride up in the chariot in the morn
       There's my brother Ben an' there's my sister Luce
       They will get the news to Uncle Bacco juice
       What a great camp-meetin' we'll have that day
       When we ride up in the chariot in the morn

Chorus:

3. So it's goodbye children, I will have to go
   Where the rain ain't fallin' or the wind don't blow
   An' your ulster coats [1], why you will not need
   When you ride up in the chariot in the morn
       But your golden slippers must be nice and clean
       An' your age must be a tender sweet sixteen
       An' your white kid gloves you will have to wear
       When you ride up in the chariot in the morn

Chorus:

1. Ulster coat = A long loose overcoat formerly made in Ulster, Ireland.

TWINKLE TWINKLE LITTLE STAR
1880

THIS CHARMING POPULAR SONG DATES BACK OVER A HUNDRED AND FIFTY YEARS TO ITS ORIGIN in England. The words were originally written as a poem by the London-born sisters, Jane and Ann Taylor, writers of children's poems and plays, and of hymns for Sunday School. Female writers were rare in those days. The music is an old French folk song, "Ah! vous dirai-je, Maman," a beautifully simple theme that inspired the works of many composers including Mozart's "Variations in C for Piano," Series 21.

The poem of the Taylor sisters was first published in London around 1804 in the book *Original Poems for Infant Minds* along with many of their other verses. The book had an immediate and lasting success. How and when the poem and music were combined is still a mystery, but the song did become popular in England around the middle of the century. It was not very long before its popularity reached growing America around 1880, and there followed several adult parodies for the next few years.

With very minor changes the music fits two other children's songs: "Baa, Baa Black Sheep" and "The Alphabet Song." There is no doubt though, that this song is thoroughly enjoyed by adults as well as children.

192

TWINKLE TWINKLE LITTLE STAR

Twin - kle twin - kle lit - tle star

How I won - der what you are

2. When the blazing sun is gone
   When he nothing shines upon
   Then you show your little light
   Twinkle twinkle all the night
   Twinkle twinkle little star
   How I wonder what you are

3. Then the trav'ller in the dark
   Thanks you for your tiny spark
   He could not see where to go
   If you did not twinkle so
   Twinkle twinkle little star
   How I wonder what you are

4. In the dark blue sky you keep
   While you through my window peep
   And you never shut your eye
   Till the sun is in the sky
   Twinkle twinkle little star
   How I wonder what you are

I'VE BEEN WORKING ON THE RAILROAD
1881

HERE IS ONE OF THE MOST POPULAR OF ALL SONGS. WHILE ITS ORIGIN IS SOMETHING OF A mystery, it seems to have originated in the South possibly before our Civil War days. Many people believe it is a genuine American folk song, some consider it of Negro origin, and many others believe it originated in some small minstrel show.

This song's earlier title was "Levee Song," and it seems to have started in this way. The building of levees (French word meaning "embankments") on the southern Mississippi was begun by the Louisiana French around 1730, and eventually this work was performed by Negro laborers who always sang as they worked. This song is known to have been fairly popular around the levees in the South somewhere in the 1830's and 40's. But Negro laborers were soon to shift their energies to the task of building railroads in our expanding country.

The first successful steam locomotive was produced in Great Britain in 1804, and first appeared in America in 1826 near Quincy, Massachusetts. But by 1850 the United States had less than 9,000 miles of track, almost all of it in the East. The West was now in need of rail transportation and we began building track west of the Mississippi in 1851. Though most of the track builders were Irish there were men of many other nationalities including many Negroes, all of whom brought their songs with them. The Negroes were so fascinated by railroads they modified many of their songs to fit the railroad setting. One of these was the "Levee Song" which began with "I've been working on the railroad."

Although railroad construction was interrupted by the Civil War, it swung back into high gear directly afterwards. By 1880 almost 100,000 miles of track were in operation and the song "I've Been Working On the Railroad" was traveling rapidly, mostly by rail. By 1881 this song was already popular over most of our thirty-eight states, making it virtually the granddaddy of railroad songs. Somewhere along the line this melody became the official song of the University of Texas (opened in 1883) under the title "The Eyes of Texas" with a brand new set of lyrics. This song was also the title of a 1948 movie starring Roy Rogers.

The first publication of the "Levee Song" was in 1900, and it began with "I've been working on the railroad." It carried a second strain which is unfamiliar to most people today. The song then began to appear in several college song books. However, since World War II a different 2nd strain was somehow added, and it stuck. It is familiar to most people although its origin is still obscure. "I've Been Working On the Railroad" is one of the greatest of all "gang" songs, and today there's scarcely a person who does not know it.

195

I'VE BEEN WORKING ON THE RAILROAD

D. C. al Fine

MY BONNIE LIES OVER THE OCEAN
1882

THIS OLD FAVORITE WAS ORIGINALLY, NO DOUBT, A SCOTTISH FOLK SONG. THERE DOESN'T APPEAR to be any record of its age, composers or its publication, although in the late 1870's a number of people were requesting at the music stores a certain anonymous song bearing this title. No one knows how it all started, but word surely got around. The story has it that a certain music publisher, seeking to capitalize on this ready-made demand, persuaded composer Charles E. Pratt to produce this mysterious song, and to write it in such a manner that people would feel inclined to join in the singing. Although it is not known, it is conceivable that Pratt may have had access to the missing Scottish folk song, but in any case, he did produce "My Bonnie Lies Over the Ocean" under the pseudonyms J. T. Wood (words) and H. J. Fulmer (music). This song, bearing real folk-music qualities, was published in 1881, and promptly rose to hit proportions.

"My Bonnie Lies Over the Ocean" soon became a favorite with college singing groups and was heard on many campuses. It made a fine "gang" song and people felt quite inclined to join in the singing. It was perfect for community singing with children as well as adults, and barbershop singers adopted it as their very own. No doubt about it, the song was a solid success.

"My Bonnie Lies Over the Ocean" (also known as "My Bonnie" and "Bring Back My Bonnie To Me") has been continually popular ever since its American publication, when we were a country of only thirty-eight states, and it will probably remain popular for a long time to come.

MY BONNIE LIES OVER THE OCEAN

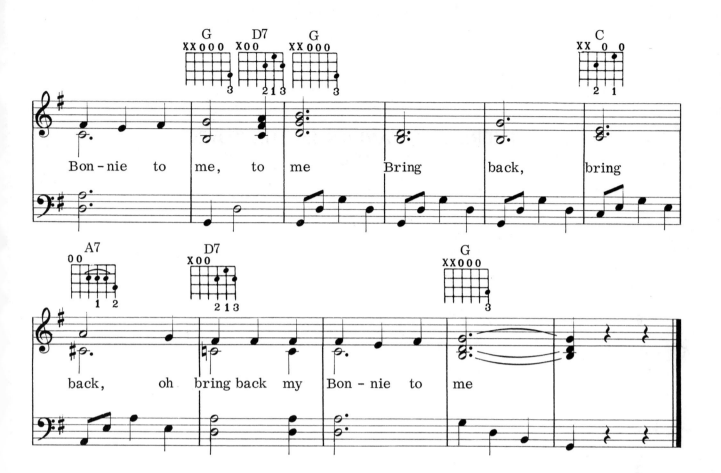

Bon - nie to me, to me Bring back, bring

back, oh bring back my Bon - nie to me

2. Last night as I lay on my pillow
Last night as I lay on my bed
Last night as I lay on my pillow
I dreamt that my Bonnie was dead

Chorus:

3. Oh blow ye winds over the ocean
And blow ye winds over the sea
Oh blow ye winds over the ocean
And bring back my Bonnie to me

Chorus:

4. The winds have blown over the ocean
The winds have blown over the sea
The winds have blown over the ocean
And brought back my Bonnie to me

Chorus:

THERE IS A TAVERN IN THE TOWN
1883

THE WELL-KNOWN FAVORITE GANG SONG "THERE IS A TAVERN IN THE TOWN" HAD ITS BEGINNING in the eastern Ivy League colleges during the early 1880's. Since then the song has been to enough colleges for a long enough time to earn several degrees of popularity.

The song was first published in 1883, the same year in which New York's Metropolitan Opera House was opened, and the era when college glee clubs were coming into their own. While the copyright bears the name William Hills, the song is believed to have been based on a Cornish folk song. It has appeared in many college songbooks.

This song caught on very quickly and it was soon heard in and out of colleges, saloons, homes, dancehalls, and streets. It became a favorite with close-harmony barbershop quartets and was often heard sung by the Saturday night boys on the corner under the gas lights. There have been several revival periods for this song including a big one by Rudy Vallee in the 1930's. We often hear and sing this song today. Its popularity is still solid.

204

THERE IS A TAVERN IN THE TOWN

hang my harp on a weep - ing wil - low tree And

may the world go well with thee

2. He left me for a damsel dark
   Each Friday night they used to spark
   And now my love, who once was true to me,
   Takes that dark damsel on his knee

Chorus:

3. Oh dig my grave both wide and deep
   Put tombstones at my head and feet
   And on my breast carve just a turtle dove
   To signify I died of love

Chorus:

WHILE STROLLING THROUGH THE PARK
1884

THIS SONG BECAME A NATIONAL HIT THE YEAR PRESIDENT HARRY S. TRUMAN WAS BORN, AN era of gaslight and horse cars in the cities, and kerosene lamps and buggies in the rural areas. Here was a vigorous period in America's development. The West was growing rapidly through the attraction of free homesteads, cattle raising, and the discovery of precious metals. National politics were undergoing important change due to the difference in needs between Easterners and Westerners. Railroads were expanding; big business was rapidly heading toward monopolies; and the American Federation of Labor was only three years old. Minstrel shows were going strong at this time, and variety shows were just beginning to give way to a thing called vaudeville which was just invented in Boston by B. F. Keith, and that is where this song comes in.

Throughout the entire life of vaudeville (almost half a century) the song "While Strolling Through the Park" was one of the favorite tunes of the song-and-dance men. They appeared on stage nattily dressed in colorful striped jackets and straw hats, carrying canes, and then went through a neat routine of singing this song and doing the two "dance breaks" provided for in the tune. On the second chorus they did the soft shoe dance in schottische tempo, occasionally slapping their hands to their knees and tipping their jauntily placed straw hats. The audience loved this kind of act and came away humming and whistling this melody. Thus the song attained a solid and lasting popularity.

The words and music of "While Strolling Through the Park" were composed by Ed Haley and dedicated to a Robert A. Keiser. Ed Haley's original title was "The Fountain In the Park," and the song was introduced to the public for the first time around 1880 by the Du Rell Twin Brothers (whose interpretation became the traditional one) at Tony Pastor's in New York City. This song was used in the 1945 movie *Sunbonnet Sue*. There is hardly anyone these days who has not heard and enjoyed this song.

WHILE STROLLING THROUGH THE PARK

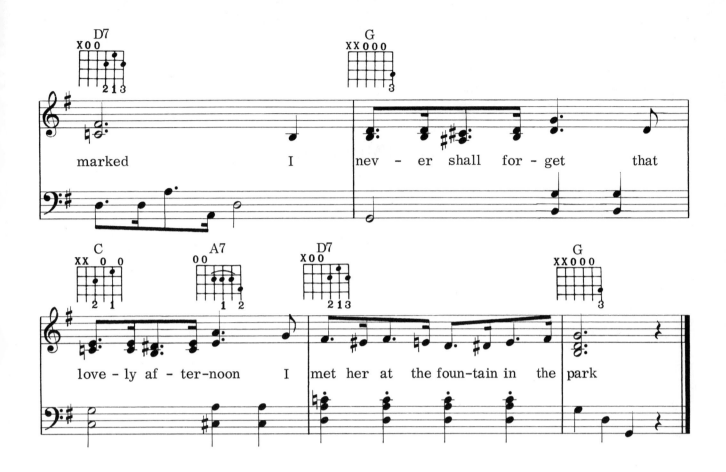

marked   I nev - er shall for - get   that

love - ly af - ter-noon   I met her at the foun-tain in the park

CLEMENTINE
1885

THIS SONG CAME ON THE AMERICAN SCENE (1883) WHEN VAUDEVILLE FIRST BEGAN IN BOSTON, and the Brooklyn Bridge was opened to the public in New York. Westward, free homesteads were still attracting people to make the long trek across the nation. Both words and music were written by Percy Montross. The song got a heavy boost toward popularity when it finally became a favorite with the smart San Francisco art colony. A group of fun and wit-loving sophisticates, they enjoyed the nonsensical appeal and lilting melody of "Clementine." Quickly the song spread to colleges, and eventually made its way to a fun-loving public who sang its many verses with gusto under the light of kerosene lamps and gaslight.

This song has had frequent revivals and is a perennial favorite. It is found in most community song books, in Boy Scout books, and in many college song books. There are any number of recordings available. It is a great "gang" song enjoyed equally by young and old, and will stay with us for a long time to come.

CLEMENTINE

2. Light she was and like a fairy
   And her shoes were number nine
   Herring boxes without topses
   Sandals were for Clementine

Chorus:

3. Drove she ducklings to the water
   Ev'ry morning just at nine
   Hit her foot against a splinter
   Fell into the foaming brine

Chorus:

4. Ruby lips above the water
   Blowing bubbles soft and fine
   But alas, I was no swimmer·
   So I lost my Clementine

Chorus:

5. In a churchyard near the canyon
   Where the myrtle doth entwine
   There grow roses and the posies
   Fertilized by Clementine

Chorus:

6. Then the miner, forty-niner
   Soon began to peak and pine
   Thought he ought-er join his daughter
   Now he's with his Clementine

Chorus:

7. In my dreams she still doth haunt me
   Robed in garments soaked in brine
   Though in life I used to hug her
   Now she's dead, I'll draw the line

Chorus:

8. How I missed her, how I missed her
   How I missed my Clementine
   Then I kissed her little sister
   And forgot my Clementine

Chorus:

LOVE'S OLD SWEET SONG
1887

CALLED "JUST A SONG AT TWILIGHT" BY MANY PEOPLE, THIS SONG IS AN EVERLASTING FAVORITE, and singing it often produces spontaneous harmonizing. It sounds like an American song —most people think it is—but it is in fact an English song.

This number was written in London, probably in the early 1880's. The lyrics are those of G. Clifton Bingham, and the melody was composed by an Irish lawyer, James Lyman Molloy. Although he practiced law in England, Molloy's greatest passion was for music. He produced "Kerry Dance," "Darby and Joan," three operas, a collection of Irish folk songs, and a host of other songs. "Love's Old Sweet Song" was his most durable and popular creation.

This song's first American publication was in 1884, the year Mark Twain published *Huckleberry Finn* and Louis Waterman invented the fountain pen. Since in those days music stores flourished throughout the country, and pianos provided the most popular type of home entertainment, "Love's Old Sweet Song" was quite widely played and sung by 1887, the year in which President Grover Cleveland dedicated the Statue of Liberty in New York harbor. Since that time the song has firmly established itself in every state of our Union. As a tenderly appealing ballad, "Love's Old Sweet Song" remains ever popular and attractive to the American people. The song was used effectively in the 1952 movie *Wait Till the Sun Shines Nellie.*

LOVE'S OLD SWEET SONG

2. Even today we hear love's song of yore
   Deep in our hearts it dwells forevermore
   Footsteps may falter, weary grow the way
   Still we can hear it at the close of day
         So till the end when life's dim shadows fall
         Love will be found the sweetest song of all

Chorus:

WHERE DID YOU GET THAT HAT
1888

THIS SONG BLANKETED AMERICA IN 1888 LIKE THE FAMOUS BLIZZARD OF THE SAME YEAR. NOT only was the song a huge success but for years afterwards the title itself became the source of little practical jokes. A person meeting a friend on the street would gaze at his hat and whistle the first six notes of this song. Passersby, hearing the whistle, would stop and stare at the friend's hat.

The composer of words and music was Joseph J. Sullivan, a fairly good black-faced comedian-song-and-dance man who had had a fairly hard time keeping himself in work. At the home of his parents in New York, during one of his layoffs, Sullivan rummaged around in the attic for something new he might use in his act. He became curious about a very tall old-fashioned plug hat he found in a trunk. When he tried it on it was too small for him, and he was quite amused with the comic effect since he was such a short chubby fellow. As a bit of whimsy, he took a little walk around the neighborhood where kids began collecting behind him shouting and yelling, "Where did you get that hat?" and several other things. This one expression impressed Joe Sullivan so much that he immediately made tracks for home, lit the kerosene lamp and began composing a story for "Where did you get that hat?," setting the whole thing to music.

Sullivan persuaded the manager of Miner's Eighth Avenue Theatre (in New York) to let him open his act with the new song. His audiences went all out for this type of humor, and wherever Sullivan was booked thereafter this song was a must. "Where Did You Get That Hat?" was published and became the national hit of the year. The song even spread to England where popular singer J. C. Heffron used it with equally good success. For years afterwards this song was performed by many other vaudeville personalities, played by bands and hurdy-gurdies, and sung and whistled by people everywhere. Today, in the mid-twentieth century, this is one of our standard songs of humor.

218

WHERE DID YOU GET THAT HAT

Playful - but not too fast

1. Now how I came to get this hat, 'tis ver - y strange and fun - ny Grand-

fa - ther died and left to me his pro - per - ty and mon - ey And

when the will it was read out, they told me straight and flat If

I would have his mon - ey I must al - ways wear his hat

1. Tile = a tall silk hat.

2. If I go to the op'ra house a-mid the op'ra season
   There's someone sure to shout at me without the slightest reason
   If I go to a chowder club to have a jolly spree
   There's someone in the party who is sure to shout at me

Chorus:

3. At twenty-one I thought I would to my sweetheart be married
   For people in the neighborhood had said too long we'd tarried
   So off to church we went right quick, determined to get wed
   I had not long been in there when the parson to me said

Chorus:

OH PROMISE ME
1890

THIS SONG BEGAN AS A FAILURE AND YET, THROUGH AN UNEXPECTED INCIDENT, BECAME ONE OF our country's most popular and beloved songs. This all happened during the Victorian age when America purchased the vast Dakota Territory from the Sioux Indians, and four more stars were added to our flag (making a total of forty-two states). "Oh Promise Me" was originally intended as an "art" song, and was composed by music critic Clement Scott and musician Reginald DeKoven in 1887. It was first published as a semiclassical song (in 1889) and nothing much happened with it. Lovers of classical music generally preferred the songs of Europe's great masters.

Reginald DeKoven, a well trained musician, was an aristocratic type of person, sincerely interested in America's musical development. While he knew ragtime and popular music, his chief interest was in opera and operettas for which he began writing around 1886. His earlier works failed to impress the theatregoing public until he wrote the operetta *Robin Hood* which opened June 9, 1890, in Chicago. Directly after opening-night performance the temperamental leading lady, Jessie 'Bartlett Davis, flew into a rage, complaining that there was not one song in the whole operetta that suited her beautiful contralto voice. She threatened to quit unless something were done about it immediately. Everyone was stunned by this outburst, and all became silent. For a few moments DeKoven was at a loss, but suddenly he got an idea. He jumped into the orchestra pit and from memory he played and sang "Oh Promise Me." At that moment Miss Davis fell in love with the song. Thereafter it was included in the show, thus preventing disaster and providing Miss Davis with a song that brought long and sustained applause from the audiences.

"Oh Promise Me" became an enormous hit in 1890, selling over a million copies. *Robin Hood* was soon forgotten but "Oh Promise Me" has steadily increased in popularity over the years. For well over half a century this beautiful song has taken its place at wedding ceremonies beside Wagner's "Bridal Chorus" and Mendelssohn's "Wedding March" —both in America and in England. "Oh Promise Me" seems destined for a long life indeed.

222

OH PROMISE ME

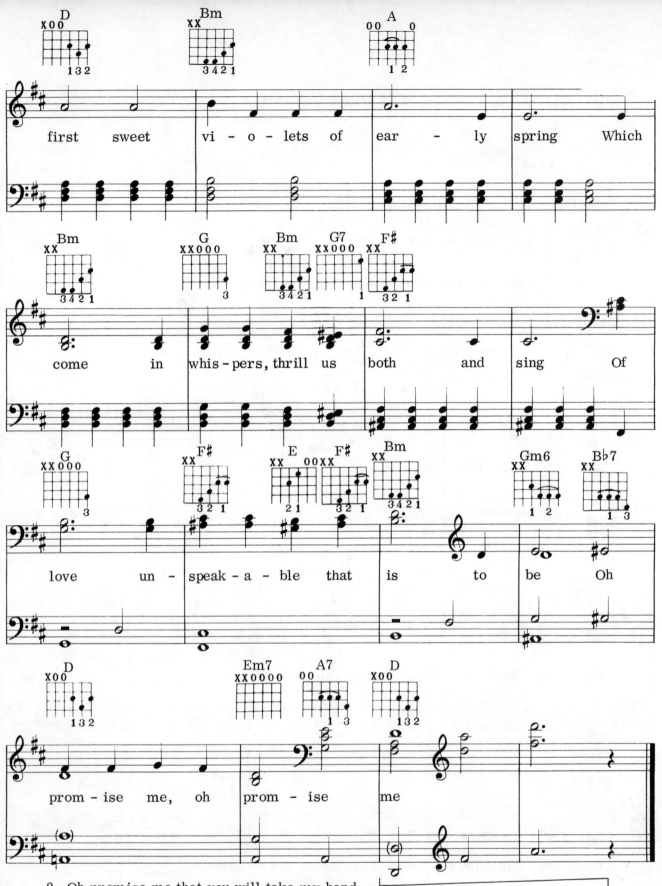

first sweet vi - o - lets of ear - ly spring Which come in whis-pers, thrill us both and sing Of love un - speak-a - ble that is to be Oh prom - ise me, oh prom - ise me

2. Oh promise me that you will take my hand
   The most unworthy in this promised land
   And let me sit beside you, in your eyes
   To see the vision of our paradise
       To hear God's message while the organ rolls
       Its mighty music to our very souls
       No love less perfect than a life with thee
       Oh promise me, oh promise me

TURN-OF-THE-CENTURY AMERICA (1890-1910)

THE TEMPO OF AMERICA'S PROGRESS PICKED UP CONSIDERABLY DURING THIS HISTORICAL PERIOD, as did the music we sang day after day. The Gay Nineties era was both exuberant and sentimental with these moods lasting well through 1910.

The twenty-year span began with the opening of the Oklahoma Territory (1890) to thousands of homsteaders, the swift growth of eastern industries which occasioned the Sherman Anti-Trust Act of 1890, covered wagons still pushing westward, and the ever-growing momentum of the women's suffrage movement. Vaudeville and musical comedy with their many new songs were gaining in public favor. Both automobiles and music publishing were in the experimental stage but on their way toward becoming important industries. The Gibson Girl fashion was spreading all over the country almost as fast as ragtime music.

The newly formed Columbia and Victor phonograph companies were striving to capitalize on Thomas Edison's recently perfected wax cylinders, with much music soon to be reproduced for millions of grateful people. Despite America's economic depression of 1893, which lasted four years, a new breed of songsmiths produced quantities of songs, many of which netted sizable profits and some of which have retained their popularity to the present day.

After the depression we plunged into the Spanish–American War (1898). Although it lasted only sixteen weeks,[1] important advantages accrued to the United States. The outstanding song hit of the war was "A Hot Time In the Old Town," which was so popular among our soldiers that the Spanish Army thought it was our national anthem. Foreign newspapers reporting on the song's importance had some trouble with the title. A literal translation of the French title back to English was "There Will Be Warm Weather In the Old City This Evening." Teddy Roosevelt and his Rough Riders sang their way up the San Juan Hill attack with this song.

During these two short decades new developments in communication and transportation sparked songs about the telephone, telegraph, steamships, bicycles, railroads, trolly cars, aeroplanes and automobiles. Player pianos appeared around 1900, played songs of the

[1] War was declared April 21 and the armistice signed August 12.

day, and won many enthusiasts. The flickers (movies) were spreading throughout most cities and towns and were shown in nickelodeons.[2] While movie reels were being changed the words of a popular song were projected on the screen and everyone engaged in a Sing-Along. Audiences loved it and gave forth with a rollicking zest. Few persons realize that radio also began at this time, with the first transatlantic message in 1902. Four years later Lee DeForest broadcast Rossini's "William Tell Overture" all the way from New York City to Brooklyn.

This twenty-year span closed with our gradual emergence from the strict Victorian influences. We became a little happier as a people and broke out with such expressions as "Oh you kid," "Get a horse," "Twenty-three skiddoo." Ragtime and the blues were in a merging transition, soon to blossom out into jazz. Ballrooms were on the rise where proper dancing etiquette required a distance of two inches between a lady and her escort. The music-publishing industry was a veritable factory turning out hundreds of songs in which a little better level of literacy was just beginning to creep in. Popular and classical music occasionally touched each other. A few of our well-schooled composers whose songs became highly popular were Ethelbert Nevin ("Narcissus"), Reginald DeKoven ("Oh Promise Me"), Charles Wakefield Cadman ("At Dawning"), Edward MacDowell ("To A Wild Rose"), and Victor Herbert and two or three others.

The close of this period saw "gang singing" and close-harmony barbershop quartets swinging into high gear. Where haircuts cost twenty-five cents men sang and listened to such favorites as "On the Banks of the Wabash," "Dear Old Girl," "Sweet Adeline," and "Down By the Old Mill Stream."

STATES ADMITTED TO THE UNION

Rank	Name	Origin of Name	Year Admitted	State Song
43.	Idaho	Shoshoni Indian words "ida" (salmon) and "ho" (tribe).	1890	Here We Have Idaho
44.	Wyoming	From the Lenape Indian place name "M'cheuwonink" meaning "great plain." Named after Wyoming Valley, Pennsylvania.	1890	Wyoming
45.	Utah	Navajo Indian name applied to the Ute tribe meaning "People of the upper lands."	1896	Utah, We Love Thee
46.	Oklahoma	From the Choctaw Indian words meaning "Red people."	1907	Oklahoma

[2] Named after the five-cent cost of admission.

AFTER THE BALL
1892

THIS WAS NOT ONLY THE SONG SENSATION OF THE YEAR 1892 BUT IT WAS THE FIRST BIG HIT in the pop tune field, having sold over a million copies. It was a time when in Benjamin Harrison's last year of the presidency America was teeming with activity, both great and small. Immigration was at a high point, Thomas Edison patented the forerunner of the movie camera, Tschaikowsky opened Carnegie Hall, women organized for the right to vote, industrial empires were being born, P.T. Barnum died, Chicago held a World's Fair, the game of basketball was just invented, and the popular music industry was just getting started.

Charles K. Harris, the composer of this song, was the first big time songwriter, although "After the Ball" was only the second song he had published. A former pawnbroker, bellhop, and banjo player, Harris witnessed two quarreling lovers leave separately after a dance in Chicago, and the scene gave him the idea for the phrase "many an aching heart after the ball." He published the song himself and managed to get a well-known singer to perform it in the highly successful show *A Trip To Chinatown*. The song was so enthusiastically received that one publisher offered him $10,000 for it, and orders for copies kept pouring in. John Phillip Sousa featured this song at the World's Fair in Chicago. Parodies were invented, and to date the song has sold over five million copies. "After the Ball" was also popular in Great Britain, so much so that when Britons heard it was an American tune they could hardly believe it. Most people know only the chorus, but the three verses (each twice as long as the chorus) bear the key to the story.

227

AFTER THE BALL

Moderately fast

1. A lit - tle maid - en climbed an old man's knee   Begged for a sto - ry "Do un - cle, please!" "Why are you sin - gle, why live a - lone?

2. Bright lights were flashing in the grand ballroom
   Softly the music playing sweet tunes
   There came my sweetheart, my love, my own
   "I wish some water; leave me alone"
   When I returned dear, there stood a man
   Kissing my sweetheart as lovers can
   Down fell the glass, pet, broken, that's all
   Just as my heart was after the ball

Chorus:

3. Long years have passed, child, I have never wed
   True to my lost love though she is dead
   She tried to tell me, tried to explain
   I would not listen, pleadings were vain
   One day a letter came from that man
   He was her brother, the letter ran
   That's why I'm lonely, no home at all
   I broke her heart, pet, after the ball

Chorus:

DAISY BELL
1893

BY 1892, WHEN THIS SONG WAS FIRST PUBLISHED, AMERICA HAD ALREADY EXPERIENCED SOME thirty-five years of change in bicycle styles. But it was not until the late 1880's—when the so-called "safety" model (*ca.* 1885) and pneumatic tires (1889) were developed—that bicycling became a fad and later a national craze. Sunday was a man's only day off from work and controversy was raised in some circles over bicycling on the Sabbath. One liberal publication stated, "A man may truly serve God in taking an envigorating spin if his heart is attuned to what is right." Around 1892 about one in seven Americans had a bicycle. Tandem bikes were popular since the girl friend could ride on the back seat, and it was the tandem bike that inspired the popular song "Daisy Bell," also called "Bicycle Built For Two," and "Daisy, Daisy."

Although this song was composed right here in America it is really English, written by the Englishman Harry Dacre (born Henry Decker), and became a hit for the first time in London. Harry Dacre had come to the United States in 1891 as many other English songwriters had, where opportunities seemed better than in England. He brought his bicycle with him, and upon landing in New York he was shocked when the customs officers said he would have to pay a duty on his bicycle. He paid the required duty under protest, but his indignation ran deep for months to come. As he became acclimated to New York and Tin Pan Alley he related his experience to many people expressing his indignation. One person simply replied, "You're lucky it wasn't a bicycle built for two," and this phrase struck a responsive note in Harry's mind. Quite aware of the growing popularity of bicycling, and particularly of women cyclists wearing billowy skirts and leg-of-mutton sleeves, Harry Dacre got the idea for a song using the theme "bicycle built for two."

After he finished composing the words and music of "Daisy Bell," Dacre took it around to music publishers. No one wanted it. Harry remembered the popular American singer, Kate Lawrence, whom he had met in London. He reasoned that if she liked his song she would sing it, and if her audiences liked it Harry might then find a publisher willing to accept it. He contacted Kate Lawrence. She listened to the song, liked it, and announced that she was leaving for a singing tour of England, the home of confirmed bicyclists. She took the song with her, rehearsed it well, and tried it out. From her very first show in London the song was a solid smash hit with every audience. Within two weeks all England knew and sang "Daisy Bell." It was even reported that wedding guests of the Duke of York danced to this song.

Now "Daisy Bell" suddenly found a New York publisher, and directly after Harry Dacre signed up many other publishers contacted him offering publication. "Daisy Bell" was an immediate hit in New York and, shortly thereafter, throughout our whole country (forty-four states). Bicycle parties everywhere were fond of singing this great "gang" song, and a few years later one bicycle manufacturer put out a model called the Daisy bicycle. "Daisy Bell" has never lost favor with the American public since it is a gay song with a happy lilt, and is perhaps one of the most typical songs of the Gay Nineties.

DAISY BELL

2. We will go "tandem" as man and wife, Daisy, Daisy
   "Ped'ling" away down the road of life, I and my Daisy Bell
   When the road's dark we can both despise p'licemen and "lamps" as well
   There are "bright lights" in the dazzling eyes of beautiful Daisy Bell

Chorus:

3. I will stand by you in "wheel" or woe, Daisy, Daisy
   You'll be the bell(e) which I'll ring, you know, sweet little Daisy Bell
   You'll take the "lead" in each "trip" we take, then if I don't do well
   I will permit you to use the brake, my beautiful Daisy Bell

Chorus:

SIDEWALKS OF NEW YORK
1894

THIS SONG IS GENERALLY CONSIDERED NEW YORK CITY'S UNOFFICIAL CITY ANTHEM. AT THE height of Al Smith's political career "Sidewalks of New York" became the Governor's political signature and was played continually throughout his campaign for the Presidency in 1928. During New York's World's Fair of 1939 the musical phrase "Boys and girls together" was heard on automobile horns.

The music was composed in the summer of 1894 by a vaudeville baritone singer, Charles Lawlor, who visited his friend, James Blake, a hat salesman, and asked Blake to write the words, something about New York. The next night Lawlor tried out the song in a nearby saloon and it was well received. The song was published soon afterwards and was first sung by Lottie Gilson (well known in those days) at the London Theatre in New York. Lawlor also used the song in his own vaudeville act.

It is said that the impatient writers, not wishing to wait for their royalties, sold the song outright for a few thousand dollars (a lot of money in those days). The song sold well over a million copies with considerable profit to the publisher. When the copyright expired twenty-eight years later, Lawlor renewed it and sold his rights again, this time for a couple of hundred dollars. This song is often called "East Side, West Side."

SIDEWALKS OF NEW YORK

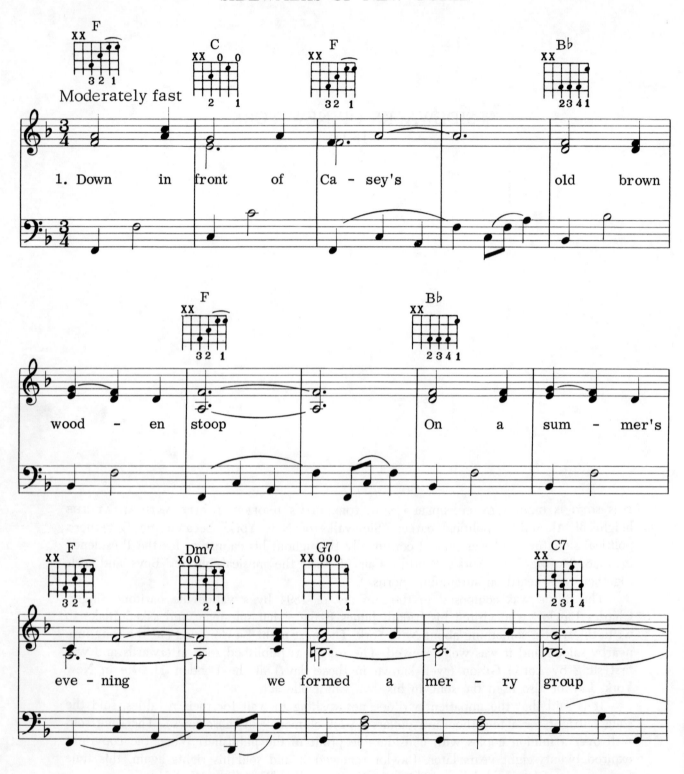

2. That's where Johnny Casey, little Jimmy Crowe
   Jakey Krause, the baker who always had the dough
   Pretty Nellie Shannon (with a) dude as light as cork
   She first picked up the waltz step on the sidewalks of New York

Chorus:

3. Things have changed since those times, some are up in "G"
   Others they are wand'rers but they all feel just like me
   They'd part with all they've got, could they once more walk
   With their best girl and have a twirl on sidewalks of New York

Chorus:

THE BAND PLAYED ON
1895

PLAYER PIANOS AND "THE BAND PLAYED ON" WERE BIG HITS IN THE YEAR OF 1895. MANY A piano roll carried this number. Immigrants were pouring into this land of the free at a heavy rate, and German street bands were quite common. In fact, that is how this song got started.

In 1895 John F. Palmer, a professional actor and occasional songwriter, was sitting around at home when he and his sister Pauline heard one of these German bands on the street. Simultaneously they both got the same idea of "let the band play on." Pauline urged John to write a song on this theme. John Palmer went to work on it. He completed both words and music, but then had no luck in getting it published. Some time later that same year he sold the song to a Charles B. Ward, who made certain minor changes for improvement. Ward got the song published and then worked hard to give it public exposure. The song was even promoted in the newspaper, the *New York World*. All this promotion, together with public acceptance of the song, snowballed it into a great and lasting success.

The lilting melody and humorous lyrics of "The Band Played On" have made it attractive to vaudeville singers over the years resulting in frequent public performances. Americans everywhere have enjoyed this song and thus it is well known today throughout the country. "The Band Played On" was featured in the 1941 movie *The Strawberry Blonde*.

244

THE BAND PLAYED ON

Matt Cas - ey formed a so-cial club that beat the town for style And

hir - ed for a meet-ing place a hall When

pay - day came a - round each week they greased the floor with wax And they

danced with noise and vig - or at the ball Each

Moderately
Chorus

For ___ Cas - ey would waltz with a straw - ber - ry blonde And the band played on He'd glide cross the floor with the girl he a - dored And the band played on But his brain was so

load - ed   it   near - ly   ex - plod - ed   The poor girl would shake with   a -

larm   He'd ne'er leave   the   girl   with   the straw - ber - ry

curls   And the   band   played   on

2. Such kissing on the corner and such whisp'ring in the hall
    And telling tales of love behind the stairs
    As Casey was the favorite and he that ran the ball
    Of the kissing and love-making did his share
    At twelve o'clock exactly they all would fall in line
    Then march down to the dining hall and eat
    But Casey would not join them although ev'rything was fine
    But he stayed upstairs and exercised his feet
    For

Chorus:

3. Now when the dance was over and the band played "Home Sweet Home"
    They played a tune at Casey's own request
    He thanked them very kindly for the favors they had shown
    Then he'd waltz once with the girl that he loved best
    Most all the friends are married that Casey used to know
    And Casey too has taken him a wife
    The blonde he used to waltz and glide with on the ballroom floor
    Is happy Missis Casey now for life
    For

Chorus:

WHEN JOHNNY COMES MARCHING HOME
1898

ALTHOUGH THIS SONG WAS BORN DURING THE CIVIL WAR, IT WAS NOT UNTIL THE SPANISH-American War (1898) that it became a national hit. Long before the Civil War this melody (almost note for note) was a touching old Irish streetsong, "Johnny I Hardly Knew Ye," which described a young girl seeing her hopelessly maimed sweetheart for the first time upon his return from the war.

The words of this song were written in 1863 by America's great Irish bandmaster (with General Nathaniel Banks' Army) Patrick S. Gilmore, under the pseudonym Louis Lambert. Gilmore had expected the Civil War to end much earlier than it actually did, and he wrote the song in preparation for a mammoth Peace Jubilee which he finally did give in Boston, 1869. This jubilee, by the way, used a 1000 piece orchestra and 10,000 voices. The song was well received both at this jubilee and also the succeeding one in 1872, but it was not until the time of William McKinley's Presidency and the Spanish-American War that the song actually reached the lips of the people. From that time on this song grew to become one of our greatest. It was used abundantly during both World Wars and in between them.

Today "When Johnny Comes Marching Home" is a sort of national institution. A 1942 movie carried its title, and it is played by brass bands, orchestras, school bands, and jazz bands. It is sung in barrooms and supper clubs, at outings, nightclubs, concerts, and in the home. It is performed by big-voiced baritones and small-voiced folk singers. It is in song books, and on radio and television. This is a song America loves and will not forget.

250

WHEN JOHNNY COMES MARCHING HOME

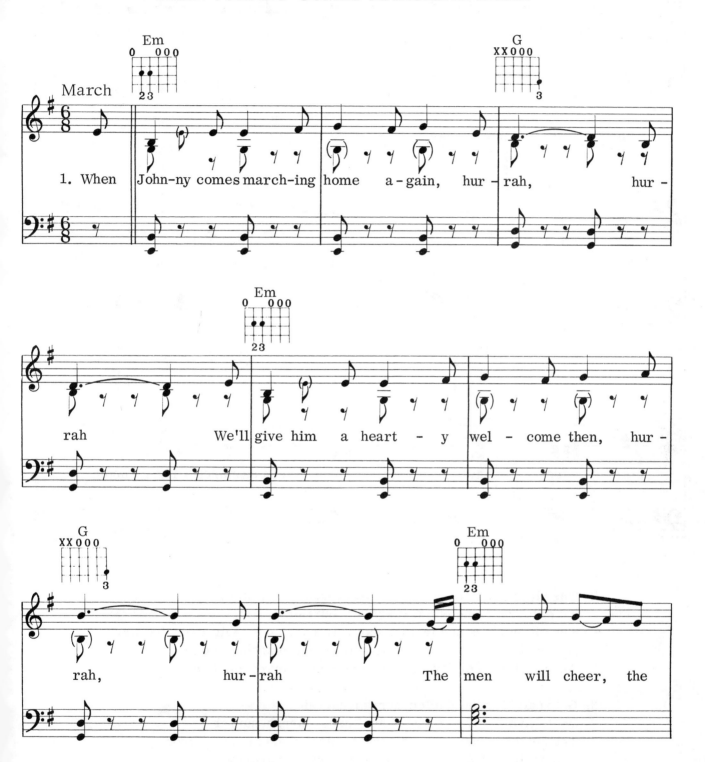

1. When John-ny comes march-ing home a-gain, hur-rah, hur-

rah We'll give him a heart-y wel-come then, hur-

rah, hur-rah The men will cheer, the

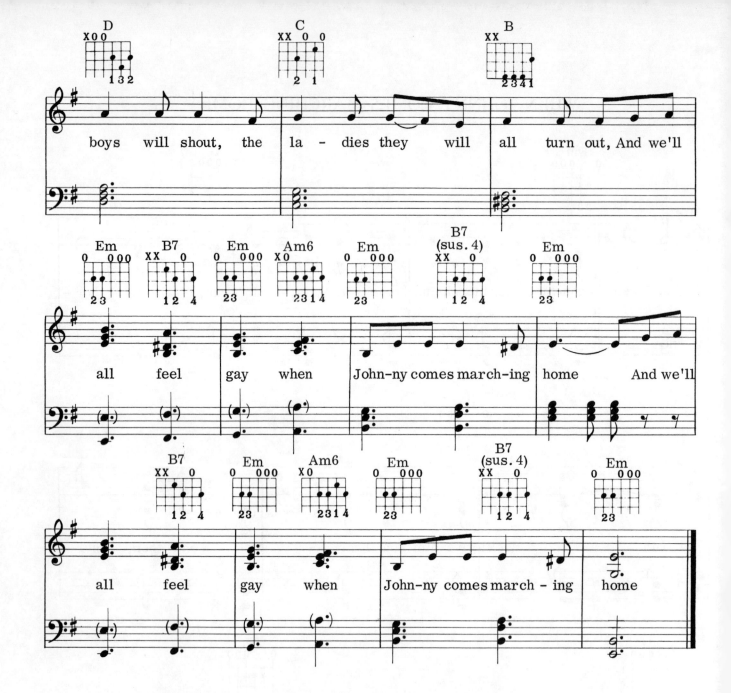

2. The old church bell will peal with joy, hurrah, hurrah
To welcome home our darling boy, hurrah, hurrah
The village lads and lassies say with roses they will strew the way
And we'll all feel gay when Johnny comes marching home
And we'll all feel gay when Johnny comes marching home

3. Get ready for the jubilee, hurrah, hurrah
We'll give the hero three times three, hurrah, hurrah
The laurel wreath is ready now to place upon his loyal brow
And we'll all feel gay when Johnny comes marching home
And we'll all feel gay when Johnny comes marching home

4. Let love and friendship on that day, hurrah, hurrah
Their choicest treasures then display, hurrah, hurrah
And let each one perform some part to fill with joy the warrior's heart
And we'll all feel gay when Johnny comes marching home
And we'll all feel gay when Johnny comes marching home

ON THE BANKS OF THE WABASH
1899

THIS POPULAR SONG IS TRULY A GREAT ONE FOR SIMPLICITY, NOSTALGIA, AND BEAUTY OF LYRIC and melody. Thus it was officially adopted as the state song of Indiana in 1913, the year President Woodrow Wilson began his first term in office. "On the Banks of the Wabash" was composed in 1896 by that prolific Hoosier songwriter, Paul Dresser, and copyrighted in 1897.

There are conflicting stories as to how this song came into being. One account has it that Paul's younger brother, Theodore (the famous novelist, Theodore Dreiser), visited Paul in New York where they took a walk in Central Park reminiscing about their boyhood days. Theodore Dreiser claimed to have suddenly urged his brother to write a song about their home in Terre Haute (Indiana) with the river running through it, adding that "home and river" songs seemed to have done well in popularity.

Another account, by conductor–composer–arranger Max Hoffman, described Paul Dresser in a Chicago hotel room working intensely on the composition with the aid of a portable organ. Hoffman reflected his personal thrill of being in the presence of a man during his time of great inspiration and creation. It appears entirely possible both stories could be true. In any case, the result Paul Dresser produced was a masterpiece of popular songwriting.

"On the Banks of the Wabash" was published in 1899 and its great success came about with amazing speed. It seems to have been the "song of the hour." People everywhere sang and whistled it clear across the country. People of Indiana in particular were beside themselves with excitement and their hearts filled with state pride. Before the year 1899 was over this song sold at least a million copies. "On the Banks of the Wabash" became standard fare for barbershop quartets, and it was performed in two fine movies, *My Gal Sal* (1942) and *Wait Till the Sun Shines Nellie* (1952).

ON THE BANKS OF THE WABASH

Chorus

moon-light's fair to-night a-long the Wa — bash From the

fields there comes the breath of new mown hay Through the

syc – a–mores the can – dle-lights are gleam — ing On the

banks of the Wa – bash far a – way

2. Many years have passed since I strolled by the river
   Arm in arm with sweetheart Mary by my side
   It was there I tried to tell her that I loved her
   It was there I begged of her to be my bride
   Long years have passed since I strolled through the churchyard
   She's sleeping there, my angel Mary dear
   I loved her but she thought I didn't mean it
   Still I'd give my future were she only here

HELLO MA BABY
1899

IN THE HISTORY OF JAZZ, SWING MUSIC PRECEDED BOP AND PROGRESSIVE JAZZ, DIXIELAND preceded swing, ragtime preceded dixieland, and this is just where "Hello Ma Baby" comes into the picture. Here was one of the first real ragtime songs printed, and it was ideal for the popular high-stepping cakewalk.[1] Ragtime music seems to have come to us from the South, up through the Mississippi River and then directly east to New York. This type of music had a pronounced syncopated beat, sounding as if the rhythm were somewhat ragged. Thus it was soon popularly called ragtime.

"Hello Ma Baby" was written in 1899 during William McKinley's administration. Frontier towns and mining camps were springing up all over the West, and entertainment was provided for by groups of traveling performers in dance halls and makeshift theatres. The composer of "Hello Ma Baby" was just such a performer who sang with various groups ever since he was a young boy. He was that great personality, Joe Howard.

Howard was twenty-one years old when he wrote this song, and his second wife (he had had about eight in all), Ida Emerson, wrote the words, although there was talk that Andrew Sterling may have contributed some to the lyrics. From the time this song was first published the public's reaction was quick, big, and nationwide. It became a million-copy song and America played it, danced it, sang it, and cakewalked it for a good many years. (A song's popularity lasted a long time in those days.) Joe Howard made a fortune with this and other songs.

The popularity of "Hello Ma Baby" subsided around World War I only to be revived again when Joe Howard performed during the 1930's in New York's night spots, and later became the M. C. on the popular "Gay Nineties" radio show, still later as a guest star on several television shows, and then again as M. C. on TV's "Gay Nineties Review."

Joe Howard's life and music were depicted in the 1947 movie success *I Wonder Who's Kissing Her Now,* which featured the song "Hello Ma Baby."

[1] The cakewalk was a contest, particularly among Negroes, and the prize was a chocolate cake. The dance was performed with the contestants assuming a proud and happy physical attitude, leaning away back and using high, snappy, strutting steps. The men generally wore high hats and made handsome use of their fancy canes, and the total effect was quite an exuberant sight. The couple judged the winners won the chocolate cake.

HELLO MA BABY

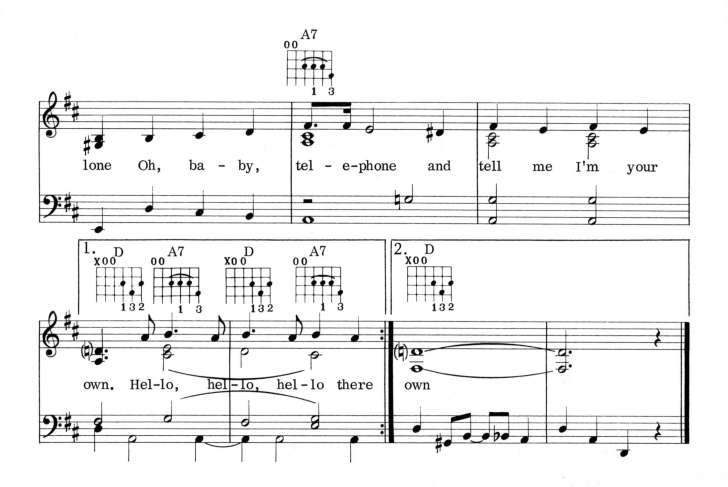

lone Oh, ba - by, tel - e-phone and tell me I'm your

own. Hel-lo, hel-lo, hel-lo there own

2. This morning through the phone she said her name was Bess
   And now I kind of know where I am at
   I'm satisfied because I've got my babe's address
   Here pasted in the lining of my hat
       I am mighty scared 'cause if the wires get crossed
       'Twill separate me from ma baby mine
       Then some other man will win her and my game is lost
       And so each day I shout along the line

Chorus:

MY WILD IRISH ROSE
1900

THIS SONG IS GENERALLY CONSIDERED ONE OF THE TOP THREE MODERN IRISH BALLADS, ALL written in America. (The other two are "Mother Machree" and "When Irish Eyes Are Smiling.") In 1899 this song's popularity rose to great heights, selling over a million copies. The year this song was composed (1899) national interest focused on such matters as adolescent boys reading *The Rover Boys* series, McKinley's administration announcing the China Open Door policy, Jim Jeffries winning the heavyweight boxing championship from Bob Fitzsimmons, Admiral Dewey's ovation in New York as the hero of Manila Bay, and Carrie Nation smashing saloons with a hatchet in Medicine Lodge, Kansas. In the larger cities the musical theatre was beginning to come into its own, and this is where "My Wild Irish Rose" was born.

The first public appearance of this song was in the musical *A Romance of Althone* (14th Street Theatre, New York), and was sung by the star (composer), Chauncey Olcott. Seven years later (1906) "My Wild Irish Rose" was again used in the musical *The Little Cherub*. The composer, born Chancellor John Olcott, was by far the most popular singer, actor, and composer of his time. Olcott's background for the writing of this ageless song included performances as a black-faced minstrel, acting experiences, and singing lead tenor roles in light opera, both in America and England. His was truly a golden voice, so moving when he sang "My Wild Irish Rose" that he became known as the "Irish Thrush," and this eventually became his theme song. A great admirer, Paul Dresser, dedicated one of his own songs to Olcott back in 1887. The song hit of 1903, "Bedelia," contains a cute reference to Chauncey Olcott in the lyric.

One of the hit movies of 1947 was entitled *My Wild Irish Rose,* and it included this song. For well over half a century this song has been a favorite gang and barbershop song. It is heard at parties, reunions, in a car, or a boat, around the piano at home, and wherever Americans of all nationalities feel like singing the oldtimers.

262

MY WILD IRISH ROSE

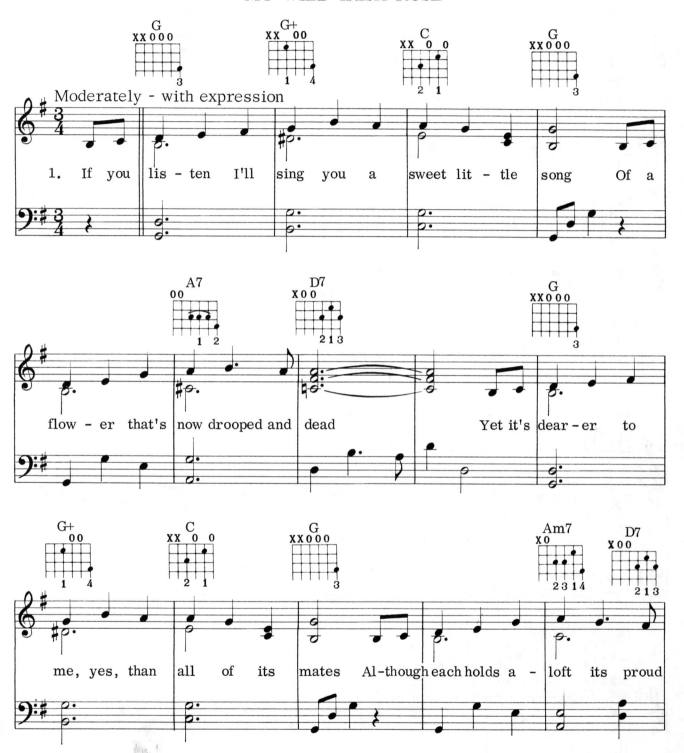

1. If you lis - ten I'll sing you a sweet lit - tle song Of a flow - er that's now drooped and dead Yet it's dear - er to me, yes, than all of its mates Al-though each holds a - loft its proud

grows   And some day for my sake, she may let me take   The bloom from my wild I-rish rose

2. They may sing of their roses which by other names
   They would smell just as sweetly, they say
   But I know that my dear rose would never consent
   To have that sweet name taken away
       Her glances are shy just whene'er I pass by
       At the bower where my true love grows
   And my one wish has been that some day I may win
   The dear heart of my wild Irish rose

   Chorus:

MIGHTY LAK' A ROSE
1901

MANY PEOPLE CONSIDER THIS SONG A CLASSIC, SINCE DURING THE PAST FIFTY YEARS OR so it has been performed chiefly by artists of the concert stage, with the music written by a classical composer. However, in the first year of its publication, this song skyrocketed to first place selling over a million copies. It was easily the greatest popular song of the day.

"Mighty Lak' a Rose" was a collaboration effort between Frank L. Stanton (words) and Ethelbert Nevin, composer of "The Rosary," "Narcissus," and numerous classical works. Nevin was born (1862) during the Civil War and unlike most pop writers with hits at an early age, he didn't get around to composing this smash hit until after the Spanish-American War. It was one of his last musical works. Frank L. Stanton was a gentle person who worked for the Atlanta *Constitution* writing all varieties of poetry. As a man of kind and empathetic feeling for his fellow beings he produced a distinguished lyric indeed for "Mighty Lak' A Rose." The original words were written in Negro dialect.

While "Mighty Lak' A Rose" is often sung at concerts it is perhaps best enjoyed at home around the piano. It is soft, quaint, tender, and beautiful. Dance band leader Vincent Lopez has for years featured this number as a piano solo. The song does have a kind of classical flavor and people everywhere have heard and sung it for well over half a century.

MIGHTY LAK' A ROSE

BILL BAILEY, WON'T YOU PLEASE COME HOME?
1902

THIS SONG BECAME POPULAR COAST TO COAST IN 1902, WHEN THE AVERAGE MAN IN AMERICA worked ten hours a day for six days a week, sat in his rocking chair in the parlor and patted his chow dog (a popular breed right after the Boxer Rebellion).

The words and music of this song were written by one of the fine song-and-dance men of the day, Hughie Cannon. Cannon was a friendly, well-liked, generous person with an "easy come, easy go" philosophy, and among his friends was a delightful, though lazy Negro named Bill Bailey.

It seems that Bill Bailey's large-size wife made a habit of throwing Bill out of the house whenever she became fed up with him. On one such occasion Bailey talked this over with Hughie Cannon lamenting that he was much too much in love with his wife to stay away from her. Cannon gave Bailey a few dollars and some advice, suggesting that since "absence makes the heart grow fonder" Bailey not go home for a few days. After Cannon left Bailey he was struck with what he thought might be a great idea for a humorous song. He fantasied Bill Bailey suddenly becoming rich and Bailey's wife begging him to come back home. Cannon hastened to write the words, setting them to music in the popular ragtime style, and giving it the obvious title, "Bill Bailey, Won't You Please Come Home?"

This song was first introduced to the public in a comedy act breaking in at Newburgh, New York. The performer was the popular black-faced minstrel John Queen, one of Cannon's friends and colleagues. The song was immediately a smash hit as evidenced by the audience's enthusiastic applause, and further evidenced by people in New York City whistling this song as they stood in line buying tickets for the show. The song's popularity spread over the nation rather quickly, and this song became an important milestone in Hughie Cannon's career.

In more recent years, since the advent of television (about 1948), this song's popularity was revived chiefly through its use by that master of the cakewalk, Eddie Jackson, who frequently appeared on television with Jimmy Durante. As a result, the song was picked up by one performer after another who sang and played it on television, radio and phonograph recordings. It is safe to say that once more this song is popular from coast to coast.

BILL BAILEY, WON'T YOU PLEASE COME HOME?

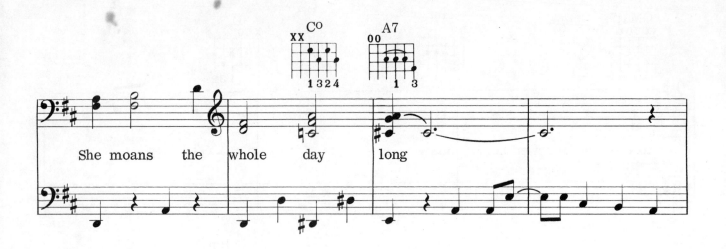

She moans the whole day long

I'll do the cook-in', dar-lin', I'll pay the rent

I know I've done you wrong

'Mem-ber that rain-y eve that I drove you out With

noth - in' but a fine tooth comb? I know I'm to blame, well, ain't that a shame Bill Bail - ey won't you please come home?

2. Bill drove by that door in an aut'mobile
A great big di-a-mond, coach and footman to hear that big wench squeal
"He's all alone," I heard her groan
She hollered right through that old screen door
"Bill Bailey, are you sore?
Stop a minute and listen to me, won't I see you here no more?"
Bill winked his eye and heard her cry

Chorus:

IN THE GOOD OLD SUMMERTIME
1902

ALTHOUGH THIS SONG WAS TURNED DOWN BY SEVERAL MUSIC PUBLISHERS, IT TURNED OUT TO BE an all-time hit with sheet copies selling in the millions. In 1902, when this song was written and published, America was already under the influence of over a century's immigration from many foreign lands. Even our language had been influenced and modified. We embraced such new words as "delicatessen" and "hoodlum" from the German, "prairie" and "automobile" from the French, the Jewish words "kibitzer" and "kosher," the Dutch gave us "boss" and "cookie," "barbecue" and "ranch" from the Spanish, "shenanigans" from the Irish, and "fedora" from the Russians. But summertime in 1902 was fun time in any language, and this is what influenced the writing of this song by two famous theatrical personalities in New York.

The renowned black-faced minstrel George (Honey Boy) Evans and comedian Ren Shields took singer–actress Blanche Ring with them to Brighton Beach for a Sunday of fun and relaxation. After a fine dinner Evans casually remarked that of all the seasons he liked "the good old summertime." Shields immediately leaped on that expression as a great song title, and Blanche Ring seconded his enthusiasm. When they returned to Manhattan, Ren Shields went to work on the song. A few days later he gave the lyric to Evans who almost immediately improvised the basic melody, and later worked it out in detail. Since Evans could not write a note of music he sought the help of Blanche Ring who wrote it down for him and also arranged it for piano.

Shields and Evans took the song around to several publishers, but none of them wanted a seasonal song which they said is "obviously" doomed to a short life of three months. Once again Blanche Ring jumped into the breach and offered to perform the song in her new musical comedy show *The Defender*. From opening night on, audiences received "In the Good Old Summertime" with genuine enthusiasm and they usually joined with Miss Ring in singing the chorus. Blanche Ring made this song and the song made her, since in this show she was making her bid for stardom. Now there was no problem in getting the song published, and shortly thereafter both the composers and publishers made considerable money on it.

Throughout the years this song never seemed to lack for a sizable popularity. The 1949 movie starring Judy Garland was named after this song. Since this is such a good gang type of song it knows no season, and it is sung and enjoyed the whole year round.

276

IN THE GOOD OLD SUMMERTIME

sign   That she's your toot - sey woot - sey

in the good old sum - mer time

2. Oh to swim in the pool you'd play hooky from school
   Good old summer time
   You would play "ring-a-rosie" with Jim, Kate and Josie
   Good old summer time
   Those are days full of pleasure we now fondly treasure
   When we never thought it a crime
   To go stealing cherries with face brown as berries
   In good old summer time

   Chorus:

BECAUSE
1902

SINCE THIS SONG HAS BEEN SO WIDELY POPULAR IN OUR COUNTRY FOR OVER HALF A CENTURY MOST people think it is genuinely American. However it is really an English song composed by writers of fairly high-level music. The words are by Edward Teschemacher and the music by a woman, Guy d'Hardelot (pseudonym of Helen Guy, or Mrs. W. I. Rhodes).

The song's first publication was in England in the year 1902. It immediately arrived in our country when American movie houses were born, with former cowboy Thomas Talley establishing the first one in Los Angeles. The dignity and sincerity of "Because" made a lasting impression on people throughout all forty-five states. Though it was not written in the style of other popular songs in that era, nor was it intended to be, heavy sales made it one of the top songs of 1902. "Because" sold over a million copies.

In the years immediately following 1902 people began using this song as a featured solo at weddings, and "Because" soon shared this honor with "Oh Promise Me" which had already been in use for thirteen years. This practice has continued right up to the present day. It seems that nearly every singer of note, past and present, has performed this song at some time or other. "Because" is today a standard pop song and a favorite with millions of Americans.

BECAUSE

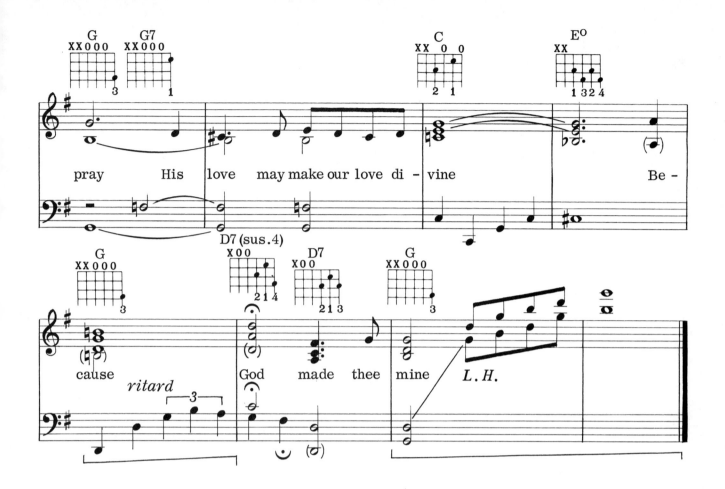

pray   His   love   may make our love di – vine   Be –

cause   God   made   thee   mine   *L.H.*

ritard

IDA
1903

THE YEAR THIS SONG BECAME A NATIONAL HIT, SELLING OVER A MILLION COPIES, WAS A BIG ONE in the history of our country. When the Union was composed of only forty-five states Orville and Wilbur Wright made their famous Kittyhawk, North Carolina, flight, President Theodore Roosevelt sent the very first wireless message to King Edward VII, Enrico Caruso made his debut at the Metropolitan Opera House while John Barrymore made his in Chicago, the first feature movie *The Great Train Robbery* was shown, baseball's World Series began, and the golden days of minstrel shows were dying out as vaudeville took over.

The composer of this song, Eddie Leonard, is considered the last of the great minstrels. He harbored great ambitions for becoming a noteworthy songwriter, but until he wrote "Ida" he did much better as a black-faced minstrel performing with his powerful singing voice and fine dancing ability.

Eddie Leonard wrote this song at a time when he was about to be fired from the Primrose & West minstrel show. It is said that the idea for this song came about through his introduction to an attractive girl named Ida, and somehow Eddie associated her name with the sweetness of apple cider. He secretly arranged with the orchestra leader to perform this number on stage in place of his regular song. When Eddie Leonard began to sing "Ida" in his "wah-wah" style (which later influenced Al Jolson) his fellow minstrels were shocked, the manager rushed to the wings to see what was going on, and Eddie put his whole heart and soul into the song. At the conclusion there followed tremendous applause from the audience, his fellow minstrels were thrilled, and instead of firing him the manager gave Eddie Leonard and "Ida" headline billing.

As soon as the song was published it became an overnight sensation. Eddie left Primrose & West and joined other minstrel groups singing "Ida" wherever he went. The song was a phenomenal hit with every audience. Other vaudevillians used "Ida" in their act, and over the years many phonograph recordings appeared. This song is firmly established as a standard in the American repertory of popular songs.

286

IDA

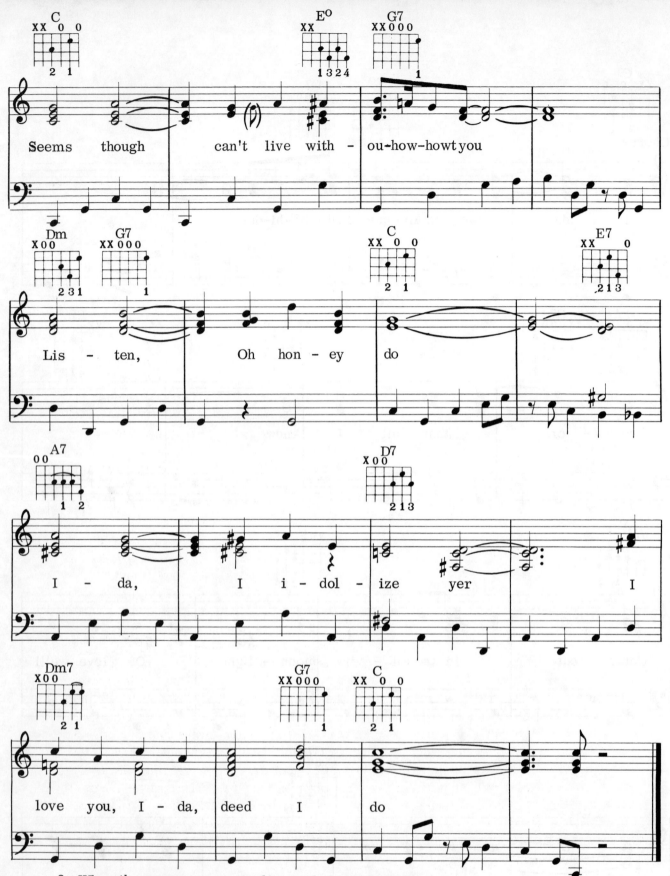

2. When the moon comes stealing up behind the hill
   Ev'rything around me seems so calm and still
   Save a gentle calling of the whippoorwill
   Then I long to hold her little hand in mine
      Through the trees the winds are sighing soft and low
      Seem to come and whisper that your love is true
      Come and be my own now, sweetheart do, oh do
      Then my life will seem almost divine
   Chorus:

DEAR OLD GIRL
1903

THIS SONG ACHIEVED NATIONAL POPULARITY IN 1903, THE SAME YEAR IN WHICH IT WAS WRITTEN and published. In this era bicycles also were nationally popular, particularly in cities, although automobiles were destined to soon take over. The Ford Motor Company came into being this very same year of 1903. Henry Ford, a former employee of the Edison Illuminating Company, Detroit, had recently been let out of the Detroit Motor Company and Ford decided to form his own company. However, Americans knew "Dear Old Girl" long before they ever heard of the Ford automobile.

This song was composed by Richard Henry Buck (words) and Theodore Morse (music). Of the two men, Morse was the more colorful and successful composer. Born in Washington, D.C., and a good violinist, Morse ran away to New York when only fourteen years old and managed to support himself from that time on. His composition, "Dear Old Girl" (written at age thirty), was a shot in the arm for Morse as a songwriter and thus many more of his compositions followed this one. The other half of the team, Richard Buck, seemed to have been a fairly good lyricist who outdid himself in this song. In 1903 "Dear Old Girl" was placed with a publisher on the brink of going out of business, and the enormous success of this song saved the publishing house from immediate bankruptcy.

In this period of history the United States was largely a country of immigrants and new Americans. Since transportation was crude by today's standards, and working hours were long, entertainment generally centered in and around the home, often at the piano. Old and new Americans alike were of a sentimental mood and songs provided appropriate expressions. Sentimental songs were much in vogue with singing groups, barbershop quartets and home harmonizers, all leaning heavily toward this type of song. "Dear Old Girl" was then, and still is, one of the favorite songs of sentiment with such singing groups, and these groups played an important role in popularizing this song. Perhaps the biggest single factor in popularizing "Dear Old Girl" was the famous minstrel-show tenor, Dick Jose. This English-born singer of enormous size and popularity, a former blacksmith in Reno, Nevada, fell in love with the song and sang it coast to coast for all he was worth. His audiences cried—and bought song copies. "Dear Old Girl" is still one of the best songs around for spontaneous harmonizing.

DEAR OLD GIRL

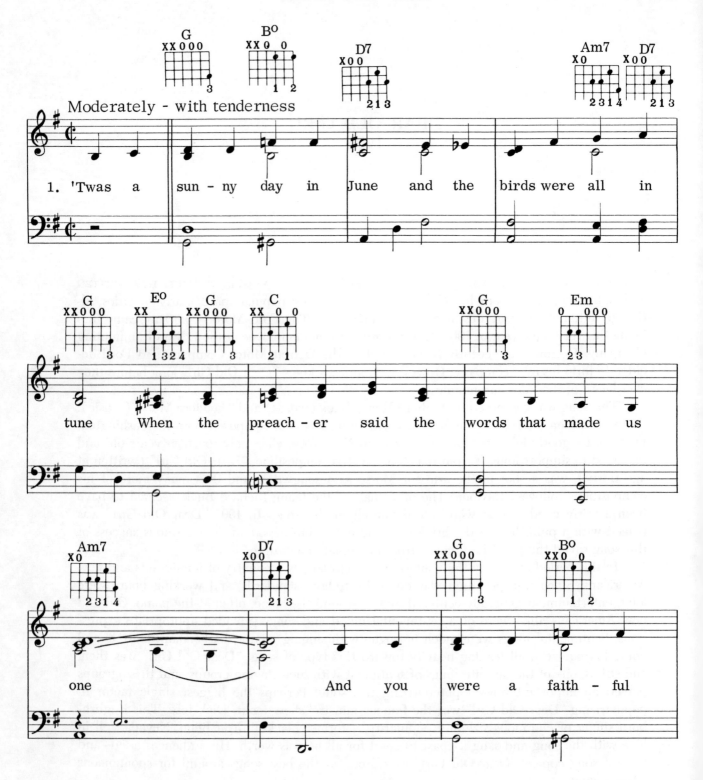

1. 'Twas a sun-ny day in June and the birds were all in tune When the preach-er said the words that made us one And you were a faith-ful

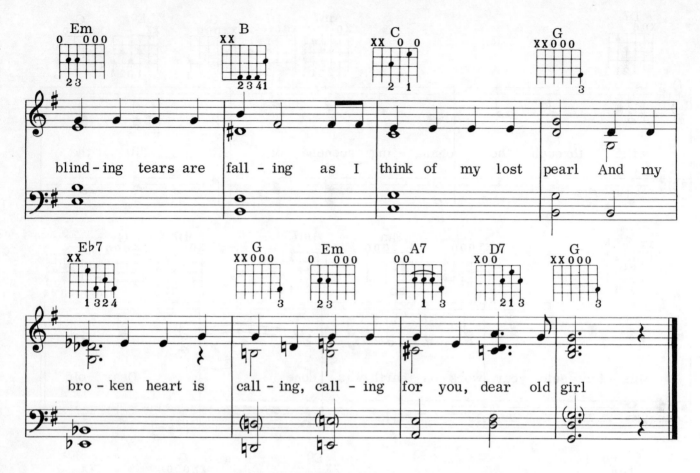

blind - ing tears are | fall - ing as I | think of my lost | pearl And my

bro - ken heart is | call - ing, call - ing | for you, dear old girl

2. All the world has darker grown as I wander all alone
   And I hear the breezes sobbing through the pines
   Once again we seem to sit when the ev'ning lamps are lit
   And the same old moon upon our cottage shines

Chorus:

294

MEET ME IN ST. LOUIS, LOUIS
1904

AT THE TIME THIS SONG WAS WRITTEN TIN PAN ALLEY WAS GAINING MOMENTUM AND WAS WELL on its way toward becoming a solid industry. America was rapidly growing up to become recognized as a first-class nation of forty-five states. New York in particular was fast becoming its chief center having just opened up its first subway and having just completed its first skyscraper, the Flat Iron Building of twenty-two stories and 280 feet high. From all over the country ambitious and gifted people converged on New York thus sharpening the already keen competition.

Two of these people were the writers of this hit song, Andrew B. Sterling (words) who had struggled to pay the rent on his furnished room, and Kerry (Frederick Allen) Mills (music) who had tried in vain to land a violin-playing job. These gifted young men felt they might capitalize on the publicity devoted to the great St. Louis exposition commemorating the one-hundredth anniversary of the Louisiana Purchase (1803). They applied their talents to this theme and the result they produced was "Meet Me In St. Louis, Louis." Their song was published in 1904, became the theme song of the exposition, and its great popularity and success far exceeded the composers' expectations.

While the exposition was a huge federal and local effort, including the first Olympic Games held in the United States, there remains today only three permanent memorials: The St. Louis Art Museum, the Jefferson Memorial, and this song. In the years following the exposition this song found its way into several stage revues. More recently it enjoyed a healthy revival as a feature number in the highly successful 1944 movie *Meet Me In St. Louis*, which even more recently has been shown on television. This song was also used in the 1941 movie *The Strawberry Blonde*.

MEET ME IN ST. LOUIS, LOUIS

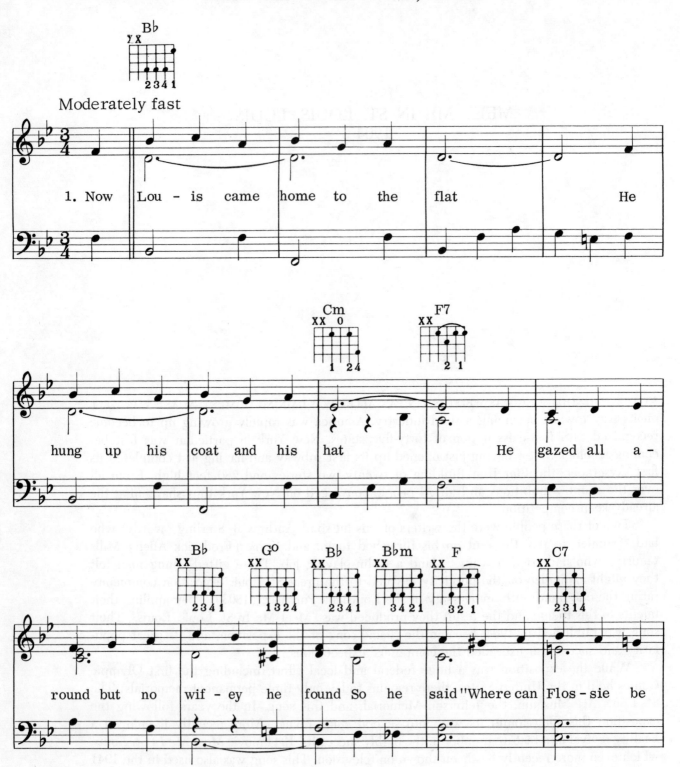

Moderately fast

1. Now Lou - is came home to the flat He

hung up his coat and his hat He gazed all a -

round but no wif - ey he found So he said "Where can Flos - sie be

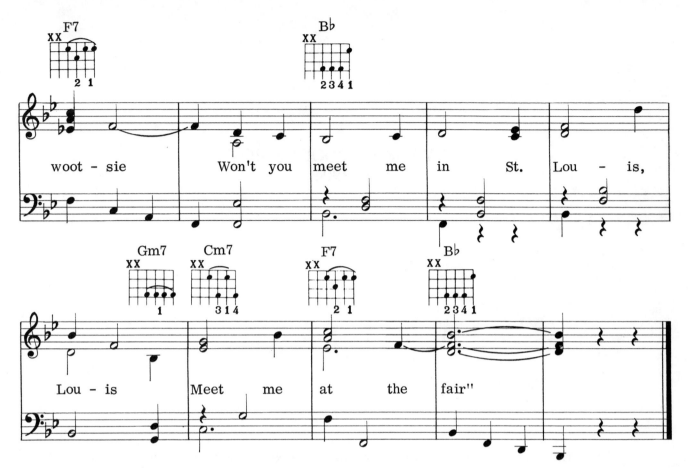

woot - sie   Won't you meet me in St. Lou - is,

Lou - is   Meet me at the fair"

2. The dresses that hung in the hall
   Were gone, she had taken them all
   She took all his rings and the rest of his things
   And the picture he missed from the wall
   "What moving!" the janitor said
   "Your rent is paid three months ahead!"
   "What good is the flat?" said poor Louis, "Read that"
   And the janitor smiled as he read

Chorus:

YANKEE DOODLE BOY
1904

TODAY THIS SONG IS WELL KNOWN BY THREE GENERATIONS OF AMERICANS. THE SONG HAS LIVED through well over half a century of historical change in our country and its popularity has always been tipped toward the up side. Its composer, one of America's theatrical greats, was that New England-born Irishman, George Michael Cohan. Cohan considered "Yankee Doodle Boy" his personal song, in which his lyric describes him as "born on the Fourth of July" (although his biographer, Ward Morehouse, states that Cohan's birth certificate shows the date to be July 3, 1878). George M. Cohan was literally a child of the theatre, since his mother Helen and father Jerry were headline vaudevillians. Like Irving Berlin and a few others, Cohan composed his songs using only the black keys on the piano.

In 1904, when young Georgie was only twenty-six, he wrote the book and songs for the musical show *Little Johnny Jones* which opened at the Liberty Theatre in New York on November 7, just one day before Theodore Roosevelt was elected president. Cohan also directed the show, in which he cast his father and mother, and in it he played his first leading role. Audiences and critics alike acclaimed "Yankee Doodle Boy" with all its flag-waving flavor, and thus it became one of the everlasting hit songs of the show. Over the years this vigorous, expansive and unselfconscious song has been a special favorite with many a well-known star, and has never failed to elicit a good round of applause.

This song was one of the big numbers in the 1942 James Cagney movie *Yankee Doodle Dandy*. The picture was highly successful here and in England, and George M. Cohan was the "Yankee Doodle Dandy." In tribute to Cohan, New York's Mayor LaGuardia proclaimed July 3, 1942, as George M. Cohan Day.

300

YANKEE DOODLE BOY

Moderately fast - with spirit

1. I'm the kid that's all the can - dy, I'm a Yan - kee Doo - dle Dan - dy

I'm glad I am, So's Un - cle Sam

I'm a real live Yan - kee Doo - dle, Made my name and fame and boo - dle

Just like Mis - ter Doo - dle did by rid - ing on a

thing a-bout a Yan-kee that's a pho — ney?

Interlude

Chorus

I'm a Yan-kee Doo-dle Dan — dy A

Yan — kee Doo-dle, do or die A

Yan-kee Doo-dle came to Lon-don just to ride the po — nies

I am a Yan - kee Doo-dle boy

2. Father's name was Hezikiah, Mother's name was Ann Maria
   Yanks through and through, red, white, and blue
   Father was so Yankee hearted when the Spanish war was started
   He slipped on his uniform and hopped upon a pony
   My mother's mother was a Yankee true, my father's father was a Yankee too
   And that's going some for the Yankee, by gum
   Oh say, can you see
   Anything about my pedigree that's phoney?

Chorus:

GIVE MY REGARDS TO BROADWAY
1904

THE COMPOSER OF THIS SONG HAD THE DISTINCTION OF RECEIVING A GOLD MEDAL IN 1940 FROM President Franklin Delano Roosevelt. He was, of course, the eminent George M. Cohan, an outstanding landmark in show business.

Cohan was literally born into show business, and as a youngster of eleven he began writing songs and parodies. At seventeen he had a bankroll of $4000, a great deal of money in those days. Very shortly thereafter he began writing, producing and directing which eventually led to the musical show *Little Johnny Jones*. Of all nineteen songs in the show "Give My Regards To Broadway" was the outstanding hit although "Yankee Doodle Boy" ran a close second. While George M. Cohan was an avid baseball fan with many players as his friends, Broadway was his life blood and this song reflects it.

America was still in a period of major expansion and vaudeville was on the increase throughout the country. The United States began constructing the Panama Canal while many song-and-dance men began using "Give My Regards To Broadway" in their vaudeville acts. This song was quite a natural directly after World War I, when American soldiers were returning to the United States, and thus the song became popular all over again.

Many phonograph recordings were made of this song, and many artists have performed it on stage, in night spots, and on radio and television. The movies have used "Give My Regards To Broadway" in at least three pictures: *Yankee Doodle Dandy* (1942), *Give My Regards To Broadway* (1948), and *With A Song In My Heart* (1952).

306

GIVE MY REGARDS TO BROADWAY

Moderately fast

1. Did you ev - er see two Yan-kees Part up - on a for - eign shore When the good ship's just a - bout to start for old New York once more? With a

2. Say hello to dear old Coney Isle
   If there you chance to be
   When you're at the Waldorf have a smile
   And charge it up to me
      Mention my name ev'ry place you go
      As 'round the town you roam
      Wish you'd call on my gal, now remember old pal
      When you get back home
Chorus:

MY GAL SAL
1905

FEW PEOPLE KNOW THAT THIS GREAT ALL-TIME SONG HIT WAS WRITTEN BY THE BROTHER OF America's famous novelist Theodore Dreiser, who substituted an "s" for the "i" in his name and called himself Paul Dresser.

A gargantuan man, Paul Dresser wrote gigantic songs and "My Gal Sal" (also known as "They Called Her Frivolous Sal") was one of his greatest, selling well over a million song copies. Dresser was quite an emotional person frequently given to shedding tears while composing a sentimental song, and no doubt this song was written during a good cry. He wrote this song when he was forty-eight years old, and it was his last. He himself had said it would sell a million copies but he did not live to see his prediction come true.

The setting of this song's national popularity was an America of forty-five states under the leadership of Teddy Roosevelt, when Western towns were springing up at a rapid rate, farming was just beginning to accept scientific application, gold was discovered in Alaska, the automobile was becoming quite an industry, subways in New York and Boston were brand new, Will Rogers began his fabulous stage career in New York's Roof Garden Theatre, and Tin Pan Alley was blossoming out into an important industry turning out such songs as "My Gal Sal."

During this period the country was bombarded with sentimental songs, and the people just loved them; but this is one of the few songs that has endured through many decades. The charm and winning attraction of "My Gal Sal" may be attributed to Paul Dresser's unique originality that avoided cliches, and to his theatrical background which included singing in medicine shows and performing as an end man with the Billy Rice Minstrels, both of which seemed to have given him good insight and sensitivity to American taste. The 1942 movie based on the life and songs of Paul Dresser was entitled *My Gal Sal,* and it featured this everlastingly popular song.

MY GAL SAL

1. Ev - 'ry-thing is o - ver and I'm feel - ing bad

I have lost the best pal that I ev - er had

'Tis but just a fort - night since she was here

al - ways will-ing to share   A wild sort of dev - il, but

dead on the lev - el Was my gal Sal

2. Brought her little dainties just a-fore she died
Promised she would meet me on the other side
Told her how I loved her, she said,"I know,Jim
Just do your best,leave the rest to him"
Gently I pressed her to my breast
Soon she would take her last long rest
She looked at me and she murmured,"my pal"
And softly I whispered,"goodbye dearest Sal"

Chorus:

IN MY MERRY OLDSMOBILE
1905

THROUGHOUT OUR HISTORY WE HAVE HAD A GOOD SHARE OF TRANSPORTATION SONGS, SONGS of wagons, railroads, sleighs, horses, bicycles, and aeroplanes. At the time automobiles were much talked about, right after the turn-of-the-century, there appeared several automobile songs. "In My Merry Oldsmobile" was one of them, and this song seems to have outdistanced all the rest for it has been popular for over half a century.

The American automobile was quite a new gadget in 1905, having been recently invented (1892), and while the expression "Get a horse" was popular, auto sales were unpopular. The story has it that Ransom E. Olds (owner of the Olds Motor Works, Detroit) decided to do something in order to gain public respect for the automobile and to open up new markets for his own product. He sent two Oldsmobiles from Detroit cross country to the Lewis and Clark Exposition in Portland, Oregon. Since there were no automobile roads in those days the assignment was hazardous. This arduous trip over mud and rugged terrain aroused national interest as newspapers gave the story daily coverage. The mission was successfully completed in forty-four days, and all America cheered. "In My Merry Oldsmobile" was directly inspired by this exciting achievement and the public interest it commanded.

The inspired composers were Vincent Bryan (words) and that celebrated showman Gus Edwards. Edwards could neither read nor write music, and his piano playing was self-taught. He was a good vaudevillian and soon conceived the idea of using children in his act. He spent long hours with them on their show material and he trained them in the art of showmanship. In his time Gus Edwards produced many stars and launched the careers of such distinguished artists as Eddie Cantor, George Jessel, Sally Rand, Ray Bolger, Eleanor Powell, Groucho Marx, Hildegarde, and a host of others. Vincent Bryan, on the other hand, was considered by Tin Pan Alley as one of the best professional lyricists of his time. His hits were many, having collaborated with several different composers of popular music.

"In My Merry Oldsmobile" was first published in 1905 and, riding on the recent publicity, became a national hit in no time. While the song did not sell a million copies in 1905, the whole country sang, whistled, and enjoyed the song. Ransom Olds not only succeeded in making the nation automobile conscious, he made it Oldsmobile conscious. For over half a century this song has been an unpaid-for commercial for Oldsmobile, and some years ago the manufacturer adopted it for its theme song. "In My Merry Oldsmobile" was used in the 1944 movie *The Merry Monihans*. This is a gay, fun song, perfect for gang singing. It is often heard on radio and featured on television. Its popularity today runs high.

316

IN MY MERRY OLDSMOBILE

Moderately fast

1. Young John – nie Steele has an Olds – mo – bile He

loves a dear lit – tle girl She is the

queen of his gas ma – chine She has his heart in a

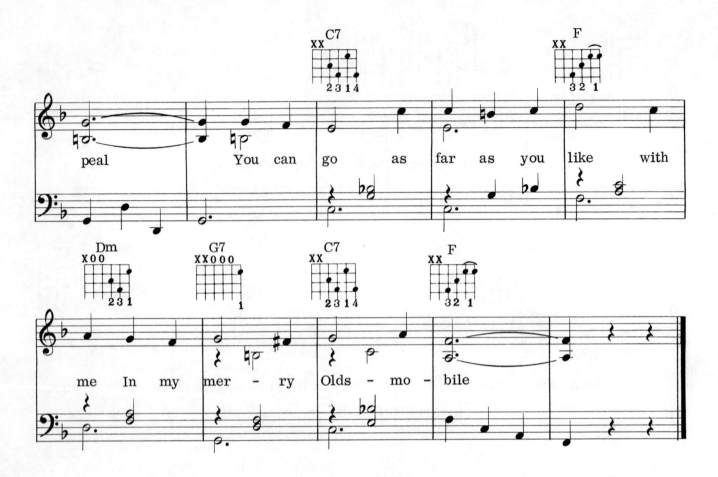

peal   You can go as far as you like with me In my mer - ry Olds - mo - bile

2. They love to spark in the dark old park
   As they go flying along
   She says she knows why the motor goes
   The sparker's awfully strong
      Each day they spoon to the engine's tune
      Their honeymoon will happen soon
      He'll win Lucile with his Oldsmobile
      And then he'll fondly croon

Chorus:

WAIT TILL THE SUN SHINES, NELLIE
1905

"WAIT TILL THE SUN SHINES, NELLIE" WAS WRITTEN BY HARRY VON TILZER (BORN HARRY GUMM) in collaboration with Andrew Sterling. Von Tilzer was one of the landmarks of old Tin Pan Alley on West 28th Street, New York City, in an era when our total population was about 76,000,000 under Theodore Roosevelt's administration. In Von Tilzer's lifetime he had written thousands of songs, over 2,000 of which were published. Von Tilzer was one of the few very successful song writers, and a source of encouragement to other composers including Irving Berlin and George Gershwin.

"Wait Till the Sun Shines, Nellie" seems to have been born simply as the result of an overheard remark. Legend has it that one rainy day Von Tilzer and Sterling, sitting in a hotel lobby, overheard a young groom trying to console his bride with the remark "Just wait till the sun shines, Nellie." Most of the story is contained in the verse, a style of song writing fairly common in that era.

This song has become a perennial favorite for over half a century. While numerous musical arrangements and recordings have been made, and all types of singers have performed it, the song itself has always retained its basic appeal to listeners and performers alike. It was used in the Bing Crosby–Mary Martin movie *Birth of the Blues* in 1941, and in the David Wayne picture *Wait Till the Sun Shines Nellie* in 1952, also in the 1942 movie *Rhythm Parade*. In the first year of the song's publication (1905) it became a solid success selling over a million copies.

WAIT TILL THE SUN SHINES, NELLIE

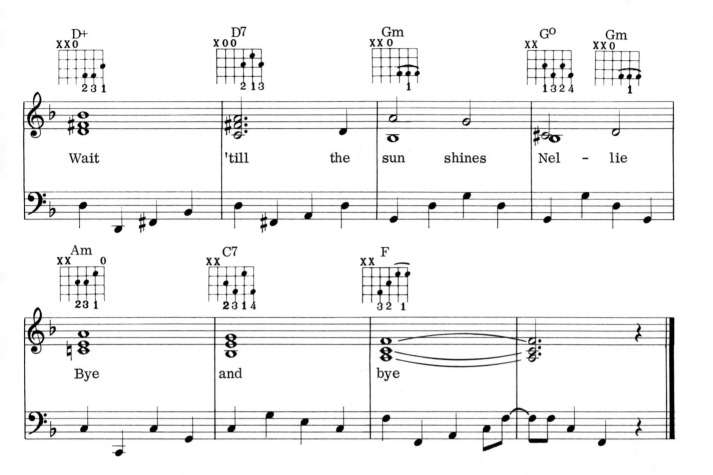

Wait   'till   the   sun   shines   Nel - lie

Bye   and   bye

2. "How I long," she sighed, "for a trolly ride just to show my brand new gown"
   Then she gazed on high with a gladsome cry for the sun came shining down
   And she looked so sweet on the big front seat as the car sped on its way
   And she whispered low "say you're all right Joe, you just won my heart today"

Chorus:

MARY'S A GRAND OLD NAME
1906

THIS SONG WAS WRITTEN DURING THE DAYS WHEN BICYCLES WERE IN VOGUE. AEROPLANES, AUTO-mobiles, motion pictures, and phonograph recordings were in their infancy. Women wore long petticoats and extra long hat pins for their picture hats; and their bathing suits were fashioned with high necks and long sleeves to which they added dainty shoes and stockings. The year was 1905; the Russo–Japanese War came to an end, Christy Mathewson (Giants) pitched three shutouts against Philadelphia, Jim Jeffries retired from the ring as undefeated heavyweight boxing champ, and this popular song was copyrighted.

The composer of this great song was that giant of the American theatre, George M. Cohan, who gave over 10,000 performances in sixty years. Cohan was only twenty-seven years old when he wrote this song for the musical show *Forty-five Minutes From Broadway* which opened at the New Amsterdam Theatre in New York City on New Years Day, 1906. George M. Cohan also wrote the book and his star of fame was rapidly rising to where he was soon to become "Mr. Broadway." "Mary's A Grand Old Name" is one of the great and everlasting songs that contributed to his fame. In writing for the theatre Cohan resisted the strong Viennese influence and tried to use material that was topical in America. Since we were largely a nation of new Americans (with immigration still at a high level) the matter of changing personal names was of current interest. Many names were Americanized while others were changed to sound more euphonious or less common. "Mary's A Grand Old Name" is based on this topical theme, and it proved to be popular indeed. Fay Templeton's performance of the song in the show was top notch. It enchanted her audiences and started her on a Broadway stage career.

"Mary's A Grand Old Name" became one of America's popular song hits of 1906 and sold many thousands of sheet copies. The schottische tempo and quality of this song made it ideal for the popular soft-shoe dance, and it was thus frequently used in vaudeville acts up through the late 1920's. Many recordings have been made, including Bing Crosby's, Fred Waring's, and George M. Cohan himself. This was a feature song in the great 1942 movie *Yankee Doodle Dandy*.

MARY'S A GRAND OLD NAME

2. Now when her name is Mary there is no falseness there
   When to Marie she'll vary, she'll surely bleach her hair
   Though Mary's ordinary, Marie is fair to see
   Don't ever fear sweet Mary, beware of sweet Marie

Chorus:

YOU'RE A GRAND OLD FLAG
1906

THIS SONG WAS COMPOSED AT THE VERY TIME WHEN PRESIDENT THEODORE ROOSEVELT WON THE Nobel Peace Prize. During the year 1906 the latest style for women included the picture hat with an ostrich plume, United States won the Olympic Games in Athens, Greece, Oklahoma was about to become our forty-sixth state, and George M. Cohan was soon to become a higher paid recording star than the great Enrico Caruso.

The composer of this stirring song was the famous George M. Cohan. He wrote it for the musical show *George Washington, Jr.* in which he himself played the leading role. Included in the cast were his father, mother, and wife. While in the process of writing songs for this show Cohan remembered having talked to a veteran of Pickett's charge at Gettysburg (1863) who pointed to the American flag and remarked, "She's a grand old rag." This gave Cohan an idea for the title "You're A Grand Old Rag." After opening night February 12 at the Herald Square Theatre in New York, Cohan received vigorous complaints from patriotic organizations charging him with degrading our flag by terming it a rag. As a dedicated flag waver, Cohan was somewhat chagrined. He promptly changed the objectionable word to "flag" and the show continued on. "You're A Grand Old Flag" was the hit song of the show. Although George M. Cohan was frequently criticized for his flag waving, the public responded with enthusiasm. There is something irresistible about a patriotic song in a snappy tempo sung by a vigorous and enthusiastic performer to an audience that loves America. In the case of this song the audience seemed more right than the critics, for it sold over a million copies.

"You're A Grand Old Flag" enjoyed a good revival directly after World War I, George M. Cohan performed the song in the 1932 movie *The Phantom President,* and the song was used effectively in the 1942 movie based on Cohan's life *Yankee Doodle Dandy.*

330

YOU'RE A GRAND OLD FLAG

Moderately - with spirit

1. There's a feel - ing comes a - steal - ing and it sets my brain a -

reel - ing When I'm list - 'ning to the mu - sic of a mil - i - tar - y

band An - y tune like "Yan - kee Doo - dle" sim - ply

sets me off my noo - dle It's that pa - tri - ot - ic

2. I'm a cranky hanky panky, I'm a dead square honest Yankee
   And I'm mighty proud of that old flag that flies for Uncle Sam
   Though I don't believe in raving, ev'ry time I see it waving
   There's a chill runs up my back that makes me glad I'm what I am
      Here's a land with a million soldiers, that's if we should need 'em, we'll fight for freedom
      Hurrah! hurrah! for ev'ry Yankee Tar and old G. A. R., ev'ry stripe, ev'ry star
      Red, white, and blue, hats off to you
      Honest, you're a grand old flag

Chorus:

I LOVE YOU TRULY
1907

THIS SONG WAS CREATED AROUND THE TURN OF THE CENTURY BY A MOST REMARKABLE AND courageous woman, Carrie Jacobs-Bond. Mrs. Bond had weathered a series of disasters over a thirty-year period that few men or women could have withstood, and yet she produced some of the finest songs this country has known.

Severely burned when only seven, at age twelve her devoted father became bankrupt and died, and she was divorced in her early twenties. Married again at twenty-five and supremely happy she was caught in the depression of 1893 and had to move near a mining camp in Michigan. Her husband (Dr. Frank Lewis Bond) whom she dearly loved died when she was only thirty-three leaving her penniless to support herself and her young son.

She struggled to make a living by painting china, renting rooms, writing music and trying to get her songs published. Finally she decided she herself would have to publish her songs, and with the moral and financial help of her friends, Carrie Jacobs-Bond entered the music publishing business around 1900. "I Love You Truly" was included in the first collection of songs she published.

Boston Opera Company's prima donna, Jessie Bartlett Davis, sang her songs, and there soon followed renditions by Chauncy Olcott, Madame Ernestine Schumann-Heink and David Bispham. In 1906 Mrs. Bond published "I Love You Truly" as a separate song, and to her great surprise and boundless joy it sold over a million copies. This proved to be the lucky turning point in her life. She had often said, "I found opportunity waiting at the door when adversity knocked."

Carrie Jacobs-Bond sang "I Love You Truly" for Presidents Theodore Roosevelt, Warren G. Harding, and Calvin Coolidge by invitation to the White House, and this song became a "must" for wedding ceremonies all over the country. Years later "I Love You Truly" became the favorite song of Helen Traubel, distinguished diva of the Metropolitan Opera. Helen Traubel's famous recording enjoyed a wide circulation.

Carrie Jacobs-Bond always felt her songs were not "arty" since she wrote them with sincerity for everyday people. In his epitaph to her, Herbert Hoover wrote "Her songs express the loves and longings, sadness and gladness of all people everywhere . . . truly folk music of the world."

I LOVE YOU TRULY

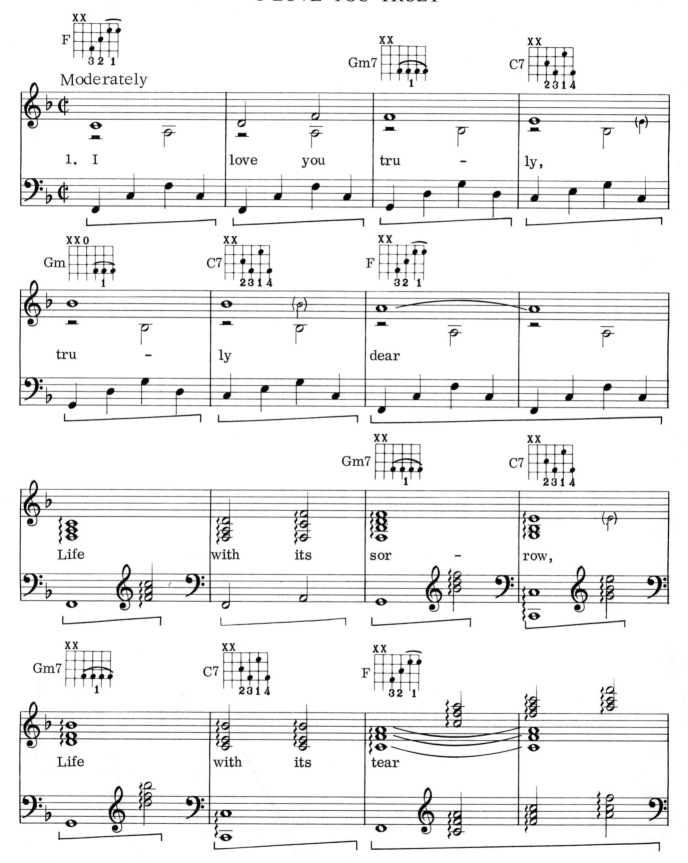

2. Ah love, 'tis something to feel your kind hand
   Ah yes, 'tis something by your side to stand
   Gone is the sorrow, gone doubt and fear
   For you love me truly, truly dear

TWENTIETH-CENTURY AMERICA (1910-THE PRESENT)

AS THIS PERIOD BEGAN, THE DEMAND FOR POPULAR MUSIC WAS GREATER THAN EVER. SHEET MUSIC sales were climbing to dizzy heights. Returning from his African hunting trip ex-President Teddy Roosevelt found women in hobble skirts and men in celluloid collars and high button shoes singing the popular songs of the day.

THE 1910's

America's hub for music publishing was in New York City on West 28th Street. By 1910 the area was known as Tin Pan Alley, a name coined a few years earlier by a writer for the New York *Herald,* Monroe Rosenfeld. Seated in a music publisher's office after having written an article on the music business, Rosenfeld was casting about for a catchy title. During a moment of daydreaming he suddenly became aware of the clatter from a dozen pianos banging away. He commented that it sounds like the banging on a bunch of tin pans. In a flash it struck him that here was his title—Tin Pan Alley.

In 1911 "Alexander's Ragtime Band" scored so heavily that it gave impetus to a new era of social dancing. America developed itchy feet. Quick-minded hotel and restaurant owners hastened to provide for dancing during mealtime. Special teatime dances were promoted and after-theatre dancing became the vogue. Even Mrs. John D. Rockefeller took lessons. However, none of this excitement reached our isolated rural areas. America's provincial people still stayed with the good old standby songs and dances which Henry Ford so admired.

The first decade in this period of history was alive with activity and song. As the movie industry gathered speed it soon discovered that censorship was riding in hot pursuit. Movie houses employed from one to several musicians to accompany the silent films. Also accompanied were the in-between sing-alongs in which everyone could participate and show off his vocal prowess. Folk-song hunting began in earnest at this time, although the search for Negro folk songs had started earlier. The total effort eventually netted us a wealth of musical Americana to which was added a good deal of folklore. When the indestructible luxury ship *Titanic* struck an iceberg in 1912 its orchestra courageously played "Nearer My

God To Thee" as it slowly slipped beneath the surface. In 1914 the Panama Canal was opened (August 15) amid much ceremony and song. Between 1915 and 1920 sheet music sold for ten cents in every five-and-ten cent store. Many songs sold over a million copies with such sales continuing even through the 1920's. World War I had its most popular songs in "It's A Long Way To Tipperary," "Keep the Home Fires Burning," "Over There," "Smiles," and a few others. The Armistice of 1918 was followed by the Volstead Act, which in turn was followed by "How Dry I Am" and thirteen years of social rebellion against Prohibition.

THE 1920's

We entered the Roaring Twenties with vigor, having exchanged the Victorian Age for the Jazz Age. Dixieland jazz was quite the "cat's whiskers," while the cat's whiskers was an important part of a radio crystal set on which amateurs tried to hear music. Gramaphones and Victrolas were more widely used than ever. No one objected to the hand-winding, since for the first time he could hear his favorite music whenever he wanted. Record sales at twenty-five cents each soared. Piano sales dropped. Directly after women won the right to vote (1920) their skirts became shorter, looser, and lower-waisted. Younger women cut their hair in bangs and many were known as "flappers," the symbol of freedom and daring. The newest dance craze was the Charleston (1923).

An important musical milestone was established on February 12, 1924, when Paul Whiteman, the "King of Jazz," gave his historic concert in Aeolian Hall, New York. Bigwigs from Broadway and musical dignitaries sat side by side, heard George Gershwin's "Rhapsody In Blue," and witnessed the decisive moment when jazz became respectable. Despite this significant occasion many important persons remained convinced that jazz was an evil that must be destroyed. One educator said, "If we permit our boys and girls to be exposed to this pernicious influence, the harm . . . may tear to pieces our whole social fabric." A physician added, "Jazz affects the brain through . . . hearing, giving the same results as whiskey."

Adventure indeed marked the 1920's. Great publicity attended Charles Lindbergh's flight (1927) across the Atlantic in a single-engine plane; and nearly as much publicity attended dance marathons, flagpole-sitting, and goldfish-eating. The "Talkies" appeared October 6, 1927, with Al Jolson in *The Jazz Singer*. This new art form was soon to use huge quantities of music, and lure many of our finest song writers and composers to Hollywood. Theatres all over the nation fired their musicians as vaudeville was replaced by the talkies. Wall Street's $15,000,000,000 slide in 1929 plunged our country into its greatest economic depression.

THE 1930's

The 1930's provided sobering experiences for most Americans, but much light was shed on our problems through President Franklin Roosevelt's frequent articulate commentaries on our nation's total direction and progress. The "Star Spangled Banner" was proclaimed our national anthem by Congress back in 1931. As radio came into more homes, giving more people free music and entertainment, sheet music and record sales dropped, as did piano sales and movie attendance.

The second half of the 1930's saw the advent of "swing" and the rise of big name bands,[1]

[1] Tommy and Jimmy Dorsey, Glenn Miller, Artie Shaw, Woody Herman, Benny Goodman, among many others.

340

thereby packing the nation's dancehalls and some of our larger theatres. Mounting enthusiasm eventually got out of hand when teenagers started dancing in theatre aisles, until local police stepped in. Many a "swing concert" was held in New York's dignified Carnegie Hall and other hallowed halls of the classics. In this same five-year period hillbilly and cowboy songs came into vogue. Americans everywhere quicky acquired a taste for the simplicity and honesty of these songs. By the end of the 1930's our most popular songs had run the gamut from the sophisticated type ("Begin the Beguine," "Lover") all the way to songs of literal candor ("Wagon Wheels," "There's A Goldmine In the Sky").

THE 1940's

The 1940's opened with America's deepest concern over the war in Europe. Hitler's lightning conquests shocked all who could read a newspaper. The German army occupied Oslo, Norway, with truckloads of soldiers singing "Beer Barrel Polka." The more popular songs of the war were "White Cliffs of Dover," "This Is the Army Mr. Jones," "Praise the Lord and Pass the Ammunition," "White Christmas," and also the first four notes of Beethoven's *Fifth Symphony*—indicating the V-sign for "Victory." American soldiers found the Army's "Hit Kit" of popular songs a great morale-booster. During the war the jukebox was born and immediately began collecting lots of nickels. By 1950 there were about a million jukeboxes in operation, playing thousands of songs and paying no royalty whatever to composers. Also during the war, songs of the theatre underwent important change when *Oklahoma* opened (1943) with a new concept, wherein songs and dance routines became a part of the plot and thus moved the story-line forward.

After the war people turned again to recordings, which received a big boost in 1948 when long-playing records came into being. At about the same time, television was just getting started and radio diskjockeys were established. By the end of the 1940's hillbilly bands and singers were in greater demand than ever before. Corn on the cob was fast becoming a part of America's musical diet. The spread of square dancing gradually brought about a national interest in folk-dancing and folk-singing, although jitterbug dancing was still popular with our teenagers.

THE 1950's

In the 1950's our musical development took a long stride forward, aided in good measure by electronics. Hi-Fi and folk-song enthusiasts multiplied by the hundreds of thousands, purchasing record albums as never before. Television provided an additional medium for musical exposure. While America delighted in hearing all kinds of music they also enjoyed making the music themselves. Since the end of World War II (1945) colleges and high schools had been placing increased emphasis on brass bands, orchestras, and choral groups. Audiences loved and supported this, which encouraged the development of many a latent talent. Musical instrument sales rose, particularly in pianos, guitars, and organs. By 1956 the jitterbug had metamorphosized into the rock-'n'-roll, although many wished it had not.

By the time our first satellite orbited (1958) record albums containing every type of music had been produced and sold. Many purchasers discovered a new excitement in studying the history and progress of jazz. Others developed a consuming interest in folk and ethnic songs. When stereophonic recording was inaugurated America's musical appetite was whetted to a sharper edge. Without a doubt we had become the world's most musically sophisticated people.

THE 1960's

During this entire period of over half a century we had gone from a nation of music makers to music listeners, and then to both music makers and listeners. Despite our current wealth of passive musical entertainment[2] people from coast to coast are leaning all the more toward making their own music.

By the early 1960's there were about 33,000,000 amateur musicians in our population of 190,000,000. Nearly one in every six people played an instrument. Over 21,000,000 played piano while 6,000,000 strummed the guitar. More than 10,000,000 school-age youngsters learned and played some kind of instrument. Virtually everyone in the country sings. And thus the future horizons look bright indeed for America's musical life.

STATES ADMITTED TO THE UNION

Rank	Name	Origin of Name	Year Admitted	State Song
47.	New Mexico	Named after Mexico.	1912	O Fair New Mexico
48.	Arizona	From the Indian word "Arizonac" meaning "little spring place."	1912	Arizona
49.	Alaska	Variation of an Eskimo word meaning "great country."	1959	Alaska's Flag
50.	Hawaii	Possiby from a native word meaning "homeland."	1959	Hawaii Ponoi

[2] Radio, television, recordings, movies, theatre, indoor and outdoor concerts, etc.

THE ROSARY
1913

FOR OVER A THIRD OF A CENTURY THIS SONG WAS THE ENVY OF ALL MUSIC PUBLISHERS, SINCE from the time of its first publication it had achieved substantial and steady annual sales from 1898 to well into the 1930's. Such popular appeal is striking since "The Rosary" is high level in both lyrics and music, a quality art song, in sharp contrast to successful songs from Tin Pan Alley.

Composition of this song began as a poem, written in 1894 by a lawyer of fine poetic talent and lots of inherited wealth, Robert Cameron Rogers. "The Rosary" was published in a magazine and as far as Rogers was concerned that was the end of it. The music was written four years later by that well-trained and noted musician Ethelbert Nevin.

It seems that a friend of Nevin's chanced to mail him a magazine clipping of the poem simply because it was a sentiment so beautifully expressed. Upon reading it Ethelbert Nevin not only thought it beautiful but became thoroughly immersed in it. Pacing back and forth, he repeated the words over and over until he had memorized them. The following day, upon returning from his music studio, he produced a completed pencil copy of the song. Mrs. Nevin said that he wrote it in "less than an hour, and never changed a note."

"The Rosary" was published in 1898 and although it sold less than 2,000 copies that year, sales and popularity steadily increased year after year. By 1913 the song had already sold well over a million copies. This song achieved national popularity in an America of 95,000,000 people.

This song's fame was so widespread that it inspired the writing of a successful British novel, and it became a favorite of the distinguished singer Madame Schumann-Heink whose audiences were enthralled with her rendition of "The Rosary." Alexander Woolcott and other notables have paid high tribute to this song. Perhaps most important is the fact that popular opinion has placed the label "great" on this song, and this is worth noting since the song has a Catholic connotation in a country that is predominantly Protestant.

THE ROSARY

HINKY DINKY PARLAY-VOO
1919

ALSO CALLED "MADEMOISELLE FROM ARMENTIERS," THIS IS PERHAPS THE MOST POPULAR SONG TO come out of World War I. As a parody type of tune there is an endless variety of verses including unprintable ones.

Armentiers is a northwest French town almost at the border of Belgium which many American and British soldiers came to know during the war. It is believed that this song concerns a real French waitress in a real Armentiers cafe.

There are several stories regarding the composer of this song. One version has it that Alfred Walden was the writer. Another version is that a Lt. Gitz Rice adapted it from "Mademoiselle de Bar-Le-Duc." A copyrighted version was published in the United States in 1924. However, the melody seems very strongly that of an old folk tune and the many verses were made up by many authors, most of whom were American doughboys, and the words were learned in folk song tradition, i.e., by word of mouth. American soldiers returning from Europe in 1919 sang this song all the way across the Atlantic Ocean, and very soon afterwards all America was singing it. Over the next few decades it settled down to become one of our standard American songs of humor.

HINKY DINKY PARLAY-VOO

2. Farmer have you a daughter fair, parlay-voo
   Farmer have you a daughter fair, parlay-voo
   Farmer have you a daughter fair
   To wash a poor soldier's underwear
   Hinky dinky parlay-voo

3. Mademoiselle from Armentiers parlay-voo
   Mademoiselle from Armentiers parlay-voo
   Mademoiselle from Armentiers
   She never did hear of underwear
   Hinky dinky parlay-voo

4. Officers came across the Rhine, parlay-voo
   Officers came across the Rhine, parlay-voo
   Officers came across the Rhine
   To kiss all the girls and drink the wine
   Hinky dinky parlay-voo

5. Officers eat up all the steak, parlay-voo
   Officers eat up all the steak, parlay-voo
   Officers eat up all the steak
   And all we can get's a bellyache
   Hinky dinky parlay-voo

6. One night I had some "beaucoup" Jack, parlay-voo
   One night I had some "beaucoup" Jack, parlay-voo
   One night I had some "beaucoup" Jack
   Till mademoiselle got on my track
   Hinky dinky parlay-voo

7. You may forget the gas and shells, parlay-voo
   You may forget the gas and shells, parlay-voo
   You may forget the gas and shells
   You'll never forget the mad'moiselles
   Hinky dinky parlay-voo

8. Captain is carrying the pack, parlay-voo
   Captain is carrying the pack, parlay-voo
   Captain is carrying the pack
   I'm hoping it breaks his darling back
   Hinky dinky parlay-voo

9. Mademoiselle heard cannon roar, parlay-voo
   Mademoiselle heard cannon roar, parlay-voo
   Mademoiselle heard cannon roar
   But all that we heard was "je t'adore"
   Hinky dinky parlay-voo

AMERICA THE BEAUTIFUL
1920

THIS, ONE OF OUR COUNTRY'S MOST BREATH-TAKING SONGS, HAD A VERY MODEST AND SEDATE beginning. A New Jersey musician and music dealer, Samuel Ward, was inspired by an old set of verses known as "Oh Mother Dear Jerusalem" and he composed the musical setting (1882) as a hymn, giving it the title "Materna" (meaning "motherly"). This song found its way into many of our church hymnals. Ward's stately music has even been used as a setting for other poems, also found in hymn books. "Materna" first appeared in print in *The Parish Choir*, July 12, 1888, in Boston, Mass.

All might have remained quite modest and sedate had it not been for the vibrant and inspired New Englander, Katherine Lee Bates. Miss Bates, who taught English at Wellesley College, was invited in 1893 to lecture at Colorado College, as was Woodrow Wilson. On her trip west she saw for the first time the abundant glories of America. Her trip culminated in an expedition to the top of Pikes Peak. Standing in that rarified atmosphere she saw "spacious skies," and "purple mountain majesties" and such an expanse of fertile country that she was moved with an exalted pride that cried out for poetic expression. She wrote the verses, but somehow two years had passed before she finally sent it to a magazine, *The Congregationalist*, which published it on July 1, 1895.

The poem created quite a stir, and for the next few years many musical settings were composed. Katherine Bates decided to rewrite the verses and this revision, the present lyrics, was published in the *Boston Transcript*, November, 1904. The poem was now talked about, written about, and received many more musical settings, including Samuel Ward's music which soon became the most popular. Miss Bates' poem spelled out so well the pride and feelings of Americans everywhere that it became the most printed during World War I.

In 1926 the National Federation of Music Clubs conducted a contest for the best musical setting to the poem. Although some nine hundred entries were submitted none seemed as suitable as Ward's "Materna," and so it developed that Katherine Bates' poem and Samuel Ward's music are today's "America the Beautiful," from sea to shining sea. It is doubtful that Katherine Bates and Samuel Ward ever met, since Ward died in 1903.

Most everyone in America knows and loves this song and it stands today as one of our highly popular national songs. It was used recently in the 1952 movie *With A Song In My Heart*, and before that the 1942 movie *Bells of Capistrano*, and in the first Cinerama production, *This Is Cinerama*.

AMERICA THE BEAUTIFUL

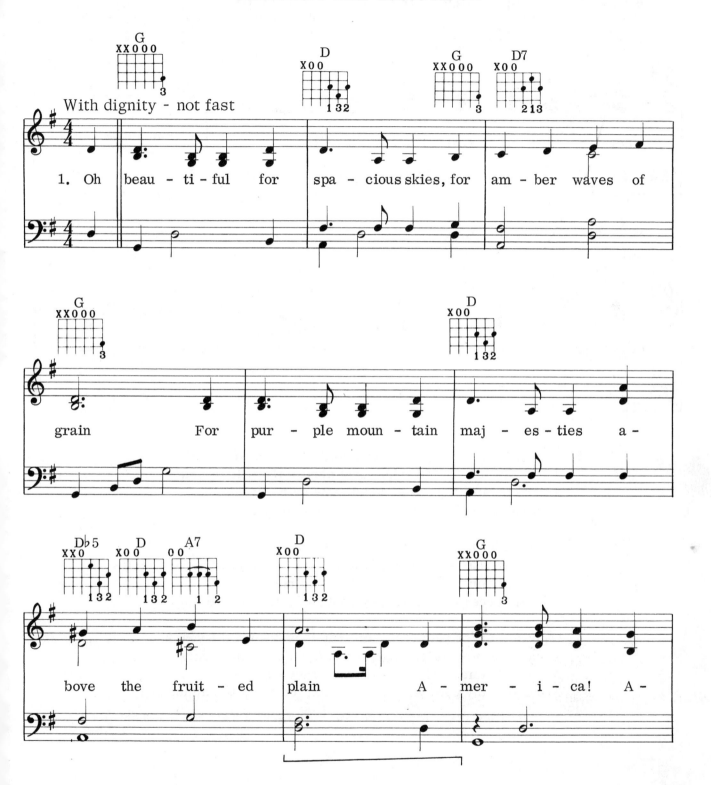

With dignity - not fast

1. Oh beau — ti — ful for spa — cious skies, for am — ber waves of grain For pur — ple moun — tain maj — es — ties a — bove the fruit — ed plain A — mer — i — ca! A —

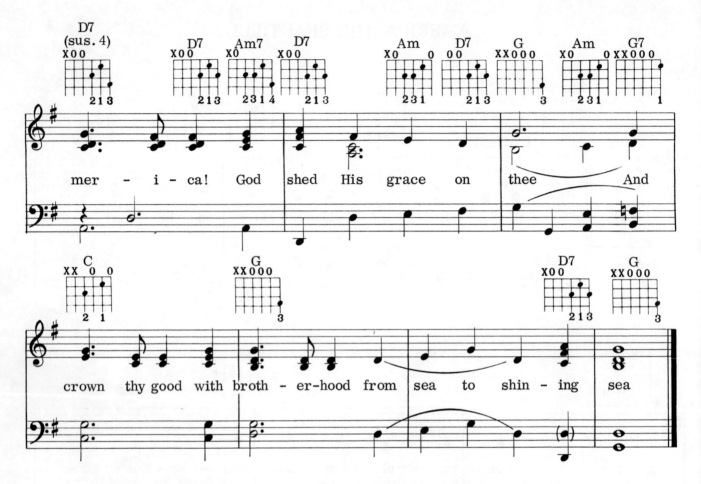

mer - i - ca! God shed His grace on thee And

crown thy good with broth - er-hood from sea to shin - ing sea

2. Oh beautiful for Pilgrim feet whose stern impassioned stress
   A thoroughfare for freedom beat across the wilderness
   America! America! God mend thine ev'ry flaw
   Confirm thy soul in self-control, thy liberty in law

3. Oh beautiful for heroes proved in liberating strife
   Who more than self their country loved, and mercy more than life
   America! America! May God thy gold refine
   Till all success be nobleness, And ev'ry gain divine

4. Oh beautiful for patriot dream that sees beyond the years
   Thine alabaster cities gleam undimmed by human tears
   America! America! God shed his grace on thee
   And crown thy good with brotherhood from sea to shining sea

SWING LOW, SWEET CHARIOT
1925

"CHARIOT" COMES FROM THE FRENCH, MEANING "TRUCK, CARRIAGE, CRADLE." THE CHARIOT REfered to in this song is not the familier Roman type. It is a small sledlike truck quite familiar to those Negro plantation slaves who used them for transporting tobacco. After Nat Turner's ill-fated revolt of 1831 Negroes keenly felt the pressure of stricter slave codes, and a legend developed whereby they visualized a huge chariot swinging out from heaven to carry their souls over Jordan (ocean) to Liberia.

"Swing Low, Sweet Chariot" was born in the heart of Sarah Hannah Sheppard of Tennessee around 1847. Mrs. Sheppard was sold as a slave and the day of separation from her baby was rapidly approaching. She vowed to throw herself and her baby into the Cumberland River rather than be a slave in Mississippi. As she stumbled in desperation along the high river road a prophetic old Negress, realizing what she was up to, approached Mrs. Sheppard. "Don't you do it, honey," she tenderly said. "Wait! Let the chariot of the Lord swing low. Listen! I will read one of the Lord's scrolls to you." Reading in pantomime, she continued, "There's a great work for this baby to do here on earth. She's going to stand before kings and queens. Now don't you do it, honey . . . just don't you do it." Mrs. Sheppard was startled, but deeply impressed. She returned home and allowed herself to be taken to Mississippi. The notion of "God's chariot swinging low" stayed with her continually until she finally gave it expression by creating "Swing Low, Sweet Chariot."

Some twenty-five years later the old Negress' prophesy came true. Mrs. Sheppard's baby, now Mrs. Ella Sheppard Moore, enrolled in Fisk University and then joined the original Fisk Jubilee Singers. As their pianist she went on concert tours beginning in 1871. These concert tours were noteworthy and quite successful, making over $150,000 for Fisk University. The climax of the tour was reached with appearances before royalty in both England and Germany. When the tours ended in 1878 Mrs. Moore began a search for her mother. Her search was rewarded and she brought her mother back to a beautiful home where Mrs. Sheppard lived out her life in abundant love and comfort. By this time "Swing Low, Sweet Chariot" enjoyed a modest popularity.

Years later, the distinguished musician Henry Thacker Burleigh gave the song a superb arrangement which was published in 1917, and since that time this song's popularity has climbed with great speed to become nationally well known by 1925.

This immortal song has been sung and recorded by innumerable artists, both Negro and white. Anton Dvorak showed the song's influence in the coda theme of his *New World Symphony*—first movement. The 1934 song hit "Wagon Wheels" bears a marked resemblance to "Swing Low," and the song even inspired a large canvas by John McCrady entitled "Swing Low, Sweet Chariot" now in the City Art Museum of St. Louis, Missouri.

SWING LOW, SWEET CHARIOT

2. Swing low, sweet chariot Comin' for to carry me home
   Swing low, sweet chariot Comin' for to carry me home
   And if you get up there before I do Comin' for to carry me home
   Tell all my friends that I'm a-comin' too Comin' for to carry me home
   Swing low, sweet chariot Comin' for to carry me home
   Swing low, sweet chariot Comin' for to carry me home

3. Swing low, sweet chariot Comin' for to carry me home
   Swing low, sweet chariot Comin' for to carry me home
   The brightest of bright days that ever I saw Comin' for to carry me home
   When Jesus washed my mortal sins away Comin' for to carry me home
   Swing low, sweet chariot Comin' for to carry me home
   Swing low, sweet chariot Comin' for to carry me home

4. Swing low, sweet chariot Comin' for to carry me home
   Swing low, sweet chariot Comin' for to carry me home
   Now sometimes I'm up and sometimes I'm way down Comin' for to carry me home
   But still my soul feels heavenly bound Comin' for to carry me home
   Swing low, sweet chariot Comin' for to carry me home
   Swing low, sweet chariot Comin' for to carry me home

THE MARINES' HYMN
1930

HERE IS THE MOST POPULAR OF THE OFFICIAL MARINE CORPS SONGS, AND PERHAPS THE FOREMOST of all service songs. Here is a song of pride. The earliest beginnings of this song trace back to 1805 when the Marine Corps flag bore the inscription "To the Shores of Tripoli." Years later, after the Mexican War (1846–1848), the inscription was changed to read "From the Shores of Tripoli to the Halls of Montezuma." It was directly after this war that the first verse of "The Marines' Hymn" was written by an unidentified Marine on duty in Mexico, and it was he who transposed the two-line Marine inscription in order to improve the metre.

Some thirty years later, around 1880, "The Marines' Hymn" received its musical setting through a modified version of "Gendarmes' Duet" (Act II, #14) from Jacques Offenbach's opera *Genevieve de Brabant*. The melody of this duet had been highly popular in Paris for some time but there was talk that Offenbach may have borrowed it from a Spanish folk song.

Although every campaign in which the Marines have participated seems to have produced new sets of lyrics for this song, three verses have remained the most popular and are now the official version. In 1942 the fourth line of the first verse was officially changed from "On the land as on the sea," to "In the air, on land and sea." Since its first printing in 1918 this song's popularity has grown with great solidity so that by 1930 "The Marines' Hymn" was familiar to almost everyone in the country. This is a great song born of a great organization and will remain ever popular as long as men "are proud to claim the title of United States Marine."

THE MARINES' HYMN

fight for right and free - dom And to keep our hon - or clean We are proud to claim the ti - tle Of U - nit - ed States Ma - rine

2. Our flag's unfurled to ev'ry breeze
   From dawn to setting sun
   We have fought in ev'ry clime and place
   Where we could take a gun
   In the snow of far off Northern lands
   And in sunny tropic scenes
   You will find us always on the job
   The United States Marines

3. Here's health to you and to our Corps
   Which we are proud to serve
   In many a strife we've fought for life
   And never lost our nerve
   If the Army and the Navy
   Ever look on heaven's scenes
   They will find the streets are guarded
   By United States Marines

HOME ON THE RANGE
1935

EVER SINCE IT HAD BEEN PUBLICIZED THAT THIS WAS FRANKLIN DELANO ROOSEVELT'S FAVORITE this song's popularity soared upward, selling over a million song copies. From that time on it became an American standard tune and has often been referred to as the "cowboy's national anthem."

This song seems to have been written in 1873 by Dr. Brewster Higley (words) and Dan Kelly (music), both Kansas homesteaders. During this period most of America, and Kansas in particular, was something of a wilderness. Rural life had people living quite some distances from each other. Schools were few and far between and people generally saw each other at church, funerals, or Saturday night in town. Dr. Higley (whose words came first) lived some twenty miles from Dan Kelly, who was known as the best guitar player in and around Smith County. They gave it the title "My Western Home."

The first publication of the words is said to have been in the *Smith County Pioneer* 1873, and the first public performance as a song that same year was by Clarence Harlan (Harlan Kansas, was named after his father). Since Higley and Kelly failed to copyright and publish their song people learned the words and music by rote. Hence several variants appeared.

This song is a favorite of many senators, representatives, supreme court justices, and others in public life. In 1947 "Home On the Range" became the official state song of Kansas. This song's popularity seems destined for a very long life indeed.

HOME ON THE RANGE

2. Where air is so pure and the zephyrs so free
   And the breezes so balmy and light
   I would not exchange my own home on the range
   Not for all of the cities so bright

Chorus:

3. How often a night when the heavens are bright
   With the light of the glittering stars
   I stood there amazed and I asked as I gazed
   If their glory exceeds that of ours

Chorus:

4. I love the wild flow'rs in this dear land of ours
   And the curlew[1] I love to hear scream
   I love the white rocks and the antelope flocks
   That are grazing on mountain tops green

Chorus:

1. Curlew = a rather large bird.

CARELESS LOVE
1937

MANY AUTHORITIES BELIEVE THIS SONG TO BE THE GRANDDADDY OF THE BLUES. IT IS SIMPLE, strong, sad, bitter, and beautiful.

Although its history is rather hazy, it seems to have originated (perhaps early nineteenth century) in the mountain areas of Kentucky, spreading to the lower lands, and then probably traveling the Ohio River to the Mississippi, ultimately fanning out through the entire South.

Because of the interchanging of this song between Negroes and whites in many towns, mountains, plantations, and valleys, the song has gone through hundreds of variations in melody and words. However, its basic qualities have always remained the same.

Toward the end of the nineteenth century, when American industrial empires were being built, this song was already well known in certain isolated areas of the South, the Ozarks, and the Mississippi Valley. With recordings of such famous singers as Bessie Smith (the late 1920's), and with frequent radio performances during the 1930's, this song became not only somewhat standardized in music and lyrics but it also became nationally popular just at the time our nation was digging its way out of the Depression through TVA and other Roosevelt-initiated projects.

Although "Careless Love" is heard today in many styles (blues, hillbilly, jazz, ballad), it is the forerunner of the blues and one of our better American folk songs.

364

CARELESS LOVE

2. Sorrow, sorrow to my heart
   Sorrow, sorrow to my heart
   Sorrow, sorrow to my heart
   When my true love and I did part

3. Once I wore my apron low
   Once I wore my apron low
   Once I wore my apron low
   You'd follow me through rain or snow

4. Now I wear my apron high
   Now I wear my apron high
   Now I wear my apron high
   You see my door and pass it by

5. Now my money's spent and gone
   Now my money's spent and gone
   Now my money's spent and gone
   No bed to put my head upon

6. Cried last night and the night before
   Cried last night and the night before
   Cried last night and the night before
   I'll cry tonight and cry no more

WABASH CANNON BALL
1938

THIS IS A FOLK SONG BORN OF A VERY SPECIAL KIND OF FOLK, THE HOBO. IT IS A GENUINE KNIGHT-of-the-road ballad with a touch of the Paul Bunyon flavor. Now hoboes are not necessarily bums, and certainly not derelicts. Most hoboes simply dislike a regulated life and prefer the illusion of being free. They do odd jobs when necessity requires it, and spend the bulk of their time in contemplation and in fantasies of fine clothes, golden riches, Utopia—and the next square meal.

When railroad-building reached full stride the latter part of the nineteenth century a whole new world opened up for the American hobo. Now he could change his locale with little physical effort, visit distant hobo friends, quickly move to a warmer climate, and still have lots of time for his leisure. Truly, railroads were God's gift to the hobo, and the speed and power of the locomotive excited every fibre of his imagination.

"Wabash Cannon Ball" is one of the products of this imagination and the song seems to have originated sometime in the 1880's. Everyone likes to believe he possesses something unique even if it is imagined, and hoboes were no exception. This song gave them something unique, a mythical Flying Dutchman sort of train, which was their very own creation. The song was learned by rote from one generation of hoboes to the next. Every hobo coming in the vicinity of the Ozarks was sure to learn this song before hopping his next rod.

Although "Wabash Cannon Ball" is a song of, by, and for hoboes, it would have stayed with them had it not been for hillbilly singers. Away back in the 1930's hillbilly singers found a place for themselves in radio and brought many "new" songs to national attention. They took a fancy to "Wabash Cannon Ball" and sang it into nationwide popularity. Roy Acuff's recording alone sold over a million copies.

"Wabash Cannon Ball" has become a standard American pop tune that may last for a long time to come. The song was featured in the 1941 movie *Rolling Home To Texas*.

WABASH CANNON BALL

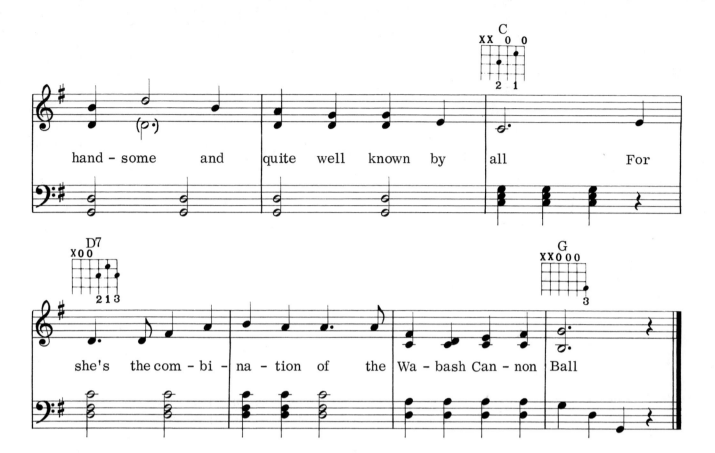

hand - some   and   quite well known by   all   For

she's   the com - bi - na - tion of   the Wa - bash Can - non Ball

2. Won't-cha listen to the jingle, and the rumble and the roar
As she glides along the woodland through the hills and by the shore
Just hear the mighty engine, and lonesome hoboes squall
While trav'llin' through the jungles on the Wabash Cannon Ball

3. Now the train it is a wonder and it travels mighty fast
It is made of shining silver and it takes off like a blast
You leave Mobile at seven, at eight you reach St. Paul
And there's a lonely whistle on the Wabash Cannon Ball

4 When she come on down from Memphis on a cold December day
As she rolled into the station you could hear the people say
"Why, there's a girl from Memphis, she's long and she is tall
And she came down from Memphis on the Wabash Cannon Ball"

5. Here's to hobo Daddy Claxton, may his name forever stand
It'll always be remembered in the courts of Alabam'
His earthly race is over, the curtains 'round him fall
We'll take him home to vict'ry on the Wabash Cannon Ball

6. Now the Eastern folks are dandies, so the Western folks will say
But they never saw the Wabash 'cause it never passed their way
We'll never take a hobo from Boston, big or small
No dandy can be taken on the Wabash Cannon Ball

BELL BOTTOM TROUSERS
1944

THIS WELL-KNOWN CHANTEY SEEMS TO CARRY ALL THE EARMARKS OF A FOLK SONG. FOR YEARS IT was learned by word of mouth and handed down from generation to generation, music and lyrics have gone through a series of modifications, variants of the original lyrics have appeared under such titles as "Rosemary Lane," "Jack the Sailor Boy," "The Waitress and the Sailor."

The original was a sea chantey by and for sailors, and dates back at least to the end of our Civil War (1865) during the heyday of America's proud clipper ships. With all its variants the song was continually popular among sailors. However, the song could never be published during mid-Victorian days because of its bawdy lyrics. Thus it remained sailor property until World War I when it fanned out to the army and our other branches of service. During this war "Bell Bottom Trousers" became highly popular among our troops and even filtered into the civilian population to some extent.

In 1943, during World War II, a cleaned-up version was composed and the song was published. Almost immediately the song's popularity soared to great heights, perhaps for three main reasons: Many people already knew the melody, the famous Vincent Lopez Orchestra frequently performed the song over radio, and the new version had quite a magnetic charm about it. Over one million song copies were sold despite the fact that we were a nation at war.

Since World War II many recording artists have selected "Bell Bottom Trousers" including Guy Lombardo, Jerry Colonna, the Merrill Staton Choir, Louis Prima, and more recently Mitch Miller (1958), Lester Lanin (1962) and Tony Pastor (1963). Within one hundred years "Bell Bottom Trousers" has gone from an unprintable sea-chantey to a delightful popular song, and is now accepted as one of the big ones in our treasury of standard popular songs.

BELL BOTTOM TROUSERS

Moderately

1. Once I thought this sail - or boy ought to have a wife

Want - ed to get set - tled down to a qui - et life

I went out with ev - 'ry girl that I could af - ford

Nev - er reached the al - tar 'cause I went so o - ver - board

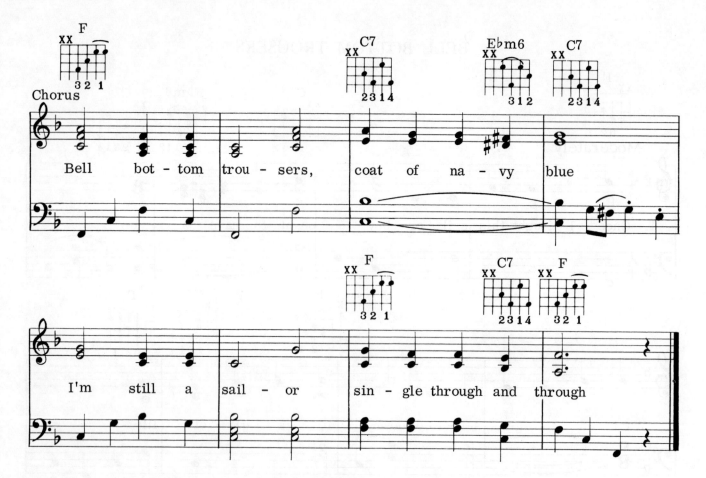

Chorus

Bell bot - tom trou - sers, coat of na - vy blue

I'm still a sail - or sin - gle through and through

2. Met a girl named Annabelle, met her in the park
   Hugged and kissed her through the night 'cause it was so dark
   But when morning came along I got such a shock
   She was tall and skinny and her face would stop a clock

Chorus:

3. I went out with Emmaline, innocent and pure
   She was so respectable, modest and demure
   When I got aboard my ship much to my dismay
   She had stolen ev'rything and even my toupee

Chorus:

4. I wrote letters to a girl I had yet to see
   She declared her love was true and she'd wait for me
   When our ship got into port how the sailors shoved
   There were forty other guys a-wanting to be loved

Chorus:

JOHN PEEL
1945

THIS IS THE SONG OF A FOX HUNT, A SPORT ORIGINATING IN THE BRITISH ISLES AROUND 1700 AND still quite popular up to the present time.

John Peel was a real person, the English novelist John George Whyte-Melville, formerly a captain in the Coldstream Guards. He was an expert hunter during the middle 1800's and was considered the laureate of fox hunting. On the occasion of his death on the hunting field in 1854, Whyte-Melville's friends attended the funeral after which they went for drinks. Here was the setting for the birth of "D'Ye Ken John Peel." After a couple of drinks one of his close friends, John Woodcock Graves, scribbled some verses in tribute to Whyte-Melville. He used the melody of an old folk song "Bonnie Annie."

It is very likely the original "Bonnie Annie" arrived in America shortly after the War of 1812, but only a small handful of people were attracted to it. Years later, when Graves' version appeared, interest picked up to some extent. Many glee clubs and college students adopted the song, and with the aid of folk-song enthusiasts the song was kept very much alive well into this century.

However, it was not until the mid-1940's that this melody became nationally popular in the form of the Pepsi Cola jingle frequently played over radio. After the jingle was discontinued the catchy melody was still remembered and enjoyed by millions, and thus the original "John Peel" lyrics were restored.

JOHN PEEL

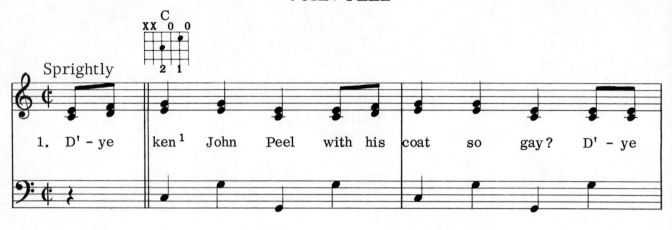

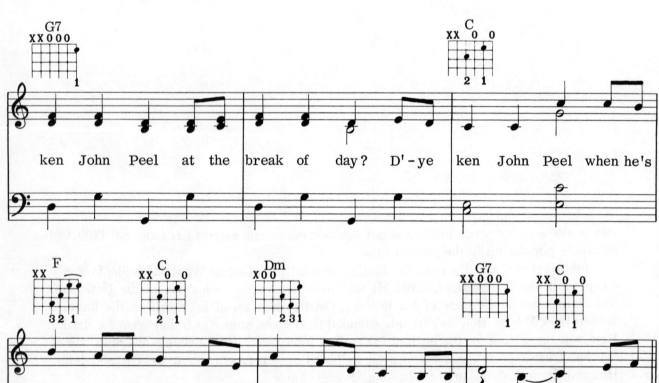

1. D'ye ken = Do you know.

2. Yes I ken John Peel, good old Ruby too
   And old Ranter, Ringwood and Bellman true,
   From a find[3] to a check,[4] from a check to a view[5]
   From a view to a death in the morning

Chorus:

3. D'ye ken John Peel with his coat so gay?
   When he lived at Troutbeck in olden days
   Now he's gone away, and so far far away
   We shall ne'er hear is voice in the morning

Chorus:

2. View hallo = The official shout of a fox-hunter when he sights the fox.
3. Find = The term used when the hounds find tne fox or his scent.
4. Check = The term used when hounds lose the scent.
5. View = The term used when the hunter sights the fox.

WHEN THE SAINTS GO MARCHING IN
1946

SOMEWHERE DURING THE LATTER HALF OF THE NINETEENTH CENTURY THIS SONG CAME INTO being as a deeply religious spiritual, probably created by those Negro folk singers who played an important role in religious ceremonies. Later, around the turn of the century, Negro musicians were beginning to come into their own as they gradually gave up playing on jawbones, bamboo tubes, and improvised drums, and switched to regular orchestral instruments. They too became a part of religious ceremonies and joined in the gospel songs and spirituals, playing them quite sedately. "When the Saints Go Marching In," however, was an exception. It seems that the Holy Rollers, a religious sect given to rather high keyed revival meetings, established the tradition of starting this song rather quietly and then building chorus after chorus until it became a frenzy of excitement.

Another tradition strongly influenced this song over the past fifty years, particularly in New Orleans. Almost all Negroes belonged to benevolent societies, fraternities, and burial clubs, and on the occasion of a death these organizations provided a funeral parade. A custom of "first and second-line" paraders developed, first-liners being the legitimate mourners while the second-liners were generally youngsters who loved music and sort of "went along for the ride." Enroute to the cemetery the parade was fairly restrained and quiet, but right after the burial musicians bowed to the crowd, hitched their suspenders and began playing as their mood dictated, which was generally free, gay, and ad lib. This was the paradise the second-liners waited for. They shouted, high-stepped, strutted, and shook everything they had all the way back to town. The most played song at such funerals was "When the Saints Go Marching In."

Thus this song had gone through a sort of metamorphosis and emerged as one of the earliest and best jazz numbers in America. The song has continuously gained in popularity, and by the end of World War II was already well known throughout the land. It is virtually the theme song of Louis Armstrong who took it to other lands including Europe, Russia and Africa.

376

WHEN THE SAINTS GO MARCHING IN

2. Oh when they come on Judgment Day
   Oh when they come on Judgment Day
   Lord I want to be in that number
   When they come on Judgment Day

3. When Gabriel blows that golden horn
   When Gabriel blows that golden horn
   Lord I want to be in that number
   When he blows that golden horn

4. When they go through them Pearly Gates
   When they go through them Pearly Gates
   Lord I want to be in that number
   When they go through Pearly Gates

5. Oh when they ring them silver bells
   Oh when they ring them silver bells
   Lord I want to be in that number
   When they ring them silver bells

6. And when the angels gather 'round
   And when the angels gather 'round
   Lord I want to be in that number
   When the angels gather 'round

7. Oh into Heaven when they go
   Oh into Heaven when they go
   How I want to be in that number
   Into Heaven when they go

8. And when they're singing hallelu
   And when they're singing hallelu
   How I want to be in that number
   When they're singing hallelu

9. And when the Lord is shakin' hands
   And when the Lord is shakin' hands
   How I want to be in that number
   When the Lord is shakin' hands.

RED RIVER VALLEY
1950

THE RED RIVER LADEN WITH RED SILT AND FLOWING THROUGH TEXAS, OKLAHOMA, ARKANSAS, and Louisiana into the Mississippi, is not where this song was born. Originally it seems to have been an old New York State song around the turn of the century called "In the Bright Mohawk Valley" from which an adaptation was made to produce "The Bright Sherman Valley" (very close to the Red River). "Red River Valley" was an adaptation of this latter tune made over into a cowboy love song.

Over the years this typical cowboy song has moved slowly and steadily up the ladder of popularity as it was frequently performed by singing cowboys on and off radio and television. By mid-century "Red River Valley" had become well known from coast to coast. Two movies were named after this song, one in 1936 starring Gene Autry, and the other in 1941 starring Roy Rogers. Numerous recordings have been made in various styles including a recent rock-'n'-roll version in 1959 which made quite a mark for itself. "Red River Valley" has taken its place as a standard song in America's repertory of cowboy songs.

379

RED RIVER VALLEY

2. As you go to your home by the ocean
   May you never forget those sweet hours
   That we spent in our Red River Valley
   And the love we exchanged 'mid the flow'rs

Chorus:

3. From this valley you say you are going
   When you go, may your darling go too?
   Would you leave her behind unprotected
   When you know she loves no one but you

Chorus:

4. I have promised you darling, that never
   Will a word from my lips cause you pain
   And my life, it will be yours forever
   If you only will love me again

Chorus:

5. Won't you think of the valley you're leaving?
   Oh how lonely, how sad it will be
   Won't you think of the fond heart you're breaking
   And the grief you are causing for me?

Chorus:

ROUND HER NECK SHE WORE A YELLOW RIBBON
1951

GENERALLY THE REVIVAL OF AN OLD SONG IS DUE TO A PARTICULAR SINGER, ORCHESTRA, RECORD-
ing, movie, or some other single agent. Such was not the case here. Revival of this song
was supported by several agents and this continued for well over a decade. The original
version of "Round Her Neck She Wore A Yellow Ribbon" was published in the late 1830's
under the title "All Around My Hat." The lyric was in dialect and the song bore the
inscription "written by J. Ansell . . . composed and arranged by John Valentine. . . . as sung
by Jack Reeve with the most unbounded applause." This song carried the same lyric idea
and construction as our current one, and it became a mild hit here and in England.

Somewhere toward the end of the nineteenth century the song was picked up by our
soldiers who changed the lyrics and modified the melody to some extent. It was used
as an army marching song and the "yellow ribbon" probably refers to the yellow piping
soldiers wore on their blue uniforms. Although the song acquired several different titles
and many parodies it remained basically the same, and the U. S. Army sang it in war and
peace thus causing its publication in 1917 under the title "Round Her Neck She Wore A
Yellow Ribbon."

During mid-twentieth century this song received several boosts in popularity. In 1949
the Eddie Miller and Tommy Tucker recordings, followed by radio performances, lifted
the song's popularity considerably, and by 1951 it was known from coast to coast. Then
followed Jerry Wayne's 1952 recording and the million-record seller of the Andrews Sisters
in 1953. In 1954 it became the theme song of the movie *She Wore A Yellow Ribbon* and
Ralph Flanagan recorded it. Subsequent recordings were by Eddy "Piano" Miller and
Chorus in 1955, Mitch Miller in 1958, and Bing Crosby in 1962. "Round Her Neck She
Wore A Yellow Ribbon" seems bound for a long period of popularity.

ROUND HER NECK SHE WORE A YELLOW RIBBON

March tempo

1. Round her neck she wore a yel - low rib - bon She
wore it fall and win - ter and in the month of May And
if you asked her why the heck she wore it She'd
say it's for her lov - er who is far, far a - way Far a-

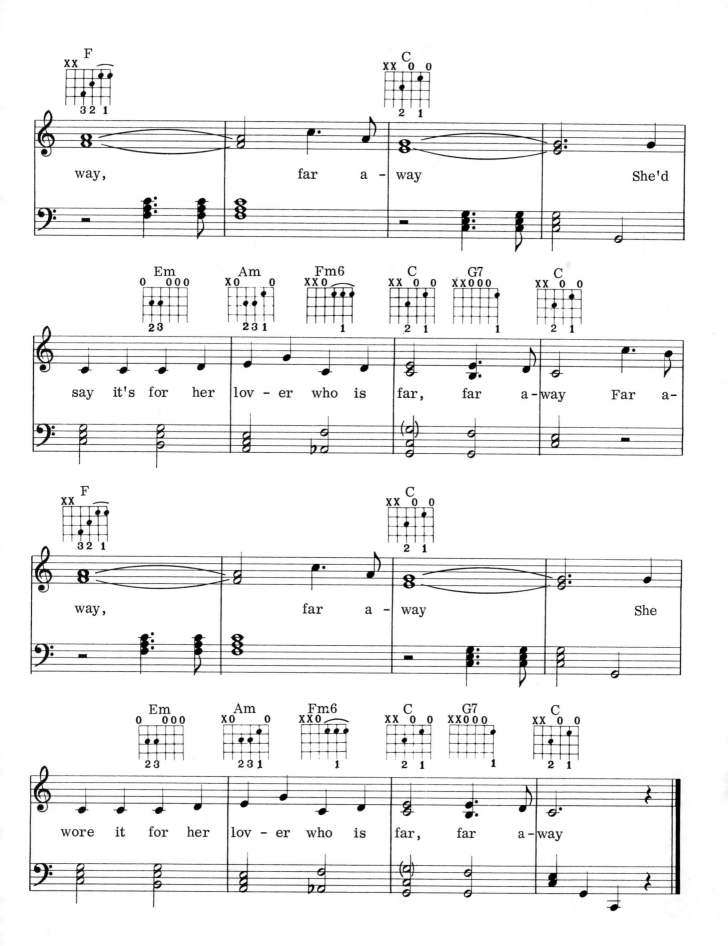

2. Round her neck she wore a golden locket
   She wore it in the night time and wore it ev'ry day
   And if you asked her why the heck she wore it
   She'd say it's for her lover who is far, far away
       Far away, far away
       She'd say it's for her lover who is far, far away
       Far away, far away
       She wore it for her lover who is far, far away

3. In her home she kept a fire burning
   She kept it fall and winter and in the month of May
   And if you asked her why the heck she kept it
   She'd say it's for her lover who is far, far away
       Far away, far away
       She'd say it's for her lover who is far, far away
       Far away, far away
       She kept it for her lover who is far, far away

4. Saved her heart and saved her sweetest kisses
   She saved them fall and winter and in the month of May
   And if you asked her why the heck she saved them
   She'd say they're for her lover who is far, far away
   Far away, far away
   She'd say they're for her lover who is far, far away
   Far away, far away
   She saved them for her lover who is far, far away

THE FOGGY, FOGGY DEW
1954

THIS FOLK SONG SEEMS TO HAVE BEGUN SOME TWO OR THREE HUNDRED YEARS AGO IN THE eastern part of England. In the tradition of folk songs it was learned by ear and passed on from person to person. Thus many variants came into being as the song became known throughout most of the British Isles. One very old Scottish version had the lyrics set to the music of "Ye Banks and Braes."

It is not clear, nor perhaps known, when or how this song came over to the United States, but toward the end of the nineteenth century "The Foggy, Foggy Dew" was quite well known in a number of regions, particularly in the Midwest. Although each region had its own version of the song the central theme always remained the same. Meanwhile the song's popularity in Britain continued to grow, spreading to Australia and New Zealand.

It was not until after World War II that Americans by and large developed a growing interest in folk singers and folk songs, and consequently most people were exposed for the first time to quite a number of "new songs." "The Foggy, Foggy Dew" was one of the more performed folk songs during the early 1950's and audiences grew quite fond of it. As a result, the song began appearing in more and more song books and recordings so that by 1954 "The Foggy, Foggy Dew" had become another one of our nationally popular songs.

THE FOGGY, FOGGY DEW

2. One night she knelt near me, so close to my side
   When I was so fast asleep
   Then she threw her lovely lovely arms 'round my neck
   And she then began to weep

   She wept, she cried, she tore her hair
   Ah me, what could I do
   So I held her in my arms, all night in my arms
   Just to keep her from the foggy, foggy dew

3. Again I'm a bach'lor and live with my son
   We work at the weaver's trade
   And now ev'ry ev'ry time I look in his eyes
   I can see the fair young maid

   Reminds me of the winter time
   And of the summer too
   And the many times I held her here in my arms
   Just to keep her from the foggy, foggy dew

THE YELLOW ROSE OF TEXAS
1955

THIS SONG BLOSSOMED INTO FULL POPULARITY OVER A HUNDRED YEARS AFTER ITS BIRTH. THE song is really quite old. "The Yellow Rose of Texas" dates back to some years before the Civil War and was probably written shortly after our Mexican War (1846–1848). Texas, and the additional territory we acquired from Mexico (California, Nevada, Utah, Arizona, and New Mexico), was much talked about in those days thus providing a good atmosphere for this song's later popularity. Originally this was, no doubt, a Negro song with the "Yellow Rose" referring to a **light** Negress.

The song was first published in 1858 bearing the inscription "by J. K." but it did not have much of a chance since the Civil War began soon afterwards. When the war ended, however, "The Yellow Rose of Texas" climbed to a fairly good popularity which seems to have lasted for about twenty years. For the next seventy years or so, during America's periods of enormous growth and maturity, this song maintained a steady but rather low level of popularity—mostly regional. Along the way the song became one of the favorites of many notable people including President Franklin D. Roosevelt.

In 1955 "The Yellow Rose of Texas" became nationally prominent. The song was revived through a fine recording of Mitch Miller's male chorus. The recording was spirited and exciting, and America's taste was ready for it. Miller's record sold enormously and within a few weeks this song swept the country. "The Yellow Rose of Texas" is back on the popular-song map to stay.

THE YELLOW ROSE OF TEXAS

Moderately

1. There's a yel-low rose in Tex-as That I am gon-na see No-bod-y got to know her No-bod-y on-ly me She cried so when I left her It like to broke my heart And if I ev-er find her We nev-er more will part She's the

2. Where the Rio Grande is flowing
   And starry nights are bright
   She walks along the river
   Each quiet summer night
       She thinks of when we parted
       So very long ago
       I promised I would come back
       No more to leave her so

Chorus:

3. Now I'm goin' back and find her
   My heart is full of woe
   We'll sing the songs that we used
   To sing so long ago
       I'll play the banjo gaily
       We'll sing forever more
       The yellow rose of Texas
       The girl that I adore

Chorus:

AURA LEE
1956

AT FIRST "AURA LEE" WAS RECEIVED RATHER QUIETLY. TWENTY YEARS LATER ITS POPULARITY took a fairly good rise and remained at that level for nearly a century. Then suddenly, in a new version, its popularity shot upward to where it became one of the top songs in the nation.

"Aura Lee" dates back over a hundred years when George R. Poulton composed the music and W. W. Fosdick wrote the words. Their song was published in Cincinnati in 1861 but it failed to generate much public interest. Years later the song began coming into greater favor as college glee clubs gained popularity during the early 1880's, and as other harmony groups were springing up. "Aura Lee" was excellent material for such groups both in its lyric sentiment and beautiful harmonizing possibilities. In the heyday of barbershop quartets this song was a natural. Thus "Aura Lee" became more widely known and appreciated for years to come.

Somewhere during the latter half of the nineteenth century the United States Military Academy at West Point appropriated the music, giving it a new set of lyrics and the title "Army Blue." The song is still traditional with the cadets and is frequently heard at Army football games.

"Aura Lee's" popularity was lifted again when the song was used in the 1952 movie *The Last Musketeer,* but the big breakthrough came four years later. In 1956 the music was given a brand new set of lyrics and entitled "Love Me Tender" for a movie bearing the same title. The song was broadcast by every radio station in the country and Elvis Presley's recording sold like wildfire. By the time Americans owned a few million copies of Presley's recording, the song was a national sensation. Of more recent years, however, people have gone back to singing the original lyrics, thus establishing "Aura Lee" as a solid standard in the popular-song field.

AURA LEE

2. On her cheek the rose was born, 'twas music when she spake
   In her eyes the rays of morn with sudden splendor break
   Aura Lee, Aura Lee, maid of golden hair
   Sunshine came along with thee, and swallows in the air

3. Aura Lee, the bird may flee, the willow's golden hair
   Swing through winter fitfully on cold and stormy air
   Yet if thine eyes I see, gloom will soon depart
   For to me sweet Aura Lee is sunshine through my heart

4. When the mistletoe was green amidst the winter's snows
   Sunshine in thy face was seen and kissing lips of rose
   Aura Lee, Aura Lee, take my golden ring
   Love and light return with thee and swallows with the spring

HE'S GOT THE WHOLE WORLD IN HIS HAND
1958

WHEN THIS BECAME ONE OF AMERICA'S TOP SONGS IN 1958, POPULAR FROM COAST TO COAST, some persons may have been somewhat surprised to learn that it was created many, many years ago. Its exact age is not certain but its roots are deep in the tradition of Negro spirituals and the song has found great favor with many a concert artist. As a spiritual of exaltation and acclaim "He's Got the Whole World In His Hand" has dignity and style.

Negro spirituals are true folk songs in every sense and are often characterized by beauty, simplicity, and repetition. Whether they came into being as spontaneous group creations or through the talent of one individual, the life of the song depended chiefly upon group approval. Obviously, "He's Got the Whole World In His Hand" received generous group approval for many generations. It has been published several times since the earlier part of this century.

Over the years this song has shown its universal appeal through performances all the way from mass revival meetings to the grandeur of the concert stage. The renowned artist Roland Hayes brought his Carnegie Hall concert (November 29, 1953) to a close with his interpretation of this song. Metropolitan Opera star Marian Anderson frequently performed this spiritual, and was among the first to record it. In 1958 there began an avalanche of recordings and performances, chiefly due perhaps to Laurie London's recording backed by Geoff Love's Orchestra and arrangement. This recording was highly successful in terms of popularity, selling over a million copies. There immediately followed recordings by Perry Como, Mahalia Jackson, The Statesmen Quartet, The Travelers, and a score of others. Some of the later recordings were by Kate Smith, Billy Williams, and Marv Johnson.

HE'S GOT THE WHOLE WORLD IN HIS HAND

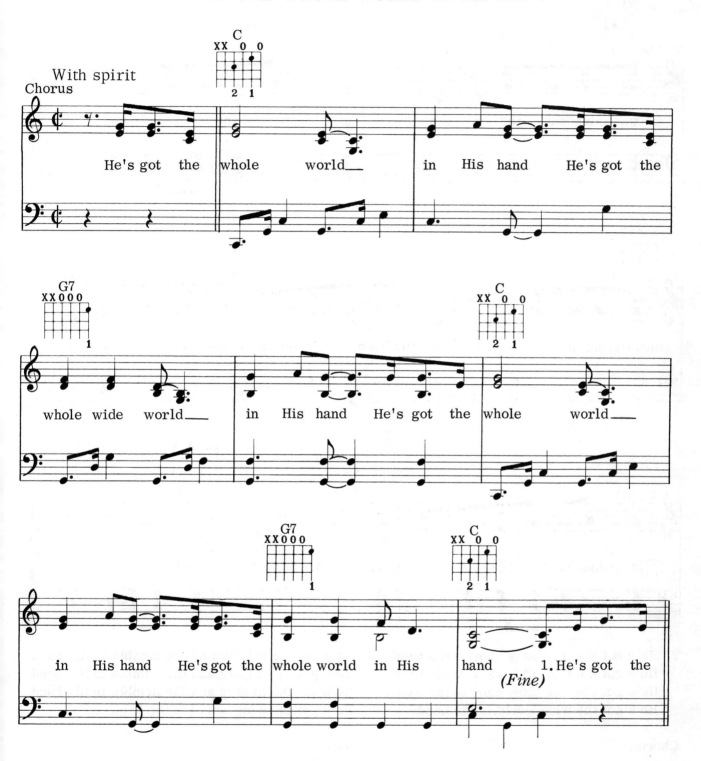

With spirit

Chorus

He's got the whole world___ in His hand He's got the

whole wide world___ in His hand He's got the whole world___

in His hand He's got the whole world in His hand 1. He's got the

(Fine)

2. He's got the tiny bitsy baby in His hand
   He's got the tiny bitsy baby in His hand
   He's got the tiny bitsy baby in His hand
   He's got the wide world in His hand

3. He's got the mighty and the humble in His hand
   He's got the mighty and the humble in His hand
   He's got the mighty and the hymble in His hand
   He's got the wide world in His hand

Chorus: Chorus:

4. He's got the kingdom up in Heaven in His hand
   He's got the kingdom up in Heaven in His hand
   He's got the kingdom up in Heaven in His hand
   He's got the wide world in His hand

Chorus:

TOM DOOLEY
1958

"TOM DOOLEY" IS AN OUTLAW BALLAD BASED ON THE REAL CRIME OF A REAL PERSON BACK IN the mountain country of northwest North Carolina in 1866. Ex-Confederate soldier Tom Dula and Ann Melton were both accused of stabbing Laura Foster to death, but at Dula's second trial (1868) he insisted Ann Melton was innocent and that he alone committed the crime. It was also revealed that Dula's attempted escape from North Carolina was thwarted by an armed man who forced his surrender. Dula's Civil War record of bravery was introduced at the trial but to no avail. He was convicted and hanged on May 1, 1868. Six months later Ann Melton was tried and acquited.

These trials became more than a local sensation and were covered by some of the major newspapers, including the New York *Herald*. The story of Tom Dula was told and retold around the hills of Carolina for many a decade. Ballads sprung up like weeds, some of which changed Dula to Dooley for easier singing. Several of these ballads were set to music, thus producing a number of variants. Of all the variants, the one we use here seems to have been the most popular in North Carolina, and it was often said that most fiddlers and banjo pickers knew it by heart. No one knows for sure just where this melody originated, but it seems most likely to have been an old Negro folk song, referred to as a "banjo tune," and it is based on the pentatonic scale (black notes of the piano).

"Tom Dooley" was learned by ear in typical folk-song tradition, and thus kept alive and regionally popular for ever so many years. Its many variants were collected and published in folklore anthologies. As public appreciation of folk songs rapidly increased during the early 1950's folk singers felt the need for newer material, and the hunt was on. Somehow the Kingston Trio came upon "Tom Dooley," recorded the song, and hit the jackpot with over a million-record sale, thus making it one of the most popular songs of the year. Subsequent recordings were by Lee Castle and the Jimmy Dorsey Orchestra in 1960, and The Four Freshmen and Tammy Grimes in 1962. "Tom Dooley" stands today as one of our most popular outlaw ballads.

TOM DOOLEY

2. This time tomorrow morning
    Reckon where I will be
    If it was not for Grayson
    I'd now be in Tennessee

Chorus:

3. This time tomorrow morning
    This soldier boy will be
    Down in a lonesome valley
    Hangin' from some white oak tree

Chorus:

4. They're gonna try Ann Melton
    Can't see no reason why
    There's only one who's guilty
    And now I'm goin' to die

Chorus:

INDEX OF TITLES AND FIRST LINES